ECLIPSO'S HAPPY QUEST

Extra special thanks to Aninha and Don for their bountiful editorial assistance, keeping things real on the happy quest in Brazil!

Choo-choo train drawing courtesy of Freepik.com
Hyacinth macaw photo courtesy of Dreamstime.com

Other novels in the Four Planet series by David Taylor
(all published by Virtual Bookworm):

A Tale of Four Planets trilogy:
Book One: Sessions with the Seer
Book Two: The Rejected Counsel of Oomb
Book Three: Centers of the Universe

Eclipso's Happy Quest:
Book One: Goosed By An Iguanodon?
Book Two: Eau De Diplodocus?
Book Three: The Saurient Express?

Eclipso's Happy Quest
Book Three: The Saurient Express?
A Novel by David Taylor
ISBN: 978-1-63868-175-5 (softcover)
ISBN 978-1-63868-176-2 (hardcover)
ISBN: 978-1-63868-177-9 (ebook)
Library of Congress Number on file with publisher.

ECLIPSO'S HAPPY QUEST

a Post-Planets Prequel by David Taylor

Book Three:
The Saurient Express?

Dedicated to Aninha and Don

"From us, resistance is born. From us come men, children, life. The woman completes herself with nature, and we have always been part of the resistance along with the men."

O-é Kaiapó Paiakan
environmental activist in Brazil

Prologue: Belém, Brazil

"Let me guess," said Ronald Howe to greet the swarthy young man holding a clipboard petition at the entrance to his and Rosa Silva's fifteenth-floor condo overlooking the Guamá River. "I was the first one you buzzed, dumb enough to say *pude subir* (come up)."

"*Não, cara!* How do you insult yourself like that?" the young man laughed.

"In case you didn't notice, I insulted you as well," Ron chuckled.

"Ron!"

"Oh-oh, I'm in for it now," Ron chuckled anew, despite the admonishment in Rosa's voice.

"Stop teasing the nice guy, and welcome him inside!"

"How do you know he's nice? Something you're not telling me?"

"Mm, that smells like the duck stew my vovó (grandma) used to make," the young man remarked as with a sweeping gesture, Ron ushered him through a short foyer, past the kitchen to the living room.

"Rosa makes the best *pato no tucupi*, no question," nodded Ron, sitting himself on the old family armchair shipped from Wisconsin. "Ah, I get it now," he added in feigned epiphany. "You caught a whiff of Rosa's cooking, and figured the petition gambit was as good as any. Take a seat," he nevertheless insisted, pointing towards a rattan sofa that featured cushions printed with watercolor pink and yellow amaryllis blooms.

Just then, breezes blew in Beep! Beep! Beep! from off the balcony.

A truck backing up?

"Bet I know what that is," said the still-unnamed visitor, leaping off the sofa for a short sprint out onto the balcony. There, he looked across the muddy Guamá at Combú Island. What drew his attention was a giant electromagnet lifting skyward a rusted-out old Cadillac.

Seen easily from Ron and Rosa's fifteenth-floor perch, the electromagnet swung the Cadillac across a dump yard to a shallow pit, the test dig for a larger and deeper landfill.

"SQUAWK!"

"Funny, isn't it, how certain noises can carry here from so far away? Am fairly certain that was a hyacinth macaw over on Combú. Yet its cawing sounded like it came from your bedroom."

"Okay," Ron chuckled yet again.

Klunk!

"You heard that?"

"How could I not?"

"After the electromagnet let go, atmospheric conditions magnified the racket from the car falling out of sight into that big hole."

"It was pretty intense," Ron had to admit.

"You know why they're dumping old wrecks there?"

"They think it's a volcano, but they ran out of sacrificial virgins? Rusted-out sedans were the next best thing?"

"Ron!!"

"No, mano!" the visitor bristled, though unable to help being amused. "That's what they call a test landfill site. But I call it bait and switch! For now, they're only trashing old autos. They can tell nearby restaurants and environmental preserves, 'You see? No foul smells, even when breezes blow over. Just industrial noise we pledge will happen only one day a week!' Soon as the project is approved, though, anything goes! The stink that carries over here will be enough to make you pass out! No longer will you be able to leave those glass doors wide open to your balcony!"

Beep! Beep! Beep!

Klunk! went another car into the provisional landfill crater.

"What is your name, anyway?" Ron asked wearily.

"Manuel Bocaiuvá; *prazer em conhecer você* (pleasure to meet you)," Manuel smiled, offering a hearty handshake. "I gather you're from the United States," he resumed in English.

"What gave away my gringolandia origins?" Ron asked whimsically, accepting Manuel's hand. "My not protesting your speaking so much English? Or my not insisting Rosa speak more Portuguese?"

Rosa sat on the arm rest beside Ron, and draped one arm round his shoulders.

"Both."

"Well at least you're honest. I'm Ron, by the way, *muito prazer em conhecê-la* (pleasure also). Okay, here's the deal. I'll sign your petition, assuming it says: Not in my backyard, neither the noise nor the stinky air, nor possible water pollution as well."

"An important additional point."

"But look, we already receive the occasional stomach-churning waft from the Marituba landfill. That is, unless it's a farting anaconda or some monster we don't know about. I can always dream. Anyway, I've read the Marituba back story. People signed petitions galore. In response, committees made recommendations, blah blah blah. The same as you're saying with this new trash pit, there was a 'pilot waste management zone.'" Ron made finger quotation marks. "Protests erupted, followed by more committees, assurances 'all stakeholders will have their voices heard,' blah blah blah. But in the end, the powers that be went ahead and did what they were hell-bent on doing in the first place."

"Ron's correct," chimed in Rosa. "So yes, we'll sign. But we're not holding our breath."

"Except when we have to, thanks to Marituba," added Ron as he accepted the petition on clipboard.

That's when they heard a staccato sound from somewhere off the balcony, like wood blocks beat rapidly together.

"Man," Manuel shook his head. "Can't get over how clearly those noises on Combú carry here. But this is an odd time of day for a cane frog to make that kind of racket."

"They usually are nocturnal," agreed Rosa. "Maybe that trash dump has them upset, also."

As if to prove Rosa's point, hot on the heels of the next klunk, the cane frog's unique croaks resumed...

...and were succeeded by an imitative noise issuing from one of the condo's bedrooms, directly behind where Rosa and Ron sat. Until "SQUAWK! *Bom día!*" capped it off.

Manuel gave Rosa and Ron a wide-eyed look by turns shocked, quizzical and judgmental.

"That's Milton Nascimento," said Ron as in, *No other explanation necessary*, though he well knew Manuel would insist.

"So, you have Milton Nascimento cooped up inside there," said Manuel dubiously, referring to a popular, multi-faceted Brazilian singer, composer, and instrumentalist. "And now you pretend he's a hyacinth macaw mimicking an irritated cane toad. Or you've got a hyacinth macaw in your bedroom, which is plainly illegal...but also *que bacana* (awesome)," Manuel concluded in practically a whisper. "Secret is safe with me. How about a peek?"

"We can explain," said Rosa.

"He's free to leave whenever he wants," Ron insisted without a trace of defensiveness as he rose from his chair. "What happened is probably unique."

"You mean how you caught him."

"But that's just it," said Ron, leading Manuel round a corner into the bedroom. "We didn't catch him. A few months ago, he flew through our balcony, and made himself at home on our midget cashew tree."

"*Bom día!* SQUAWK!" squawked Milton Nascimento, looking Manuel straight in the eye. Nascimento's talons clutched a bright orange cashew fruit so tightly, they pierced its skin. They also kept him firmly perched on the branch of a small but sprawling cashew tree planted in a huge yellow ceramic pot.

Under other circumstances, Manuel might have marveled at the cashew tree. However, the hyacinth macaw dominated his attention, as one of the most magnificent creatures he'd ever beheld. The macaw's rich blue plumage set off dramatically the lemon-yellow stripe that circled each eye, and ran down his curved beak as well.

"Yours is no disgrace, SQUAWK!" Milton Nascimento squawked at Manuel this time.

"You're already in his good graces, sir," insisted Ron while the hyacinth macaw left off from staring at Manuel, for a bite of the cashew fruit. "He's quoting from an English progressive rock band named Yes."

"Yes? I've heard of them," said Manuel. "But why mimic an English band, and not his namesake, Milton Nascimento?"

"He loves Milton," said Rosa. "But he usually only bobs his head to his songs. He rarely repeats any of the lyrics."

"Yes music is what we think drew him to our balcony in the first place," went on Ron. "I played 'Yours Is No Disgrace' one evening while we were sitting out on the balcony, and he suddenly flew in, landed on our cashew tree. He repeated 'Yours is no disgrace' several times, then helped himself to the cashew fruit."

"That's when we still had our tree in the living room," Rosa added.

"He came for the music, and stayed for the cashews?" asked Manuel, incredulous.

"That's about it," Ron nodded. "Ever since, once he decides a guest is no threat, he sings, 'Yours is no disgrace.' He's also a big fan of *Sagrado Coração Da Terra*."

"He hums along to their records," said Rosa.

"They're a symphonic rock group from near Fortaleza."

"Never heard of them."

"Ditto; first learned about them from a friend in the United States who collects experimental music."

"They play the most beautiful melodies on violin and synthesizers," rhapsodized Rosa.

"If you can spare the time…"

Klunk!

Manuel would have happily spared the time for *pato no tucupi* while listening to *Sagrado Coração*. The new klunk they heard from across the Guamá River, alone, wouldn't have been enough to derail his acceptance of Ron's generous invite. Just another trashed wreck. However, the clatter that ensued, of something enormous collapsing, sent a minor tremor through the condo.

Milton Nascimento tried to mimic said clatter while Manuel, Ron, and Rosa rushed from the bedroom through the living room out onto the balcony, sandals flip-flopping all the way. And that beautifully shaded hyacinth macaw abandoned his effort soon enough to keep up with them. As always, his wings flapped majestically slowly, where Ron was concerned.

Ultimately, Milton Nascimento joined Ron and Rosa, plus their petition-wielding guest, Manuel, at the balcony railing. He perched there to attend carefully to the spectacle developing across the Guamá River on Combú Island.

Clouds of brown dust billowed from the landfill as though, the three human onlookers reckoned, they were rising from a volcanic crater. So thick, they briefly obscured the electromagnetic crane from view.

Meanwhile, the sudden massive ground shift that produced the tremor also produced a shrill metallic screech by smashing together multiple car wrecks. And from amidst this harsh din emerged a thunderously deep roar.

Rosa, Ron, and Manuel exchanged anxious sideways looks. *That can't be a monster crying out, can it?*

"Godzilla's cousin disturbed by the landfill?" Ron asked, only half joking.

Godzilla was a Japanese movie monster awakened by an atom bomb blast in the Pacific, and supercharged with radioactivity. In the film, he laid waste to Honolulu, Hawai'i, enroute to the United States mainland to instinctively exact vengeance on those who invented the bomb. But he was tamed by slender extraterrestrials who looked like gray versions of a popular purple toy with extra-stretchy arms and legs, named Roobanda.

The movie, *Godzilla*, further popularized speculation that outer space beings were behind the periodic disappearance of innumerable weapons across the Earth. And that those same beings were the ones who left behind solar panels, transistorized phones, and other artifacts decades ahead of current technology. The world was far different from what it might have been, without such mysterious intervention.

Among those raptured-away weapons, incidentally, were a couple of atom bombs the United States government was rumored to have wanted to explode near Tokyo, Japan. The idea was to scare off certain people in the Japanese government from their imperialist designs. Of course, when squadrons of Japanese fighter jets likewise mysteriously vanished before they could ever take to the skies, so much for a surprise attack on Hawai'i.

"My mother believes monster snakes the length of two flatbed trailer trucks inhabit the deep interior near the border to Ecuador," said Manuel. "But one of those would probably sound more like this: Sissss!"

"Sissss!" went Milton Nascimento.

"Whatever it is," Manuel went on, though he couldn't help laughing over the hyacinth macaw's mimicry, "I better check in with the Alliance. That's an environmental protection consortium consisting of several indigenous tribes. Could be a significant new development here. What I'm thinking," he went on as leaving the balcony to traverse the living room, "is that we heard river water flood a sudden sinkhole from digging that landfill."

"So those car wrecks they've dumped in there might pollute the Guamá," Rosa speculated while wondering why her normally talkative, snidely remarking husband had gone quiet.

"Acid leeching from dead batteries, transmission fluids, radiator fluids; imagine how much worse when they start dumping heavy-duty industrial waste," said Manuel to endorse Rosa's concern as he opened the front door.

"Sorry you won't get to try Rosa's *pato no tucupi*, plus hear *Sagrado Coração*. Maybe if you drop by another time, provided that sinkhole hasn't swallowed us by then..."

"*Com certeza* (for sure)," said Manuel with his back to the loving couple, and already well out the door to the elevator.

Despite Ron resorting to his typical dark humor, this time about the sinkhole, Rosa couldn't help sensing the wind taken out of her beloved husband's sails. "I know you, Ron, and something's not settling well," she said, following after Ron on his beeline back out to the balcony.

"You may think I'm out of my mind, or already suspected that long before now," said Ron looking over the balcony railing. He focused intently on the landfill crater the other side of the Guamá River as breezes carried off the final remnants of dust that billowed out.

There was a growing flurry of human activity in the surrounding area, including a fire truck and police car that drove off.

"*Por cierto* I knew you lost your mind eons ago, my big gray macaw," responded Rosa, affectionately wrapping her arms round Ron's waist, and looking up at him with cherishing eyes. "That's why I married you, so we could be crazy together. What is this about?" she concluded, following his intent gaze across the river.

"Just before that roar, or whatever it was, thought I saw a tail whip from side to side out of the landfill. Then lost it in the dust clouds. Wasn't big enough for Godzilla, but it did look scaly reptilian green. Happened so fast, you would have missed it if you blinked at the wrong time."

"*Meu Deus* (My God)!" Rosa gasped.

"I must have been hallucinating."

"Oh, no! You are too cynical for hallucinations!"

"SQUAWK! SQUAWK-SQUAWK!"

"Now what are you in a tizzy about, Milton Nascimento?" Ron asked.

The magnificently large, blue-feathered macaw with yellow-ringed eyes was staggering like a drunk from side to side along the balcony railing. He spread his wings low, and dipped his head repeatedly as though, Rosa imagined, he were digging into something.

"Has he finally reached courtship age?" asked Rosa.

"Great; we might have to make room for a second guest soon."

Chapter 1

Augustine "Augie" Matias was ready for most anything, peeking out the window of the Turok Tours bus inside a parking lot close to Baltimore-Washington International Airport. For example, Sherman Peabody was about to emerge from girlfriend Cecilia's car. But Augie wouldn't have been the least surprised had Sherman's airbag, strapped to him like a suicide bomber's vest, accidentally inflated. And then Cecilia either pushed him bouncing out of her car like a boulder-sized balloon, or punctured his airbag.

Puncturing Sherman's airbag, of course, might have propelled him flying out of her car like the deflating parade-float-sized Brachiosaurus balloon back in West Africa. For glorious moments, that odd spectacle had Augie believing Eclipso's expedition finally came across a surviving sauropod dinosaur. Albeit a sauropod dinosaur that, however wingless, rocketed through the air on its impossibly powerful flatus exhaust, like a mythical dragon.

What Augie did not expect was Sherman accompanied by someone behaving even more oddly than himself.

After Sherman emerged from the front passenger seat, his companion emerged from the rear seat. That fellow's notably stiff manner made Augie wonder whether he suffered back issues. Scrunching his chin into his neck the same as Sherman scrunched his own chin, he followed Sherman round the car's rear, up beside the driver's window.

"Jesus Sauropod Christ!" swore Sergeant Fred Frankly seated beside Augie. Fred was one of three space travelers marking time with the Eclipso expedition until they could be transported back to year 2064 from 1982. "Is the entire freakin' Peabody clan committed to keeping their chins glued to their necks?"

Meanwhile, Cecilia rolled down her window to give Sherman one last kiss before leaving. And as she rolled it back up, Sherman's new sidekick also moved in for a kiss, shattering it with the greatest of ease.

"'Cilia Honey, are you okay?!" asked Sherman distraught, his chin lifted as far off his neck as Augie had ever seen it.

"I'm fine! You two go along!"

Cecilia sped off before Sherman could protest.

Sherman's companion turned his head from side to side with a puzzled expression, until he broke into an exaggerated-looking frown. And after what Augie would have sworn sounded like grinding gears, he said to Sherman, "I am sorry for breaking the window."

"Well done on that apology, sir."

As "sir" beamed with an exaggerated grin, Augie couldn't discern even a single drop of blood on his forehead where it burst through the car window.

For boarding after Sherman, "sir" eschewed simply taking the steps. Rather, he turned his back on the bus, and crouched down into a fetal ball out of Augie's view. Pursuant to which, he literally rolled up the stairs. Whereupon he uncurled and with a hop, rose to his full six-and-a-half-foot height, towering over Sherman.

"Friends," said Sherman, while Augie felt more than justified sensing something strikingly unnatural about the tall guy, "you might have noticed I am not alone this time."

"Yes, I might not have been too drunk to notice," snarked Irene McDowell from an aisle seat, her chin lifted regally high.

Augie could have sworn he heard a faint whir as various expressions played across the tall guy's face. When a nodding frown was the final outcome, Augie mused it might as well have been two lemons and an apple that came up on a slot machine.

"I am sure we all appreciate your sobriety," parried Sherman. "But regardless of whichever state you *are* in, Ms. McDowell, what you see here beside me, some might call a robot. I would argue he is so much more, though. Via cascading logarithmic programs that enfold all the latest quantum physics applications gleaned from our time travelers' gifts in place of weapons, I have endowed him with artificial intelligence, or let's simply call it 'AI.'"

Sherman lifted his chin off his neck to look the AI robot's way.

Mr. AI returned the look, albeit most stiffly.

Sherman resumed scrunching his chin into his neck.

The AI robot continued the monkey see, monkey do, likewise scrunching its chin back into *its* neck.

Augie figured flesh-colored latex covered a metal and plastic frame chock full of gears.

"Truly fascinating," breathlessly affirmed time traveler Ali Magabu, who stood up from his window seat for a better view. "You must be thinking, Mr. Peabody, that your AI companion will prove useful to your dinosaur search?"

"Charly – that's his name – "

With a subtle head tremor accompanied by faint whirs, Charly broke into a silly-wide grin and nodded.

"...has already been inculcated with all our amassed cryptozoological data thus far. In addition, he carries an encyclopedia's worth of general knowledge. As well, his empathy program should keep him pleasant to work with."

"How could anyone else ever be more pleasant to work with than you, Sherman?" Irene snarked anew. But she had to roll her eyes when she noticed Scott McDonald, with a serious crush on her, anxiously give Sherman a jealous look. *Yes, that's right, Scott; I'm more attracted to a guy with his chin perpetually glued to his chin than to you.*

"I try my best, Ms. McDowell. To finish answering your question, Dr. Magabu," went on Sherman, "Charly should be able to integrate new data with previously downloaded data at prodigious speed. And yes, that could prove indispensable for locating any living non-avian dinosaurs out there to be found. Perhaps also deal with those hoaxers attempting to sabotage Eclipso's quest. But talk is cheap. Let's hear more from Charly himself."

"Talk is cheap, unless it's coming from the AI robot's mouth?" Irene whispered to journalist Laura Gómez seated beside her.

"Charly, would you like to introduce yourself?"

Click...whirr... "Yes, I would."

After several seconds elapsed with Charly offering nothing further, Sherman added, "Please introduce yourself."

On another faint whir, Charly turned Sherman's way and said, "Thank you." Then he looked down the bus aisle at everyone intensely scrutinizing him, and said, "Let me introduce myself."

Another long silence prompted professional skeptic Stephen Feldman, totally unfazed, to say, "Okay; we're all ears."

With more clicks and whirs, Charly tilted his head from side to side. Several more expressions played across his face until he settled on quizzical. "You don't look all ears," he droned. "My sensors have identified arms, legs, noses, and other features in addition to ears. Oh, wait..." ...click...whirr... "...an idiomatic expression; got it." Click...whirr... "My name is Charly. I am an artificial intelligence entity. My major interest is cryptozoology, especially as pertains to the possibility of surviving non-avian dinosaurs. I look forward to detection and

examination of any and all data relevant to this subject."
Click...whirr... "But I am also fitted with an empathy
program, by which I will strive to make you comfortable in
my presence."

On yet another whir, Charly turned his attention to Irene.
"What is your name, if I might ask?"

"You might well ask. My name is Irene McDowell."

"Irene is a nice name."

"I bet you say that about all the names."

Click...whirr... "No," Charly shook his head. "Your name
is the first one I've had the opportunity to say that about.
And anyway, my holistic quantum programming
guarantees I will react that way to only certain names."
Click...whirr... "But I don't want to bore you."

"No danger of that," Irene whispered huskily out the
corner of her mouth to Laura seated beside her.

"What is your favorite color, Irene?"

"Bright bloody red. What's yours?"

Click...whirr... "I don't actually contain any blood. But
my joint lubricants are shaded a semi-translucent golden
olive."

Sherman resumed scrunching his chin into his neck.

Augie was of the impression that if Sherman could have,
he would have curled up into a fetal ball and rolled out of
there, the same way Charly rolled backwards onto the bus.

"I meant *your* favorite color, not the color of your blood.
Is a favorite color something your holistic quantum
programming confers on you?" Irene managed to ask
without busting out laughing.

Click...whirr... "Whoops! My bad. Ha-ha. My favorite
color is purple." Click...whirr... "Therefore, we don't have
that in common. But variety is the spice of life."

"Wow, you sure know how to sweet-talk a girl. What are
you doing later, Big Boy?" Irene asked, again in her husky
voice. She enjoyed testing the limits of the AI robot's

abilities so much, she could only roll her eyes again, when she noticed Scott's frantic look. *Seriously? You're worried a machine might steal my heart?*

Whirr...whirr...whirr... "Later, I will be doing the same things I'm doing now: collecting evidence of non-avian dinosaur survival, and trying to behave empathetically." Click...whirr... "Ah, yes. You're wondering whether I might be interested in ritual behavior leading to sexual copulation later this evening." Click...whirr... "I am very flattered. However, I am not equipped with a penis for insertion." Click...whirr... "Maybe-"

"Turn it off. Make it stop," pleaded Irene, suddenly very spooked.

Before Sherman could lift a finger, Charly unlatched his left ear and swung it aside. He revealed a circuit board he tapped with his forefinger until a very long, dying-down whir ended in a sharp click. Upon which Charly slumped over, and fell forward onto the bus aisle floor with a loud THUD!

"I am the first to admit there might be a few bugs still to be worked out," said Sherman in what struck Augie as a defensive tone. "For certain, before the next time Charly interacts with us, I will have deleted all his imitative behaviors, such as scrunching his chin into his neck."

"You might want to at least temporarily sequester your AI's empathy program," suggested Stephen.

"Charly won't feel bad about that?" Irene couldn't help asking.

Chapter 2

Once more, Vicky Copplestone-Matias found herself in the front office at Green Pastures Elementary School, en route to the conference room for a we-need-to-speak-to-you with curriculum specialist Diane Mueller and principal Dr. Marsha Klondike. Her stomach used to tie in knots over such meetings. But now, she couldn't help being reminded of old *Roadrunner* cartoons. *What have they ordered from the Acme Corporation this time?* she mused with detached whimsy.

Typically, Roadrunner traversed desert landscapes at such remarkable speed, she left a dusty jet contrail in her wake. And Wild E. Coyote tried to catch her, ordering extraordinary contraptions from the so-called Acme Corporation. But his quest was in vain, always blowing up in his face, often literally.

Over the past spring and summer, Diane employed her own contraptions to throw Vicky out of the education profession rather than eat her for dinner, Wild E. Coyote's ultimate goal with Roadrunner. But same as in the cartoon, they kept backfiring.

One meeting was about to initiate Vicky's formal dismissal from teaching. Only, a distraught mother barged in at the last minute. She wanted to thank Vicky for the joyful moments her unorthodox class provided a beloved son in his final days before a freak brain aneurysm horrifically took his life.

Another time, parents stood on the verge of calling for Vicky's pedagogical hide. But they found themselves wonderfully mesmerized by a chapter in Eclipso's dinosaur search that climaxed in a cautionary lesson on the virtues of skeptical inquiry.

So, what was the new scheme? What ridiculous new contraption did the box from the Acme Corporation contain this time?

Yes, there definitely was a cartoonish aspect to Diane's behavior. And something else helped Vicky remain calmly centered as Diane and Marsha welcomed her into the conference room with broad grins. That was the replenishing good time she had with Augie and their daughter Liz in early August, 1982, after Augie returned home from Cameroon.

The Copplestone-Matias clan took a leisurely drive down the Florida Keys. Along the way, they stopped at a dolphin research center, where Liz received a peck on the cheek from one dolphin after giving her a tummy rub. In Key West, they searched for the best Key-Lime-Pie ice cream scooped high into a freshly baked waffle cone.

True, Vicky could tell Augie's mind often wandered elsewhere. A perfect case in point was when standing waist deep in sea water, waiting for the dolphin trainer to call Dafne over for tummy rubs. Augie scanned the far horizon not so much for telltale dolphin fins as for a relic Plesiosaurus to reveal itself, Vicky felt certain. He wanted a snake-like head to soar skywards on a serpentine neck, producing a dramatic silhouette. And the rest of the trip, he didn't exactly keep his worry secret. He fretted over what next for Eclipso's quest, as shrouded in mystery as that supremely eccentric, reclusive billionaire kept his thoughts on the matter. *He wasn't going to pull the plug on the whole operation, was he? On account of the hoaxers?*

Nevertheless, there were enough happy memories, including with Augie, to leave Vicky feeling she could easily deal with any new nonsense her school administrators might dish out. Though she also wondered: Was joyful family travel more important for fueling her work towards the greater good? Or was putting up with workplace nonsense more important for being able to afford joyful family travel? Or were both perspectives true, simultaneously?

Pleasantries about Diane and Marsha's own vacations disarmed Vicky initially. Such small talk couldn't possibly be prelude to Diane launching a new attack on her professional future, could it? Or maybe it could; principal Marsha Klondike finally said, "I hope we're meeting with you, Vicky, before you've gotten too far along with your classroom preparations."

"Oh?" *Gulp.*

"Nothing bad," Marsha went on. "Rather, it's a classic case of: Be careful what you wish for."

Vicky couldn't help notice Diane look at Marsha askance on the "nothing bad" part of her remark. That threw Vicky off from otherwise reacting, *The Beatles already warned me.*

Earlier that year, the first Beatles album was released featuring Yoko Ono and Linda McCartney as full-fledged members, alongside the rest of the band. John Lennon penned the title track for that concept work entitled *Be Careful What You Wish For.*

"Here's the deal," Marsha again. "Parent and student demand for your particular fourth-grade class has gone completely off the charts. Clearly, the big deal is your world studies unit focused on your husband's exploits in search of an impossibly alive dinosaur. Math and reading, not so much."

Diane made what Vicky considered her sour-lemon suck-face. *Mismanaged math and reading,* Vicky imagined Suck-Face adding, if Suck-Face didn't fear pushback from Marsha.

"It didn't seem fair, um, looked like lots of headaches for us if only a third of the fourth graders got to experience your husband's project while the rest, um, lost out."

Didn't you mean to say, "while the rest were spared"?

"What we're looking at, Ms. Copplestone," said Diane in her severely formal manner, on a nod from Marsha to pick up where she left off, "is relieving you of a fourth-grade section."

"Not relieving her, Diane," corrected Marsha. "You will still be full-time, Vicky."

"Yes, of course," Diane squealed in her girlishly hi-pitched voice Vicky noticed she resorted to, whenever especially nervous. "Nobody's talking about cutting back your hours."

Especially since you can't get away with that legally without showing just cause, Vicky so wanted to remind her.

"We're looking at a redesign of your schedule," Diane explained. "You'll be able to focus exclusively on the, um, interdisciplinary study benefits from following those dinosaur expeditions. Should make life much easier for you."

"Your class will be an elective," Marsha translated, "tentatively entitled: A Cryptozoological Quest."

"If that's alright with you," Diane added. "The title is certainly up for negotiation."

But not my removal from regular teaching duties, one step closer to out the door altogether; got it.

Chapter 3

Somewhere in western Pennsylvania, a stand of tall yellow birches concealed a castle-sized mansion. There, Augie Matias surprised himself at how nostalgically comforting he found sitting back at Eclipso Sunray Smith's swamp-embedded conference table.

True, Sherman Peabody was now accompanied by his latest contribution to the dinosaur-searching cause, an artificial intelligence entity named Charly. And three actual, additional people claimed to be time travelers from Earth's future, responsible for weapon stockpiles vanishing, with nonviolent artifacts left in their place. They had Eclipso's blessing to join his team until their partners in purported history tampering could retrieve them.

Otherwise, though, it was the same gang Augie first met several months earlier, for dinosaur searches in Papua, New Guinea and Cameroon, West Africa, that ended in farce.

There was Scott MacDonald, the authority on all things related to the alleged West African beast named mokele-mbembe. He still labored to look uninterested in Irene McDowell the same time he kept checking her out. And failed miserably.

There was professional skeptic Stephen Feldman, his wry grin reminding Augie of an alligator's set jaw line.

Journalist of the paranormal and other "woo-woo," Laura Gómez, had pen and notepad ever at the ready. And University of Maryland Professor Roberta Quiñones seated beside her smiled as wanly as before. Augie wondered whether she'd ever open up about her personal troubles.

Then there was the happily married couple, Harriet and Harry Letterman. Their legendarily impressive cryptozoological data-gathering made their Down Syndrome seem the most trivial of footnotes. They smiled joyfully as ever. But Augie did notice with a bit of concern that when Harry tried to place his hand over Harriet's, she lifted it away, unlike on previous occasions. Albeit gently and still smiling, Harriet nevertheless exuded disgruntlement, Augie felt.

Nothing complicated about cryptozoological museum curator Bernie Coleman's smile, though. Augie suspected he was tickled simply to be there, alive and healthy at his ripe old age. Plus, Eclipso's fresh infusion of no-strings-attached cash saved his museum back in Portland, Maine from shutting down.

Which returned Augie to consideration of the time travelers. They accompanied Eclipso's search team home from West Africa aboard the steam-powered, football-field-sized drone named Cloud Nine. Augie was led to believe they would hang out with Eclipso at Ankylosaurus Mansion until the quest resumed. Or they would vanish back aboard a starship named Smoke and Mirrors, as they claimed to keep expecting any moment. So how did they end up boarding the Turok Tours bus alongside everyone else? And why did one of them, Marine Corps Sergeant Fred Frankly, have his voice break into an occasional squeak when he commented on Sherman's robot? Like he was going through puberty twenty years too late?

Fred and his two sidekicks from the future, officers Ali Magabu and Kevin Smith-Park, were reticent to share what they did after they turned down Eclipso's kind offer to rest and recuperate at his mansion.

What happened was, they tried to hurry up their return to 2064, and it didn't go well.

Aboard the starship Smoke and Mirrors (or purportedly aboard the starship Smoke and Mirrors, Stephen would have insisted), First Officer Buddy Leung, expert in all things astrophysical, had expounded early and often on time travel conundrums. There was one conundrum in particular, whenever the three officers journeyed to the past for switching out weapons in favor of solar panels and the like. Namely, they eliminated the need for that journey in the first place. But having been at the center of the conundrum, their memory remained intact regarding what they did. Meanwhile, the Smoke and Mirrors returned them through a space-time wound to their present, 2064.

The away team's mission to expunge surveillance cameras from amidst the latest looted weapons was a special case. They didn't realize those cameras were there until after the heist. This meant they had to travel back before the heist was completed, to surgically excise said cameras while surrounded by versions of themselves frozen in space time, like statuary. Otherwise, video of the starship could have fallen into the hands of arms dealers. That would have given those mercenaries far more information about how their destructive money-makers were disappearing than Fred and company wanted them to have. Which was none.

During the mission to tweak an already-altered past, the Smoke and Mirrors starship couldn't just hang around and wait. No, to avoid unwanted detection, it had to hide out in a space-time rift at the edge of the solar system. There, starship Captain Helena Taylor hoped the away team would simply reappear back on board since their successful mission meant they didn't need to undertake it in the first place. That had happened sometimes before, so why not this time? Otherwise, the starship would have to rescue them from the past, probably find them frozen into a completed-time state.

Obviously, the more-desired outcome didn't happen. Instead, the away team found itself caught up in a search for living dinosaurs. It was a search partially financed, ironically enough, by profits Eclipso Sunray Smith made exploiting the technology left behind by them. Among other hi-tech marvels, cellphones were introduced to Earthling civilization decades earlier than otherwise would have been the case.

Fred and company found the dinosaur search mildly entertaining. But as the days wore on with still no rapture back to 2064, they were growing impatient. And so, during the weeks off before the search was to resume, they hatched a desperate scheme to spring themselves back to their present, some eighty years later. For that scheme, they leaned heavily on what they had digested from Buddy Leung's time-travel explications.

The idea was disarmingly simple, really. One of them would locate his closest ancestors, probably one set of great grandparents. Then he would creep closer and closer to them, literally bend his branch of the family tree, in a fourth-dimensional sense, until it suddenly flung all three of them back to their present aboard the Smoke and Mirrors. At least that's what Buddy told them they might try in a pinch. But not even engineer Kevin Smith-Park understood the least bit of Buddy's quantum-physics-based reasoning.

Anyway, Fred was the one who found a set of great grandparents first, on his father's paternal side. His great grandfather was stationed at Myrtle Beach Air Force Station. Air Force Officer Francis Frankly and his newly-wed wife, Mildred, were attending a dance at the local U.S.O. on a steamy mid-August evening.

Crouched behind a stand of nearby palm trees, Fred recognized Francis and Mildred as one of the couples dancing under the stars. They were trying to "Walk Like An

Egyptian" as the Bangles tune went, released four years early on the altered timeline.

Fred and company ventured out, away from the palms, tiptoeing closer and closer...until Fred suddenly shrank so much, his belted pants dropped to around his knees, and his shirt felt several sizes too loose.

"What the French-fried f---!" Fred cussed in a voice that broke girlishly hi-pitched. He hoisted his pants up around his waist and nearly tripped over their legs on his hasty retreat back behind the palms.

"It was truly wise of us to give up on that plan as fast as we did," Ali commented later. "Otherwise, we might have needed to change your diapers, Sergeant Frankly."

Fred Frankly's return to his adult-sized proportions took far longer than it took for him to shrink to pre-adolescence. But thankfully, when they left for Eclipso's mansion, the only remaining side effect from his quantum mishap was his occasionally cracking voice.

As for the ever-ebullient Alistair Frump, if he suffered any setbacks over the multi-week layoff from Eclipso's quest, they sure didn't show. His big welcoming grin suggested he was ready and raring to resume scouting out remote locations around the world for his dream golf course, where golfers could realistically expect to glimpse a surviving non-avian dinosaur, or at least hear one fart. That's a line of evidence Sherman Peabody developed in Cameroon, West Africa. Which is to say, before a Thanksgiving-Day-Parade-Float-Sized dinosaur balloon made a farce out of Eclipso's quest.

Here they all were again, back at Ankylosaur mansion with three time travelers and one artificial intelligence robotic entity growing their numbers. They awaited the undaunted Eclipso's imminent proceedings, his diminutive mother standing guard behind where he sat at the head of the conference table.

Of course there was also the far more diminutive Bonsai Gator. Full-grown at pencil length, Bonsai stood erect on his two hind legs, impossibly so where Stephen Feldman was concerned. He probably awaited the next reggae version of a Beatles tune performed by the six-piece cover band, Yellow Dubmarine.

Until the music started, Bonsai Gator usually sat up to his oversized eyes in a miniaturized swamp lush with bonsai vegetation that occupied a good deal of the conference table. With so many special, honored guests, though…

Eclipso's first order of business was to address Sherman's A.I. robot. "Sherman Peabody tells me your name is Charly. How do you like that?"

Click…whirr… "Neutral; it provides zero additional data regarding the possibility of non-avian dinosaur survival to the present day."

"Um, I programmed him with empathy logarithms, but they're not working very well yet. I turned them off, for now," explained Sherman. His chin squished against his neck seemed to Augie more an expression of embarrassment than usual. "Every part of his being is currently obsessively devoted to searching for a living non-avian dinosaur. All stimuli are single-mindedly evaluated as regards their value to that search, nothing more. Isn't that correct, Charly?"

Click…whirr… "There is nothing in your comments and question that brings me any closer to discovering a living non-avian dinosaur."

"Splendid," commented Eclipso, though in what Augie perceived as a guarded tone. "Nevertheless," he went on in as severe a nasal voice as Augie had yet heard from him, "we have a problem."

Eclipso's mom and Bonsai Gator nodded in unison.

"You mean," said Stephen, "even bigger than the problem that some of you think Bonsai Gator was actually nodding agreement with you, rather than sizing up one of your bonsai swamp's dwarf dragonflies?"

"You mean, bigger than no problem at all, Mr. Feldman?"

Augie imagined that had Eclipso's question dripped from his mouth, it would have been acidic enough to corrode a hole through the thickest metal.

"As for the *real* problem," Eclipso continued, "there is a saboteur in our midst."

Everyone besides Eclipso found themselves involuntarily eyeing everyone else. Augie mused they could have been sizing up each other as suspects in a murder mystery. Or wondering who farted in a suddenly foul-smelling room.

"Allow me to jump ahead, Eclipso, since any second now, we might finally vanish from here back to our present," bulldozed Sergeant Frankly. "Fake dinosaur tracks in New Guinea, a fake dinosaur balloon float, minus the parade, in West Africa; two consecutive hoaxes does seem too much of a f-n' coincidence..."

"Maybe," dubiously reacted Stephen. "There have been far more confirmed crop circle hoaxes than that, in England alone. Couldn't fabricated dinosaur evidence become the next big fad?"

"Whether or not that's the case, you truly suspect someone here might know something about it, Mr. Sunray Smith, sir?" asked Ali.

"I am almost certain of it. We've managed to stay out of the news up to now, aside from innocuous local press regarding the classroom exploits of Augustine Matias's wife," nodded Eclipso.

"Both hoaxes were preceded by a mysterious, slow-moving light in the night sky," said Harriet. "There is that." And for once, she did not conclude with an affirmation of loving solidarity between her and her husband, Harry.

"Perhaps our mischief makers have developed an air-born transport vehicle as quiet as our Cloud Nine, for delivering their hoaxing paraphernalia," suggested Eclipso. "And it happens to light up at night, to see where they're going of course."

"Not necessarily," Augie shook his head. "On New Britain Island, the rumbles and wind gusts were probably loud enough to drown out a helicopter even. And think about the loud racket from all those nocturnal critters on the Sangha River."

"True," Eclipso conceded. "But we also cannot discount another possibility. As noted before, off the coasts of New Guinea, fishermen have complained about a strange, bat-like creature stealing their catch at night. It bears a remarkable resemblance to certain presumed-extinct flying reptiles. And from parts of the Congo issue reports of a similar, even larger creature occasionally known as the kongamoto."

"And," added Dr. Roberta Quiñones, "both creatures are said to have glowing bellies. Could be bioluminescent plankton they pick up from diving like pelicans into certain waters."

"Exactly," Eclipso nodded emphatically. "We must consider the logical, common-sense notion that if both habitats sustain surviving populations of non-avian dinosaurs, they might also sustain surviving Pterosaurs."

"Well while you're at it," said Stephen, the only thing holding his irritation in check being the easiest million dollars he could ever hope to earn, "you don't want to ignore the possibility those lights emanated from flying giraffes. They smeared bioluminescent mud on each other's bellies. Those of their ancestors that didn't, they crash-landed in the dark before they could have children. Just another 'logical, common-sense notion' you need to consider."

Eclipso met Stephen's drawn-out sarcasm with a long, squinting stare while holding yet another humus-dipped pretzel beside his face. He might as well have been holding a most elegant tea cup, Augie mused, especially given his extended pinkie finger. And he had a supporting cast. His mother ever at guard behind him also stared squinty-eyed at Stephen, her lower jaw in motion like she was a cow ruminating on her cud. This, while Bonsai Gator kept his own eyes peeled on Stephen, and slowly shook his head how Augie could only interpret as disapprovingly.

Where most others in attendance were concerned, the tension felt every bit as thick as weeks ago, on the Sangha River in West Africa. That was when they anticipated, any second, a relic Diplodocus might lift its snake-like head out of the brackish waters, on a neck the width of a grown man's torso. Currently, though, apprehension concerned how Eclipso would react to Stephen's latest snark. A relic dinosaur rearing its head out of the swamp-embedded conference table was not really in the offing.

Anticlimactically, Eclipso finally muttered, in his very nasal voice, "Well that's just ridiculous."

"Oh," went Stephen. He stifled himself from continuing, *Surviving Pterosaurs with glowing bellies, and surviving dinosaurs evading definitive notice in multiple locales for countless centuries, that's okay. But you draw the crazy-talk line at flying giraffes!*

"Unless," Eclipso continued, "you're aware of unearthed giraffe skeletons that include wing bones, as per Pterosaur fossils."

"You've got me there," admitted Stephen.

Augie mused to himself that Stephen was literally deflated, didn't contain enough hot air to propel his body flying about the conference room like that sauropod dinosaur balloon had gone flying across the Sangha River.

"So," Eclipso looked away from Stephen to address his more general audience as in, *Now that I've taken care of that,* "if you were expecting me to discuss where next on our search for surviving non-avian dinosaurs, I'm sorry to disappoint you. That won't be a thing."

The group as one cast eyes of startled disappointment Eclipso's way, even including Bonsai Gator. That's when Eclipso's enigmatic mother gave him a significant poke in the back. Pursuant to which, he hastened to add, "Any discussion, that is. There won't be any of that. But soon as you're back aboard Cloud Nine, the quest will most certainly resume. Only, you will not be apprised of *where* it will resume until your arrival there. That will give the hoaxers zero time to prepare. Moreover, please be advised your every communication with anyone outside our special little circle will be closely monitored for the duration of this particular leg of the quest. And if that doesn't put an end to the nonsense, further measures will be considered. Let's just say that for the innocent, may they continue to enjoy the lasting peace of a clear conscience. But may the guilty experience constant inner torment until they cease and desist, if not also confess their transgressions.

"Now, if for whatever reason this plan of action makes any of you too uncomfortable to continue, you can bail right now. And still keep the million dollars I deposited in each of your bank accounts merely for having tried, even if you played a knowing part in the sabotage."

Once again, Augie saw looks exchanged as in a murder mystery. Presumably, the innocents wondered who "dunnit" while the guilty wondered how long they could still get away with it. *And,* in Augie's case the wonder was also over whether some other associate of his, outside the immediate group, might be responsible. Not his wife Vicky, however. Yes, she did occasionally express frustration.

After all, he wasn't around for her and daughter Liz as much as he might have been, if there weren't so many cryptozoological expeditions and before that, fossil hunts. No way, though, would she ever ask him to scale back. Especially this dinosaur search, with Eclipso paying every member of the expedition a fortune, lack of success notwithstanding.

What Eclipso's new approach did have Augie wondering was whether there might be someone in his wife's sphere of interaction up to no good. Next time they spoke, he'd definitely need to raise that ugly specter.

Augie had no idea fellow explorers centered suspicion on people close to them in ways he couldn't possibly suspect Vicky.

Scott MacDonald's brother, Donald, for example, certainly gave Scott plenty of reason to wonder just exactly what he was up to.

"Well praise the Lord, that's all we need to know, isn't it, my big bro'?" enthused Donald after Scott finished debriefing him about the West African adventure. "Set aside that crazy balloon. You have that lizard's scale left on a mid-river sand dune, unlike any known crocodile or alligator scale, you said. And a fart someone recorded that had to have come from a large reptile. Include the second set of three-toed tracks in New Guinea you said the track-hoaxing machine couldn't have also made...it's a slam dunk!" Donald spread his arms wide in celebratory mode, a familiar yet still unsettling crazed look in his eyes. "Dinosaurs are alive and well, all over the Earth! Praise Jesus! Mission accomplished for Eclipso! Everyone can go home and stay home!"

Scott wanted to push back hard on his brother's assessment. For starters, while the evidence gathered thus far certainly seemed tantalizingly suggestive, nothing definitive had been established. The "slam dunk" regarding non-avian dinosaur survival was still nowhere in sight. And even if the "slam dunk" became everywhere in sight, there would nevertheless be lots more to learn.

Scott was growing to suspect a major problem with organized religion, or at least with Christian evangelical fundamentalism. Namely, there was this implication that once you embraced its basic tenets, "that's all we need to know," as his brother put it. The rest was unessential trivia.

Part of Scott really wanted to hammer Donald, ask what he was afraid of. Did Donald think if he dug too deep, what he discovered might call his new-found faith into serious question? Moreover, did he understand that searching for a relic surviving non-avian dinosaur was not simply about winning an argument? That such a discovery would just be the start? And certainly, it would do absolutely nothing to undermine the theory of evolution? No matter, whether some mystical life force propelled evolution, as Scott himself believed, or not. Nothing in the theory said old species couldn't keep on keeping on alongside evolving new species. Otherwise, for example, all fish as predecessors of land-going creatures would have gone extinct hundreds of millions of years ago.

What continued to hold back Scott from really going after his brother on these matters was the same as always. Undeniably, Christian fundamentalism had helped Donald leave behind a self-destructive drug addiction. It had literally saved his life. And so, Scott accentuated the positive in his reaction to Donald's time-to-move-on re the dinosaur search. "If we can add to our knowledge of these magnificent creatures," he said gently, "we will appreciate God's creation that much more, as God gave us the brains to do."

"Yeah, okay," Donald nodded dubiously. "Say," he added like something really energizing just occurred to him. "I'm meeting with a friend around seven. Think you can join us for dinner? Um, they would like to meet you!"

Charmaine O'Reilly seemed to Scott a perfect fit for his brother. She hung on Donald's every word about the mushroom business. Moreover, she referenced her religious faith nearly every other sentence. ("The Lord sure has blessed us with such a fine refreshing breeze today for the middle of August!")

But they'd hardly put in their menu orders when Donald suddenly announced, "Oh, whoops! Forgive me Jesus! I just remembered: Supposed to conduct a youth Bible study group starting a half hour from now! If you can have my grub boxed to go..." He handed over a twenty-dollar bill to Scott. "...I'll eat later. You two take your time, enjoy."

He was out the door before Scott could offer a word of protest, starting with that twenty-dollar bill. No way would he use it, given the million dollars plus that Eclipso gifted to his bank account.

Charmaine could not have looked more uncomfortable, fussing over her wavy blond hair while seated across from Scott in a secluded booth. He wondered whether it sank in for her the same time it sank in for him, that his brother was up to a clumsy bit of matchmaking.

Scott found himself almost as touched as irritated by his brother trying to gift him what he most wanted for himself, namely a romantic relationship with Charmaine.

The other thought was nothing but irritating, a question really. Clearly, Donald wanted Scott home permanently from any more dinosaur searches. Maybe he feared further such investigation might lead to the dreaded conclusion that non-avian dinosaurs did not survive to the present day, after all. However, could such fear have driven Donald to employ expert hoaxers for continually sabotaging Eclipso's quest?

Of course, there was the little matter that Scott hadn't yet admitted to Donald his infatuation with Irene. Wasn't the sort of thing he could very well do before he fully admitted it to himself. But naturally, he had zero romantic interest in Charmaine...the same as Irene re Skip's lovelorn designs on her. They also left her wondering, like Scott with his brother, just how far Skip was willing to go.

Even had the next destination in Eclipso's quest been shared with Irene well before she departed, she had already long since decided that this time, she would keep it secret from Skip.

"Tell me, girl," Skip started over a champagne flute stuffed with panko-fried asparagus at the tapas bar in downtown Frederick, Maryland, "did my water bottle hold up through Cameroon? Is it ready to take the next journey?"

"The bottle you gave me, you mean, which makes it *my* bottle?" Irene asked pointedly. "Didn't get to bop it over the head of any Allosaurus. So yeah, it's ready for several more trips, if necessary." Crunch! she went at an asparagus head.

Skip flinched and winced involuntarily, for which he wanted to slap himself silly. Nevertheless, he went on, "So there's this other girl..."

"Other girl? Who's the first girl? Because I'm no girl. Someone knocked at your door selling cookies?"

"I was hoping, um, Rosa could join us, but she had volunteer work."

"'Um, Rosa'? Was her volunteer work refusing to sit in the back of buses?"

Skip writhed about on his bar stool like he was trying to wriggle free of the trap he'd set for himself, Irene mused. Then finally, he whined, "She deserves a whole lot more respect than that! But don't misunderstand; she means nothing to me! Nothing!"

"Well, that's some serious respect you're showing her, yourself, if I never heard it," snarked Irene while thinking, *Yeah, it's hard for someone to mean something to you when they don't exist in the first place.* She couldn't help mischievously adding, "She does sound nice enough, you shouldn't string her along if she really means nothing to you. For sure, she doesn't have to worry about me." *Would that there was some other young lady roaming around like Bigfoot out there, to distract him from me!*

"So, you won't get violent with her?"

"Why would I do that?"

"C'mon!" Skip squeaked, supremely frustrated over Irene not demonstrating the least bit of jealousy.

"Okay," said Irene, playing dumb, "you'd like me to beat the crap out of her?"

"No!!"

"Well then, we're agreed."

Next thing Irene knew, Skip was out the front door, yelling at himself, "Skiiiip!"

Irene was left wondering: Might a guy willing to expound upon a non-existent competitor for his romantic attentions also be desperate enough to prank the dinosaur search, simply to keep her nearby?

Meanwhile, Dr. Roberta Quiñones came very close to a flat-out accusation of sabotage against her significant other.

"Any chance this Eclipso character will put his search on a long hiatus because of the hoaxers?" was Daniela's initial response to Roberta's capsule summary of the West African misadventure. She posed this question just as she pulled into the parking lot of their College Park, Maryland condo, having driven Roberta home from the bus station beside the Baltimore airport.

"You're hoping for a long hiatus?" Roberta couldn't help bristling as she stepped out of Daniela's pickup truck, and heard multiple dogs barking up a storm. It peeved her no end that Daniela would sum up all she related with that one question, as much as she craved her love after being away so many weeks. And she couldn't let it stop there. "Do you think hoaxes might convince Eclipso to stop the search altogether? Is that your wish?!?!?!"

Daniela angrily slammed shut the driver's side door of her pickup, and shouted loudly enough to be heard above her pooch's continuing arf-arfs, "I don't care what Eclipso does next! For your sake, I hope you all stumble across enough surviving dinosaurs to pack a zoo! I really do, Roberta honey," she softened tearfully. "But you don't know how hard it is here without you. I'm up every morning at six to walk Charles and Phillip before I open the pet shop. And hardly a day goes by that I don't have to cover for another employee who quit without giving advance notice. Or screwed up so bad, the bozo over my head should have fired his ass. And when I get home, there's always something. Last week, the hallway toilet overflowed and the plunger didn't unclog it. I had to call a plumber who insisted on cash only. I'm not complaining..."

By this portion of what Roberta creepily sensed was a well-rehearsed speech, Daniela had come alongside her, put an arm round her waist. Rather than feeling genuine affection, though, it seemed to Roberta more like Daniela was making sure she didn't stray from approaching the front door to their condo. "I just wish you were here longer. That's all."

So we can have more of this whoopty-do fun that has me wanting to call a taxi? Roberta couldn't help despairing bitterly. She wriggled free of Daniela's guiding arm and, turning towards her, asked firmly, "You want me here longer for what, exactly?"

Dachshunds Prince Charles and Prince Phillip barked all the more excitedly as they sensed Daniela and Roberta's ever-closer presence.

"Well, you've shut the door on more adoptions!" Daniela complained harshly, shouting again to be heard above the increasingly frantic dachshund barks that had neighbor lights winking on.

"If that's something you want to take full responsibility for, have at it! I'm not going to stop you!"

"Roberta, you know I can't just drop everything like you do with your dinosaur search, to pursue something *I* really want to do, for a change," Daniela reacted in a voice Roberta found eerily monotone, flat. "Someone has to always be here for our children," she added while opening the front door to their condo.

"I thought the pet store, and..." Roberta suddenly felt overwhelmed by the futility of arguing any further. Daniela's absurd lurch from talk of more adopted dogs to lamenting how pet care, care for "our children," was holding her back from pursuing whatever she really wanted to do... When Daniela originally asked if she could shack up with Roberta, she begged her to also welcome her two pet dachshunds. The promised understanding was that Prince Charles and Prince Phillip were her responsibility, not Roberta's. Any help Roberta pitched in, Daniela would consider "above and beyond."

"Who's a good boy? Who's a good boy?" playfully asked Daniela, whipping Prince Charles and Prince Phillip into even more of a frenzy. They leapt about like they were on a trampoline, when they weren't racing back and forth in the foyer.

"Who's a good boy??!!" growled someone male from a nearby window. "I'll show you who's a very bad boy if you two freaks don't shut up your damned mutts!!"

Slam! Daniela kicked the door closed behind her as she went down on her knees for Prince Charles and Prince Phillip to lick her face, their tails wagging a mile a minute. "Such a royal greeting! Such a royal greeting!" Then seeing the two pooches leave her to sniff and snort at Roberta, who remained standing, Daniela added, "See how much they miss you?"

Yep, nothing says 'royal greeting' quite like excitement pee sprayed everywhere. "Look, I'm beyond exhausted," Roberta lied in lieu of the pee stuff, and headed for the nearest couch to flop down.

"Can I get you something? Are you okay?"

Roberta pulled a bottle of green tea from her backpack. "Just allow me to..."

"Let's find you a *Scooby-Doo* cartoon," said Daniela to the dachshunds, leading them to her and Roberta's bedroom.

Thereafter, whenever Daniela checked in on Roberta, Roberta faked being totally conked out asleep. All that while, she sought within herself the resolve either to recommit to their relationship, maybe even suggest joint counseling, or to make a clean break from Daniela. Anything but this endless purgatorial indecision, using the dinosaur search to postpone the inevitable.

Roberta Quiñones was struck by just how much of a mess the condo had turned into, without her around to enforce routine cleanup. Her lover talked big about holding down the fort while she was gone. But Roberta could see into the kitchen that the sink burst full of unwashed pots and pans. And a pizza box stuck out from under the trash can lid, as though the trash can itself were some filthy Christmas stocking of the damned, Roberta imagined. She also had to wonder how many bottles had been thrown in there that should have gone into recycling.

Closer to the couch where she pretended an exhausted collapse, Roberta spotted corn-chip crumbs, dog hairs, and heaven-knew-what scattered everywhere. Clearly, the beige carpet hadn't been vacuumed for the longest while. Perhaps not since she last did it before heading out to Papua, New Guinea.

Then there were the discarded videogame boxes on the floor beside Daniela's chair of choice, for way too many late-night sessions in pursuit of just one more *Petunia Pretzel* level before retiring to sleep.

Will have to scrutinize the next credit-card statement extra closely, Roberta told herself as she absent-mindedly pondered the Celtic design of entangled Welsh dragons on the pendant of a silver necklace, Daniela's gift. That was on the eve of departure for Papua, New Guinea. Given out of pure love, or to guilt Roberta out of leaving her permanently?

No such agonizing for Laura Gómez, where work associate Tom was concerned, Tom who happily handled her *Out There* column for *The Puffington Post* while she was on most secretive assignment. She hadn't the least concern the copper bracelet he gave her was anything other than an expression of his total infatuation with her. Yes, there was the fig leaf excuse of investigating claimed "woo-woo" health advantages from wearing certain metals. But that simple, no-strings-attached joy he exuded on her stopping by his office…

"Señorita Gómez! This is an unexpected pleasure!" Tom rose to his feet enthusing after Laura entered and gently shut the door behind her. Under other circumstances, colleagues would have followed her in. But not lost on any of them was a romance brewing, best lent some privacy. "Please," he motioned towards a chair facing his desk. "Did you bring any photos we could use of you horseback-riding a Triceratops?"

"I could have flown aboard a Diplodocus balloon the size of a Thanksgiving-Day-Parade float, as it deflated."

"Oh-oh; not another hoax."

"Another hoax, Tom. That's okay; Eclipso is intent on eluding whoever it is, next leg of the search. There might even be a saboteur in our midst."

"'A saboteur in our midst'; wow, that sounds like an espionage adventure. But I see you're still wearing the copper bracelet. Haven't completed my article on that yet, so do you have anything interesting to report? Protection from those hoaxers? Or other conferred benefits?"

"Haven't had any dandelions growing out of my ears since you gave it to me, Tom."

"That's good; I know those were becoming such a nuisance."

"One thing it hasn't protected me from, though." Laura pulled her chair closer to Tom's desk, close as she could. Then she leaned over, suggestive he should lean over as well, for sharing something most confidential.

When Tom obliged, she planted a lingering kiss on his lips. "Oh," he gasped. "So, it's a bracelet with those kind of benefits? Better keep it on, then."

"Wouldn't dream of taking it off," she responded breathlessly into his ear.

Eclipso recruited only one couple to be aboard Cloud Nine for ventures into hoped-for dinosaur habitats. Yet sadly, their short respite from the search proved very unsettling, all the way around.

Harriet Letterman fully anticipated her parents would seize on her and Harry's couple of weeks home to make the case for their abandoning the project altogether. What she didn't expect was that her husband would agree, in any way, shape or form. Even worse, he did so right in front her parents, Sally and Stu Rosenberg.

"Goodness," Sally reacted in her trademark girlishly high-pitched voice as, round the kitchen breakfast table, Harriet concluded her recounting of their West African experience. "How unfortunate, what happened with that balloon. But I'd say they're very lucky it didn't crash-land on their heads."

"Or capsize their boat," Stu added. "You two are pretty lucky as well; what if that thing had collided with Cloud Nine?"

"Oh, no worry there," said Harry in his groaning voice, with a dismissive hand wave. "Samuel Longbottom would have easily flown Cloud Nine out of the way."

"And our altitude was too high for it to reach us," said Harriet to Harry's nodding, bespectacled grin.

"But didn't you say there was a mysterious, slow-moving something also at a high altitude, that glowed? That your team wasn't sure wasn't a giant bat or bird?"

"Actually, we were wondering whether it might be a flying reptile such as a Pterodactyl," corrected Harry.

"A Pterodactyl," Sally repeated with her girlish voice gone breathless.

"Then what if a Pterodactyl had attacked Cloud Nine?" asked Stu.

"That would have really been something!" enthused Harriet with her own bespectacled grin.

Harry appeared a bit taken aback, to the parents' encouragement.

"This is the point, guys," Stu went on. "There are so many things that could have gone dangerously wrong! Things we haven't even addressed yet! For example, what if one of your crew had contracted some serious contagious disease, such as the Ebola virus, and spread it to you?"

"We didn't hear about anybody with Ebola anywhere near us," Harriet reacted defensively. Then she paused, waiting on Harry to chime in. But when she saw his eyes darting from side to side, like he had to think about what her Dad said, she added, "And we were inoculated against malaria and other diseases. Isn't that right, Harry?"

"Mmm-hm," Harry confirmed rather wanly.

Quick to pick up on Harry's seeming inner turmoil re the safety issue, Sally peppily asked, "With all your hi-tech equipment, couldn't you provide support remotely on a computer, from the safety of your own home? For the most part, didn't you remain aboard Cloud Nine, away from the center of action?"

"That's true," Harry agreed, with far more enthusiasm than he confirmed they'd been vaccinated. He added, "I think your mom has a point there, Harriet sweetie." Harriet's attention to the charismatic charms of Alistair Frump fueled him with jealousy.

"If their third trip is anything like the first two, they won't be anywhere near our time zone!" bristled Harriet turning to Harry. "They could be needing our in-put middle of the night where we are. And then there would be the time delay for our response! We need to be on the front lines, when and where the discovery might happen! That completes who I am!"

Pursuant to which conversation, Harriet had to ask herself: Would Harry be capable of helping the hoaxers, just to stay home rather than travel?

"Yes, of course, Sherman Peabody; please feel free to speak up at any time," Eclipso reacted presently, waving a half-eaten pretzel in the direction of Sherman's timidly raised hand.

"And I thank you for that, sir. I was just thinking on how the element of quantum uncertainty you've introduced fairly mirrors the uncertainty as to our ultimate goal. Quantum physics suggests that an electron is at no one particular location until it is measured. Rather, it's at multiple locations simultaneously. Or rather, there is a probability wave function for where it might reside, the lowest probability being in a distant galaxy."

"That would make perfect f-n' sense, I suppose, if I were smokin' enough wacky tobacky," grumbled Sergeant Frankly. "You ought to get together with our first officer who figured out time travel! See who can blow the other's mind more completely! Jesus Reptilian Christ!" he swore, noticing Bonsai Gator seeming to shake his head disdainfully at him. "For a critter I could probably flatten with a fly swatter, you sure are one judgmental-looking S.O.B.!"

With a sigh, Sherman went on, "In the same way, where next for our dinosaur search resides in many possible locations until Eclipso chooses one for us. Wherefore the parallel uncertainty of our common goal. Non-avian dinosaurs might be surviving at several different locations, simultaneously, until our quantitative investigations measure it at one particular location."

"Or measure it at *no* particular location," amended Stephen. "Under which circumstance such a creature exists nowhere at all. Perhaps your Artificial Intelligence Entity, Charly, would like to weigh in on that possibility?"

Charly looked to Augie like it gave a start, as if being woken from a nap, followed by a whir and a click. "I am not aware of any new evidence that bears on the question of non-avian dinosaur survival, especially any evidence that weighing would help to analyze."

"The old evidence is so much bull excrement, I hope you know," snarked Stephen.

Click...whirr... "I did not know. Was the bull suspected of having feasted on non-avian dinosaur flesh, prior to the execration? And did subsequent DNA analysis of the excrement turn up possible dinosaur DNA?"

"I was speaking of bull excrement in the figurative sense."

Click...whirr... "So was an analysis run searching for figurative DNA?"

"Please shut yourself down, Charly," sighed Sherman.

Whirr...click!

Chapter 4

"If you keep standing guard, Milton Nascimento, we'll have to rename you The Sentinel," playfully warned Ron.

The majestic hyacinth macaw perched statuesquely still atop the railing of Ron and Rosa's fifteenth-floor condo balcony. Far as they knew, he'd been there endless hours. He appeared intently focused on something far side of the muddy Guamá River.

Was it the landfill pit, looking like a yawning abyss ever since the sudden sinkhole there? As reported on local news? Or was another hyacinth macaw beckoning Milton Nascimento? Leaving him conflicted into paralysis between the easy, cashew-abundant shelter of his human caretakers, and the dangers of returning to rainforest adventure?

"If he spots something – or someone – he really wants, maybe he's going to leave us?" Rosa wondered.

"Then I'll buy you a legal canary, in a cage so he has to stay, and you can torture him whenever you want."

"Maybe I'll put *you* in a cage, *caro!*"

"Ai!"

Just then, they heard a clarion call down below on Avenida Portugal from the *trem da alegria* (train of joy). A steel-drum, calypso version of Beethoven's "Ode To Joy" blared from the lead car built to look like a small-scale version of an old-style steam locomotive.

Ron was reminded of distinctive music announcing the arrival of an ice cream truck to his suburban neighborhood near Racine, Wisconsin on scorching-hot July afternoons, when breezes blew in from the west rather than off Lake Michigan. The tune was usually "Turkey In The Straw."

"Is the *trem da alegria* what you've been waiting for, Milton Nascimento?" Ron asked the hyacinth macaw still perched statuesquely still beside him, as he looked down over the balcony railing at the parked *trem* taking on passengers. "If so, you better hurry up so they don't leave without you."

Milton Nascimento simply bobbed his head to the endlessly repeated calypso version of Beethoven's "Ode To Joy" summoning the faithful to party.

Meanwhile, alongside the lead car with open-air, flat-bed carriages in tow, a variety of super-hero-costumed figures boogied up a storm.

"Ron *caro*, I feel like I'm seeing something strange without knowing exactly what it is," said Rosa sounding more excited than concerned. She joined Ron at the railing, the opposite side of perched Milton Nascimento.

"Me too...again. Wait," he pointed at the costumed dancers. "Look; there are two Katydiddlys!" *And one's long green tail, whipping from side to side like a metronome, just dissolved from view!*

"That's right!" exclaimed Rosa, about the two Katydiddlys at least.

"SQUAWK!!"

In the alternate universe of mysteriously spirited-away weapons caches worldwide, Katydiddly was a popular comic-book superhero. The origin story went that Jane Bland led a humble existence as an exceptionally caring hospital nurse. That is, until one day a katydid, a bright green grasshopper-like insect, nibbled at her earlobe. It was an oddly special katydid, accidentally exposed to special cosmic rays when a tornado freakishly whirled her into the ionosphere before just-as-freakishly lowering her back to the ground. Thanks to that katydid's fateful nibble, Jane developed extraordinary powers, in addition to shape-shifting into a human-insect hybrid. She could hop over anything in a single bound, even a mountain range. And she could spit out a brown substance that produced a sticky thin filament for seizing bad guys, then swinging them around until they surrendered.

No sooner did Ron return to the balcony with his binoculars than Rosa pushed them aside. She looked into his eyes with a glint in her own by turns exhilarated and affectionately loving. "Let's go!" she said.

"You mean–"

"*Espere por nós! (Wait for us!)*" Rosa shouted over the railing.

"We're just going to let Milton Nascimento stay alone on the balcony?!" Ron asked, though already halfway to the door, Rosa towing him along.

"If he leaves us, he leaves us!"

*

Ron and Rosa ran the gauntlet of dancers in superhero garb, plus that extra Katydiddly. They were still boogieing hard to a calypso version of Beethoven's "Ode to Joy."

Aboard the *trem da alegria*, Ron and Rosa found themselves in the company of the usual suspects. Those included a group of Japanese tourists, a Brazilian couple with their eager young son and daughter, and a teenaged Brazilian couple who could keep neither their hands nor lips off each other, even while boarding.

"That looks like fun," said Ron, pointing at the smooching couple. "Want to give it a try?"

As Rosa slapped Ron on the arm, the smoochers' impassioned writhing-about writhed them falling off their bleacher seat. With a big klunk!, they found themselves sprawled on the floor of the open-air flatbed car. Which meant they not only missed seeing Superman thrust his hips in an obscene tribute to them – as if they wouldn't have missed that anyway. They also missed seeing the Japanese tourists cover their faces, modestly trying to conceal their amusement. And most importantly – what really got Rosa and Ron's attention – they never saw the two Katydiddlys board the *trem*.

Crouching like two behemoth toads, the one Katydiddly leapt onto the same flatbed car where Rosa, Ron and the smoochers were located. Then the second one followed suit in what struck Ron as an impossible maneuver. It leapfrogged the first one, without knocking into the roof of the flatbed car.

Rosa and Ron, clutching the top of the backrest ahead of them as tightly as had they boarded a roller coaster, exchanged wide-eyed looks. Should they be terrified, or happily thrilled?

The first Katydiddly to hop onto the open-air flatbed car consulted with Superman too softly for them to overhear above the steel drum din of the calypso "Ode To Joy." But Ron figured it was something to the effect of, *Who the hell is that second Katydiddly?*

With a here-we-go bell-ringing, the *trem da alegria* moved slowly underway, and Superman approached the second Katydiddly. By then, that apparently green-costumed superhero duplicate was clinging to the outside frame of the flatbed car, with seeming ease. With so much seeming ease, in fact, Ron was reminded of an Anatole lizard clinging to a wall. Above all the continuing racket, he couldn't discern what Superman said to Katydiddly 2. But he was certain it had to be something to the effect of *Where did you come from? Are you sure you were assigned to the correct* trem? *I thought there was only one of each superhero assigned per* trem.

Whatever Superman said, Katydiddly 2 reacted simply by baring teeth unusually long and sharp for any human. Whether or not they were costume teeth, Superman made an okay-just-asking gesture, and quickly backed off.

Where Rosa and Ron were concerned, things eventually got even weirder, far weirder than the *trem da alegria's* usual trippy strangeness.

Among the more typical *trem da alegria* hi-jinx, the superheroes would hop off, do something outrageous, then run hopping back on board again. This time was certainly no different.

Superman, for example, deboarded near a little boy contentedly licking his chocolate ice cream cone. He scooped the ice cream off the cone, and sprinted over behind a guy in swim trunks, obliviously surfing the internet on his smart phone. Superman pulled wide open the rear of the trunks, dumped in the scooped-off ice cream, let go, and hurriedly retraced his steps to the stunned little boy. Crouching down beside him for seriously intoned apologies, he gently handed him a rubber snake.

Once Superman leapt back aboard the *trem*, it sped up to outpace the enraged guy running after him, said guy's swimsuit dripping a trail of chocolate ice cream.

There were on-board hi-jinx as well.

Christmas-tree-style lights brightly illuminated the interior of Rosa and Ron's open-air flatbed car in the rapidly descending equatorial darkness, as Katydiddly 1 climbed onto one of the metal poles supporting the car's arcing roof. Katydiddly 1 swung around on the pole to hang outside, partially cloaked in night shade. Then, as the *trem da alegria* passed several road signs, loud thumps suggested the green superhero got unwittingly slammed against them.

Ron assumed an illusion at work he still couldn't figure out, despite how many times he'd seen it previously. In other words, that wasn't any weirder than normal.

Weirder than normal was all about the second Katydiddly. It appeared to mimic the first one, clinging to one of the metal poles, and hanging outside the open-air flatbed car at an angle. Only, Katydiddly 2 clearly ducked each road sign in passing, to keep from being clobbered, no optical illusion about it. Still, though, to Rosa and Ron's utter bafflement, there were thumps similar to the thumps from the first Katydiddly. Moreover, with the first Katydiddly, each road sign remained perfectly still, despite the oversized insectoid head seeming slammed against them. However, those signs clearly wobbled from side to side, each time a thump accompanied Katydiddly 2 passing them by...like something powerful slapped them hard.

Kids aboard the *trem da alegria* pointed and giggled at the first Katydiddly seemingly pummeled senseless by street signs. The smoochers came up for air on only the very first thump! And the Japanese tourists cringed with every thump! as though they themselves were being sideswiped by the road signs. They had no idea the strangest was yet to come, albeit typical for the *trem*.

On an especially loud thump!, Katydiddly 1 appeared knocked off its perch altogether, somersaulting across the ground beside the track-less *trem da alegria*. Not to fear, though: Superman to the rescue, albeit pausing to snatch a pair of purple panties out of thin air.

As from a volcanic eruption, clothes were spewing skyward from the bleacher seat where the smoochers descended to the floor. The panties were among them.

Superman leapt off the *trem da alegria* onto the first Katydiddly's shoulders.

The male smoocher, his face all but lost amidst his tousled hair, looked up dazedly over the backrest. But a hand wielding inch-long fingernails, intricately painted to look like stained glass windows, quickly pulled him back down below again. *Might as well be octopus tentacles dragging him to his fate*, Ron mused.

Ron and Rosa noticed Katydiddly 1 carrying Superman on his shoulders alongside the *trem*, Superman swinging the panties around triumphantly in the air. That is, until he leapt off just long enough to pull them down over a police officer's head, before leaping back onto Katydiddly 1 again.

By the time the police officer untangled himself from the panties, the *trem da alegria* was already well down the road.

That's when Ron and Rosa heard coming from a distance, cutting through all the *trem*'s party-time commotion, a squawked rendition of a refrain to Milton Nascimento's love song, "Anima," repeated over and over.

"*Te quero ver,*
 Te quero ser alma."

(I want to see you, I want to be your soul.)

Rosa and Ron turned each other's way and exclaimed simultaneously, "That's our Milton Nascimento!"

"Something crazy in the atmosphere carrying his voice this far," remarked Ron, shocked to hear the macaw quoting Nascimento at such length.

"Not so far," countered Rosa, pointing. "Look, *caro*, we're going right beside our condo!"

"I'm following the second Katydiddly who bared those scary teeth. She's just leaped off- Wait; where's she headed?!" Ron couldn't keep a hint of alarm out of his voice.

To Ron's unexpected relief, Katydiddly 2 scampered back on board the *trem*.

Superman still riding piggyback, Katydiddly 1 tightrope-walked the railing of a short bridge the *trem da alegria* was crossing, over a small tributary from the Guamá River. Halfway, though, Katydiddly 1 acted as though having lost balance, and suddenly disappeared off the railing. But

Superman hopped off Katydiddly 1's shoulders, leaned over the railing, and blew her a kiss, then ran jumping back aboard the *trem*.

Most passengers aside from the smoochers were left by turns gasping and giggling. Then Katydiddly 1 suddenly materialized out of the darkness, running to catch up to the *trem* as its speakers blared the Bee Gees' disco tune, "Stayin' Alive." That's when Rosa and Ron realized they'd lost track of Katydiddly 2.

"There!" Ron pointed towards a three-story warehouse, home to an impressive variety of food, clothing, and souvenir stalls, everything from honey-roasted cashews to stuffed-animal cartoon characters such as the ever-popular *Abraços Girafa* (Hugs, the Giraffe). Beyond it loomed one side of Rosa and Ron's high-rise condo facing the Guamá River.

"What am I supposed to see?" asked Rosa, straining to discern anything special or unusual.

""You're going to think I'm crazy, *caro*,-"

"'Going to'?" Rosa laughed.

"Okay, what I meant to say is, you're not going to hear any good reason to not continue to suspect I'm totally insane," Ron quipped as his sweetie gave him a reassuring hug. "Could have sworn I saw that second Katydiddly make an impossible leap from the market warehouse roof to the side of our condo building, then scamper upwards like a lizard!"

"Ai!"

"'Ai' indeed. Just before I lost it in the darkness, also could have sworn I glimpsed a long tail! For the second time tonight!"

"Ahhhhh!" "Uhhhhh!" came ecstatic cries rising from where the smooching couple had sunk from sight.

"So it took my strange creature report for you guys to finally climax?" Ron shouted.

Rosa was about to give Ron the hardest slap on his arm she could muster, plus lecture him on how he should not be so crass in the presence of children and foreign tourists aboard the *trem da alegria*. But soon as she made eye contact with him, something dawned on both. "Milton Nascimento!" they shouted at each other simultaneously, anew, and leapt off the *trem* to race for their condo.

*

"Milton Nascimento is still out on the balcony railing," said Rosa. "He appears okay. But look, *caro*; he's doing this dance side to side like he's swooning."

"I *would* look, but something's happened to our sofa," said Ron having just turned on the living room lights. "I think Milton Nascimento was a very bad boy!"

"SQUAWK!!"

"Not our Milton Nascimento!" protested Rosa re-entering the living room from the balcony. "You hear how upset you're- Oh!" Rosa gasped, seeing how badly the rattan sofa's middle cushion was shredded. Torn-out stuffing formed a circle there.

"Milton Nascimento!" Rosa shouted at the still-swooning hyacinth macaw as she stomped back out onto the balcony towards him. "Have you been ripping apart our sofa to make a nest? You should have asked so we could provide you with all the twigs you needed! We even could have added silky ribbons, if you wanted a splash of color to impress your sweetie!

"Umm, Ron?" said Rosa with an abrupt change of tone as in, *Something's got me worried.*

"What, did some magician aboard the *trem* make your bra disappear, again?" Ron asked, trying to make light of Rosa's concern even before he knew what it was, as he joined her out on the balcony.

"Look carefully at Milton Nascimento's beak and claws," Rosa said, ignoring her husband's snark. "If he was the one destroying our cushion, shouldn't he have snared a stray thread or two on them?"

After Ron joined Rosa's careful inspection of the macaw's claws and beak, he looked up the same time she did. "Not Katydiddly 2?" he asked incredulously.

"No!" Rosa shook her head dismissively. "There must be another macaw nearby who answered Milton Nascimento's mimicry of the love song, or saw him doing his mating dance, or both."

"And she paid him a courtship visit, to show him that if they're going to live under our roof, she needs to redecorate? I think we should consult our local bird lady, Aninha!"

Chapter 5

The football-field-sized, steam-powered drone, Cloud Nine, was descending through the middle of a raging rainforest thunderstorm.

Augie Matias and company not only heard crashes of thunder, albeit muffled. They saw lightning flashes at strobe light frequency. Those flashes illuminated torrents of rain on the control center's panoramic view-screen. But for all that, Cloud Nine's stabilizing propellers held the drone so steady, Augie and company felt like they might as well have been slowly descending an elevator.

Plenty soon enough, the storm was spent. Clouds other than the single enormous one generated by Cloud Nine dissipated rapidly, and equatorial sun shined brightly on a muddy tributary of the Amazon River. Dense jungle stretched as far as the eye could see. And a large, circular hut accompanied by smaller, tin-roofed structures lined one riverbank, a few canoes tied near shore.

A Yanomami shabono? Augie asked himself. He recalled a communal building he frequented years ago while digging for what he hoped would be post-Mesozoic dinosaur fossils in Amazonia.

Suddenly, the display of what spread out underneath Cloud Nine shrank over to the left half of the view-screen. The right half showed Bonsai Gator swooning in time to a reggae version of "Tomorrow Never Knows" by the Beatles, performed by the Beatles reggae cover band, Yellow Dubmarine.

"Turn off your mind, relax, and float downstream…" went John Lennon's dreamy lyrics.

"I am so so sorry, my dearest Bonsai Gator," Eclipso Sunray Smith addressed the pencil-thin gator standing pencil-erect on his two hind legs, his little tail providing balance. "I see how contentedly you are floating on the music stream. The time has come, however, for our big reveal on the next step of our quest you believe is such a good idea."

As the reggae-fied Beatles tune cut off, Bonsai Gator slumped over while still standing on his hind legs. He made a shrugging motion with his two front legs since he really didn't have any shoulders. And off-screen, he trundled back down into the miniature swamp with which Eclipso's expansive conference table was embedded.

"Poor little guy," folk myth specialist Irene McDowell couldn't help remarking, looking on from Cloud Nine's control center view-screen.

"Look," said professional skeptic Stephen Feldman, freighting that one little word with loads of exasperation, "Bonsai Gator isn't bummed out over Eclipso cutting off the music. Most likely, he had his eye on one of those miniaturized dragonflies. He was going after it whether the music cut off, or not."

"Who said anything about Bonsai being bummed out?" Irene asked, playing totally innocent.

"Didn't you just say, 'poor little guy'? C'mon! I could see you feeling sorry for him because Eclipso turned off 'his' reggae Beatles!"

"A wee bit defensive, are we? Doth protest too much?" Good fun getting under Stephen's skin, where Irene was concerned.

"Okay," Stephen huffed and puffed, mission accomplished for Irene. "Bonsai Gator is one of the intellectual giants of our time, and ought to have been enrolled at Cambridge alongside Magdalena." He referred to the teenage girl who guided Eclipso's team through a hoax-ridden dinosaur search on New Britain

Island off the north coast of Papua, New Guinea earlier in the year.

"Bonsai Gator to Cambridge?" scoffed Eclipso, gesturing with a half-eaten, humus-smeared pretzel in his Ankylosaurus mansion. He sat thousands of miles away in west central Pennsylvania, his mother standing stalwart behind him, as always. Although, Augie noticed her suddenly stop moving her jaw like she had been chewing on something. "That's crazy talk," Eclipso scoffed some more. "Bonsai could never abide their dress code."

"You mean the part about wearing anything at all," chuckled aspiring golf-course developer Alistair Frump, also from on board Cloud Nine alongside Irene and company.

"Exactly! And they wouldn't be too keen on his carrying a portable swamp along with him, wherever he went."

Timid cryptozoology museum curator Bernie Coleman wanted to ask, *Is a portable swamp even a thing?* But by the time he worked up the gumption to open his mouth, before he could utter a peep, Eclipso went on, "Samuel Longbottom has brought you into a steady hover above a tributary of the Amazon River. The exact location will remain a secret for now. That should thwart our pestering hoaxers, or at least give them far less time to prepare. Ah, I can see your eyes pop out, Dr. Matias. Of course, I know all about your dig for post-extinction-boundary-layer dinosaur fossils. Care to elaborate for our fellow partners in crime?"

"Scott, Bernie, Roberta," said Augie obligingly as he turned away from the view-screen to face his colleagues, "think I already shared this with you three, at least. Several years ago, I journeyed to a region in the Amazon very similar to what we're seeing down below us now. Searched a rock outcropping there, for fossil evidence a small number of dinosaurs survived to the early Miocene, some twenty million years ago. Well, the pieces of large reptilian vertebrae the locals described turned out to be from a thirty-foot-long prehistoric anaconda, a significant discovery in its own right. Other than that, we found a single tooth from a duck-billed dinosaur named Hadrosaur. It was lodged inside the fossil rib cage of a Megatherium, a giant prehistoric ground sloth. However, the Miocene strata contained slivers of Cretaceous strata. So, we couldn't say for sure the tooth wasn't reworked to the Miocene from the Cretaceous."

"And now we will search for a living non-avian dinosaur that reworked its way into the present along the Amazon River, rather than digging for old bones, yes?" enthused Eclipso.

"Wait," said Stephen in what Bernie would have described as his party-pooper voice. "Anywhere in the Amazon, you're treading very close to the Yucatan peninsula, ground zero for the catastrophic asteroid impact sixty-five million years ago. For dinosaur survival, at least you could argue that Africa, and New Guinea especially, are a good distance away."

"But even closer to the impact zone, zamia cycads from the early Mesozoic thrive along the north coast of Puerto Rico," pushed back Dr. Roberta Quiñones from the University of Maryland. "Not to mention numerous iguanas, frogs…"

"All of which obviously repopulated there from far more distant, less-impacted locations," Stephen pushed back on the push-back.

"Surviving non-avian dinosaurs couldn't have also eventually repopulated there? I mean to the Amazon? Further away than Puerto Rico from the Yucatan?" Irene leapt in.

"Instead of getting bogged down in that argument," intervened journalist Laura Gómez, "I'd like to hear from you, Eclipso, on specifically what brings us here. This certainly has to be about more than one twenty-million-year-old Hadrosaur fossil tooth that might be far older."

Eclipso took a deep breath, to brace himself for broaching a matter still most painful for him. "Very well, then," he said at last. "I've mentioned before that shortly after my dear wife, Agnes, delivered Bonsai Gator to me, a sinkhole swallowed her near the Amazon River. She was on temporary diversion from our search for pygmy non-avian dinosaurs in the South Pacific.

"Reports had emerged of something enormous burrowing underneath a *Yanomami* settlement some hundred eighty miles south of Belém, Brazil. With Crusader Rabbit zeal, Agnes combed that entire region for the beast. In the process, she hoped to help the locals stave off developers from clearing the nearby rainforest jungle for a cattle ranch. Said ranch would supply burger meat to fast-food restaurants...and its cows would send lots of additional methane gas into the atmosphere, contributing to the nascent global warming crisis.

"The best thinking at the time was that rather than any dinosaur, a relic surviving monster snake – a Titanoboa, perhaps – was doing the undermining. We know Titanoboas roamed Colombia fifty million years ago, with bodies the circumference of a school bus. One of them might have created the sinkhole into which my beloved Agnes - Sniff! - disappeared, never to be seen again. Although none of this has been confirmed."

"I am profoundly sorry for your loss," said Stephen in a sincerely somber tone. "But before you go blaming an impossibly large extinct snake for that sinkhole, there are other far more plausible scenarios to consider. You must be well aware the land adjacent to any large body of water such as the Amazon is especially susceptible to sinkhole development. Simple erosion processes, dissolved limestone for example, are all the explanation needed. And those developers you mentioned, I've read that in remote, lawless parts of the Amazon rainforest basin, they are especially prone to violence for thwarting environmental activists. Wouldn't put it past them to have used underground explosives to produce a sinkhole, just as certain undesired people walked by."

Eclipso's long silent stare at Stephen Feldman was mediated by the view-screen video transmitting from thousands of miles away. But that did nothing to dilute how unsettling Stephen found such regard.

"Mr. Feldman," Eclipso said at last, still gesturing with his partially eaten humus-lathered pretzel, "I assume you've seen a shark fin dart through water?"

"Okay."

"Not it's not okay if you've never seen-"

"Okay, yes, on TV I have seen video of a great white shark fin."

"Then imagine that instead, you see a two-story, wood-framed hut move through a swamp."

"On a flatbed trailer? No problem."

"Not on a flatbed trailer, Mr. Feldman. Not on anything but the swamp itself. That's what two eyewitnesses described from the exact same location where minutes earlier, Agnes vanished into a sinkhole that rapidly filled with swamp water. Those witnesses could hear the water rushing in just before the hut started to migrate."

Click...whirr... "I'm not hearing anything relevant to the search for a living non-avian dinosaur," suddenly complained Sherman Peabody's robot named Charly. That is, if it could be called complaining rather than mere observation, emotionally detached like the artificial intelligence entity's monotone, robotic voice.

"I've reactivated you to simply take in the present conversation, Charly. Not to give your own input yet,"

Sherman advised the casually dressed, unblinkingly wide-eyed character standing beside him.

"That is not relevant information, either," Charly responded, again sounding monotone, if not absolutely deadpan.

Sherman clicked a button on the nape of Charly's neck, and Charly slumped over as though with really bad back posture.

"I would have asked my AI to turn himself off," explained Sherman. "But I believe he was getting stuck in a feedback loop where instead of following my command, he would have said it wasn't relevant to the dinosaur search, either."

"What does 'AI' stand for again?" asked Irene dubiously.

"Far as I'm concerned, it stands for Artificial Idiot," muttered Sergeant Fred Frankly.

"We're wasting time, people, as generous as I'm intent on being with that most precious gift in aid of our quest," said Eclipso. "Not to panic you or anything like that, but Bonsai Gator has indicated a certain sense if not of urgency, then of not wanting us to take too long."

"Not urgency, but 'not wanting us to take too long,' wow," remarked *Puffington Post* journalist Laura Gómez as she scribbled furiously. She envisioned eventually writing her tell-all book about Eclipso's dinosaur quest.

"Yeah, couldn't you feel the panic in Bonsai's latest reggae dance moves before he returned to that swamplet or whatever-the-f--- we should call it?" Fred vented yet again. He fervently wished any second to find himself reawakening back aboard the starship Smoke and Mirrors, eighty years hence.

"Aninha Floresta is not a name I imagine would mean anything to you," Eclipso plowed ahead, unfazed. "But 'floresta' is Portuguese for 'forest.' And forest she is, spirit of the forest working hard to thwart would-be cattle ranchers. Ever since Agnes vanished, she has been my main contact for all Brazilian things cryptozoological. Just last week, she reached out to me with a report of a decidedly dinosaurian bent."

"Another eighty-million-year-old Hadrosaur fossil tooth found worked into twenty-million-year-old Miocene rock strata?" Stephen snarked as usual.

Again, Eclipso gave Stephen one of his withering stare-downs, then said, "Yes, of course: an eighty-million-year-old fossil tooth that's been producing tremors at nineteen-day intervals near a gold-prospecting area of Brazil, over the past three months. And coincidentally close by where the sinkhole swallowed up Agnes. Only there's no fossil tooth involved, and Aninha reports something else that makes this situation of special interest to us.

"The working explanation-"

"Which before we hear it, I'm just guessing is what you should stick with," Stephen snarked anew.

After a weary sigh, Eclipso pointedly picked right back up where he left off, saying, "The working explanation was a relic Titanoboa molting, or undergoing one of its other biological cycles. Egg gestation, perhaps."

"Okay, I rescind what I said about sticking with the working explanation."

"She also raised the possibility a herd of relic Glypto-donts-"

"Glyptodonts?" interrupted Irene. "You mean those prehistoric armadillos the size of a rhinoceros?"

"Exactly," confirmed Eclipso, pointing what was left of his pretzel at his view-screen, Irene's direction. "The thinking goes that just like our widely-extant armadillos, any surviving Glyptodonts habitually burrow. Perhaps a bunch of them are moving through, or rather directly underneath, the *Yanomami* settlement in question. But they only have the stamina to dig so many feet at a time, taking nineteen-day breathers in between."

"Could I please see what's behind door number three?" wearily asked Stephen, alluding to television game shows.

"You won't much care for that any better than the two other possibilities I've outlined," said Eclipso. "Something more substantial backs it up, though. And that's what brings us there. You see, it wasn't only those periodic tremors that prompted gold prospectors to flee the area, and left would-be cattle ranchers extremely frustrated. Aninha spoke with the wife of one prospector who told her something quite amazing. Her husband claims that one night, he not only saw an ostrich-sized dinosaur run in front of his fellow prospector's pickup truck. He also saw the head of a far larger dinosaur emerge from the ground, coincident to one of the earth tremors. Said tremor tossed his associate's pickup crashing onto its side. Then the smaller dinosaur disappeared into the larger one's mouth. And so did his associate."

"That's absurd!" complained Stephen. "How much Amazonian moonshine were they drinking? Or maybe they ingested some especially hallucinogenic mushrooms?"

"Neither. In fact, the wife reports that before her husband related his terrifying experience, he exhaled in her face to prove he hadn't been drinking. Plus, she said he came home much earlier than usual, clearly upset to an extreme."

"Sure," nodded Stephen. "Say his mining company fired him earlier that day. He would have had plenty of time to drink himself silly, sober up 'til no trace of booze was left on his breath, and then make it back home earlier than usual. What part of that explanation is anywhere near as implausible as a still-extant underground dinosaur causing earthquakes, sinkholes, and a two-story hut's migration through a swamp like a roaming shark fin?"

"There was a particular feature of the reported ostrich-sized dinosaur that adds a note of special credibility. The gold prospector in question told his wife it was partially feathered, as though a giant bird were half-way plucked, or suffered something comparable to mange. Mange is a peculiar skin disease that leaves some dogs and other furry creatures with patches of bare skin."

"Wait," said Stephen. "It was ostrich-sized, with feathers. Any thought given to the possibility it was, indeed, an ostrich that escaped someone's ranch, imported from Australia? Under the heading of if it looks like an ostrich, is feathered like an ostrich..."

"But remember it was only partially feathered," countered Scott MacDonald.

"Correct," confirmed Eclipso on view-screen. "What's more, it was reported to have had a long reptilian tail. That's not a feature of any ostrich with which I'm familiar."

"That feature could have been imagined, filled in from what he freaked himself into misapprehending he saw."

"But what about that giant dinosaur head that swallowed it in one fell swoop?" Bernie Coleman worked up the gumption to ask, albeit in his typically soft-spoken gentle voice.

"That's where the hallucinogenic mushrooms came in," Stephen was quick to respond in what Augie found a most flippantly irritating manner. "Far more likely that, than a Subterranean-o-saur causing earthquakes, comparable to what the Japanese used to superstitiously fear from monster catfish, centuries ago."

"Okay, let's suppose the Godzilla-sized dinosaur head was fueled by a panicky imagination more than anything else," said Augie. "In reality, whatever geological forces were at work caused an upheaval of swampland covered in green slime. As that upheaval subsided, it devoured the smaller creature in question, like quicksand."

"I'm good with that," nodded Stephen.

"Let's see if you're also good with this," Augie continued. "There is growing consensus among zoologists, regarding how so many reptiles and amphibians survived the Earth's deep freeze after an asteroid struck near the Yucatan peninsula sixty-five million years ago. It was their ability to hibernate for long periods of time. Even revive from a semi-frozen state, like iguanas do in Florida after rare deep freezes. Isn't it possible that whatever is causing those tremors every nineteen days has roused a remnant dinosaur population? From a long-enough sleep to shame Rumpelstiltskin? So, now's our chance to finally pin this down as in: the third expedition's the charm?"

Before Eclipso could respond, while Stephen closed his eyes and shook his head in extreme vexation, Harriet Letterman took her husband Harry by surprise. Without even raising a hand to be called on, she added, "We learned in West Africa that *something* strange is happening underground. That tunnel you explored along the Sangha River, Scott, I wish I could have explored also: Wasn't it too large for a hippopotamus to dig? And didn't part of it collapse like a sinkhole, right under your feet?"

"I would have liked to have been there too, sweetie-pie," said Harry, placing a hand tentatively over Harriet's hand, which she promptly batted away.

"Again, that was along a river, the Sangha River," Stephen valiantly, where he was concerned, observed. "Just like the tremors, and a moving hut, and a monster mouth swallowing an ostrich-like creature happened near a tributary of the Amazon River."

"Mr. Feldman, let's imagine you can prove ground movement related to river erosion is all we're really talking about in these situations. You will do our dinosaur quest a real service, as we will stop wasting time on a dead end," said Eclipso. "Into the bargain, if you could also give more definition regarding exactly what happened to my Agnes..."

"Of course, as you well know, Eclipso, I suspect there are nothing but dead ends where this quest is concerned," Stephen felt obliged to remark. He wanted to add something to the effect of, *If the possibility of your wife's survival is what you're after, I certainly don't want to be a party to giving you any cruel false hope.* But he refrained, figuring such a comment would also be cruel. Ditto for the observation that under rainforest conditions, Agnes's body had probably long since decayed away. At best, there might be a surviving strip of clothing, or piece of jewelry if she was into that sort of thing.

"We must never lose hope," would-be golf-course developer and Eclipso's financial partner, Alistair Frump, did say without a qualm in the world. "But about this business of a snake monster, or a herd of Glyptodonts, undermining a place with enough regularity to set a calendar! At first, I thought: That is not the sort of thing likely to send even the most eccentric of eccentric multi-millionaires flocking to a golf resort. On further cogitation, though, it occurred to me: Periodic upheavals, with the ground swelling like a balloon, and maybe Snakezilla occasionally lifting its head out, why that could become the new Old Faithful!"

Click...whirr... "I'm hearing too much idle speculation that provides zero useful information in the search for surviving non-avian dinosaurs," Charly robotically lifted himself out of his slumped-over posture to report.

"Too soon, people?" Sherman looked around to ask.

"Definitely too soon," Irene rushed to respond. "Assuming Charly is loaded to the hilt with detection and analysis devices galore, why not wait to reactivate it, him, whatever, until we're back out in the field?"

"Agreed. Charly, you can de-activate yourself."

Click...whirr... "I am well aware of that, Sherman...my friend."

"So do it. Now."

Click...whirr... "Roger that." Pressing a button on the nape of his artificial neck, Charly slumped over again, terrible posture.

*

Samuel Longbottom timed the descent of the mist-enshrouded Cloud Nine to coincide with an early afternoon gentle rainforest shower. That's when, on a daily basis, a naturally spawned cloud deck was in the habit of lowering. The idea was not to draw attention to the unusual spectacle of a cigarette boat loaded with Eclipso's amply paid search team descending out of Cloud Nine's self-generated mists, down to the tributary's smoothly running waters.

The *Yanomami* settlement where Augie and company would pow-wow with environmental activist Aninha Floresta lay just round a bend in the tributary. Aninha herself saw no sense in her compatriots being spooked by witnessing something that could prompt the more superstitious among them to worship the Eclipso team as oversized *Xapiripe* spirits...or want to execute them for being devils. Best that the *Yanomami* meet the search team bringing their boat ashore rather than descending from a cloud. Over the following days, Aninha could bit by bit explain to the local shaman. Especially that her foreign friends were opposed to rainforest clearing, because of how that might decimate possible relic dinosaur populations. Once he understood that, she was optimistic he would make sure they were treated well by fellow villagers.

Moreover, Aninha fully anticipated the greeting the search team would receive.

Back on shore, not more than fifty yards from the cigarette boat, Raul Viana, self-appointed leader of "rainforest development," emerged from a stand of several large ferns, pushing them aside.

Augie reacted by revving up the boat for quick departure, if deemed necessary.

That's when Raul brought a blow-dart gun near his lips. Aiming directly at Augie, he said, "You need to shut down that outboard motor, *senhor*." While Augie obeyed, Raul spread apart his arms and shouted to still be heard above the fading rain shower din, "What is this?! More surrogate imperialists from the United States, here to thwart our progress?!"

"You call burning down the rainforests, filling the planet's lungs with smoke, progress?!" angrily thundered Aninha Floresta, emerging dramatically from amidst a different thick stand of ferns not far from where Raul stood. Her massive figure dressed in black adorned with flamboyant bird-of-paradise and lilac flower designs made a huge impression on Augie. *She's not messing around.*

"Outnumbering you cannibal sympathizers who want to hold back Brazil from her glorious destiny, that's what I call REAL progress!"

"'Cannibal sympathizers'?! Ironic coming from a guy threatening them with a blow dart!" Aninha continued to brazenly thunder, even as Raul aimed his blow dart her way. "What is your blow dart arrow dipped in? A neuro-toxin fatal a minute after piercing the skin?! Or are you going with some especially hallucinogenic mushroom extract?!"

"She knows he doesn't dare harm her. Else every *Yanomami* in South America will be after him," Samuel confided to Augie via an earpiece.

"Should I have my partners in progress do target practice on your foreign interlopers, Aninha?!"

As Raul spoke, several heads popped out from amidst the ferns beside him, each one wielding a pistol.

"But first, let me guess," Raul went on. "They're capitalizing on those monster stories drunken fools have circulated, to scare people away from cattle ranching here."

"I don't know how anyone can capitalize on tremors every nineteen days that are out of everyone's control!" Aninha just kept thundering. "But yes, my friends from abroad, fellow citizens of our planet, are here to investigate! By the way, you're outnumbered!"

With that, sun broke through the lifting cloud ceiling, shining brightly on several *Yanomamis* who poked their heads out from virtually everywhere, it seemed to Augie. Their every last blow dart was poised at Raul's relatively limited number of associates.

Raul tucked away his own blow dart in his beige long-sleeve safari shirt, like it was a pen.

"Now, if you're really interested," Aninha went on, "you're welcome to join us in the shaman's *shabono*. With what I've heard about the possible presence of a *mapinguari*, you're probably lucky you haven't gotten one of your land surveyors shredded apart like so many salad greens!"

"The *mapinguari* is one of those creatures the *Yanomami* warn about in certain parts of the Amazon, especially if you go traipsing through jungle at night. Of course, it won't be 'official'," elaborated Irene, making finger quotation marks, "until some white guy says it exists. Has quite a resemblance to that elephant-sized, long-clawed ground sloth named Megatherium, supposedly gone extinct throughout South America ten, eleven thousand years ago."

Click...whirr... "Still not sensing any useful information on surviving non-avian dinosaurs," robotically reported Charly in his monotone voice.

"But at least the flatus emission detector is functioning properly?" asked Sherman.

Click...whirr... "Capybara emissions predominate presently," he reported. "But no trace of unidentified reptiles that could be dinosaurian."

Shaking his head, Fred muttered, "I don't need no damned flatus emission detector to detect the sheer B.S. I'm hearing!"

Chapter 6

"Please, Vicky, take a seat," said curriculum adviser Diane Mueller as she motioned Vicky Copplestone over in front of her desk. "How can I help you?"

As pleasantly as Diane smiled, Vicky intuited, to enraging effect, that her arch-nemesis at Green Pastures Elementary School already well knew what she was there about. Diane was playing dumb out of pure spite.

"Something I didn't quite understand when I signed off on offering my interdisciplinary unit as an elective."

"Well, you- What was that exactly? Excuse me." Diane covered her mouth and made a noise that she tried to camouflage as a cough.

Vicky could tell Diane was stifling a chortle. Moreover, that she might be about to say something to the effect of, *Well, you shouldn't have signed off until you DID "quite understand" every last bit of the fine print.*

Vicky reminded herself about the million bucks her hubby Augie collected from Eclipso, just for active participation in the most thorough search, ever, for a surviving non-avian dinosaur. But that didn't help enough; she could still feel the steam coming out of her ears as she responded, "The way you and Marsha posed the situation, numerous students, *with their parents' blessing*, wanted into my class. The five sessions I was allotted should have filled up and then some. The overflow would require fudging the upper limit on one or more of the class sizes. Remember saying that?"

"Mm-hm," Diane nodded noncommittally. She bit her lower lip to keep from busting out laughing.

"So as of now, with only five days left before opening, those five sections range from five registered down to only two."

"Ohh," ohhed Diane. She made what Vicky regarded as a lame effort to sound empathetic.

"Last night at Magruder's, picking up a few things on the way home, ran into a student named Emme Feuillet, accompanied by her mom."

"I know Emme; she had this terrific exhibit on volcanoes at the science fair last spring."

Vicky also remembered that exhibit, but wasn't going to be sidetracked. She went on, "Emme very politely introduced herself. She even apologized for intruding on my grocery shopping. Then she told me how sorry she was that she wasn't going to be able to sign up for my elective. She said that would have required giving up physical education, chorus, or art. Since she dreamed of one day joining Cirque du Soleil, she didn't see how she could afford to sacrifice any of those."

"Of course."

"It wasn't an 'of course' for me," Vicky finally couldn't help bristling. "Did not sink in before, that students only got to choose three electives. If they select mine, they have to unreasonably give up phys ed, art, or music."

"I thought that was clear," Diane said in an assertive manner that led Vicky to suspect she had rehearsed saying just those words to her, every moment to fantasize she got.

"Okay, I guess my groups will just be that small then. At least that means I can give my students lots of extra attention."

"But if they're that small, might be a problem. Let me dig out your revised contract."

"Well, it won't be a problem my keeping full-time employment; that much I do remember as a 'definite,'"

Vicky couldn't help bristling anew; the way Diane rummaged about a pile of papers on her desk somehow felt so phony. Why would her contract be sitting out there at all, rather than filed away days ago?

"Ah, here we are; it was on top of this mess."

"Yep." *As though you had no idea this moment was coming, and hadn't kept my contract there on purpose.*

"Let's see. I believe there was a provision..." Diane turned the contract partway Vicky's direction so they could study it together.

Haven't you already memorized the key provision by heart?

"Here it is: 'In the event student registration does not meet the ninety per cent benchmark, the employee's extra-classroom duties will be expanded proportionately. In the event student registration does not meet the fifty per cent benchmark, the employee's status will be reclassified as 'itinerant,' though maintaining current salary level. Employee will be expected to perform clerical duties at Central Office proportionate to the percentage the student registration in the elective falls below the hundred per cent benchmark. However, failure to reach at least fifteen per cent of the benchmark enrollment will require cancellation of the elective. The employee will do full-time clerical work at Central Office for at least five months while other options are explored.'

"Well," Diane turned her head away from both the contract and Vicky, afraid she'd bust a gut, "I'm not sure the numbers you mention quite reach fifteen per cent. But there are a few days of registration left. And I believe there are about seventy-three students who haven't finished their elective selection yet, so... We'll revisit this on Friday, and either way I'll contact Central Office to let them know."

As though you haven't already. "About seventy-three," huh? *"About" would have been seventy to eighty, something to that effect if you didn't know EXACTLY how many were yet to register!* "To be continued," Vicky opted to say curtly. She rose rapidly from her chair and turned to leave with no further remark.

"Good luck!"

"Oh, please excuse me," said Vicky; Diane's insincere wish might as well have been a violent push out the door, for how much it infuriated and distracted her. Consequently, she almost ran head-long into a spry young lady approaching the curriculum adviser's office.

"That's okay," the young lady reacted in a girlishly hi-pitched voice. "Wait, are you Vicky Copplestone?"

"I am."

"Lori Merriweather here," Lori said, barely managing to shake Vicky's hand without spilling her arm full of curriculum-stuffed ring-binders on the floor between them.

"You're the new fourth grade teacher?" *New enough to the county that for fear of your job security, you'll let Diane control your every move? Even if it goes against what you've learned about best education practices during college training?*

"I'm so sorry haven't had a chance to pick your brain yet; all these professional in-services are so time-consuming, still playing catch-up with my classroom prep! But I've heard lots of amazing things about your husband's international travels helping teach kids a little bit of everything!" Lori gushed. "With that special elective if you have enough register,-"

Oh, Diane's so excited about the possibility I won't meet even the lowest benchmark, she couldn't help spreading the word.

"-hope we can coordinate."

"Let's hope."

"Lori?"

The way Diane Mueller leaned her head out her office doorway, Vicky found herself imagining it attached to a long, snake-like neck in turn attached to an elephantine torso with an alligator's tail… *Mueller-mbembe, roaming the bureaucratic swamps of Montgomery County Public Schools.*

"It's only me!" Lori gushed again, though this time with a nervous edge.

"No, this is great!" Diane fawningly emoted in a girlish voice even more hi-pitched than Lori's had been, to a shrill extent. But then realizing Vicky was still standing there, she turned her way and said with brittleness, "Lori and I have a lot to discuss, and very little time to discuss it."

The grin on Lori's face turned more plastered-on than heartfelt as she hunched her shoulders to awkwardly squeeze her way in between Vicky and Diane to enter Diane's office.

Slam!

The closed door did not muffle Diane's voice enough, back to fawning shrill, that Vicky couldn't make out her saying, "That flower-print blouse looks so fetching on you!"

Whatever Lori responded was too soft for Vicky to understand, but Diane's subsequent shriek of laughter…Vicky was certain Lori didn't exactly prove herself, all the sudden, to be one of the world's great stand-up comedians. *Far more likely, Diane just couldn't hold it in any longer, how absolutely thrilled she is over the prospect of finally shutting down my too out-there instruction, far as she's concerned.*

Chapter 7

"Okay, here we go...again," sighed Stephen Feldman, not long after he filed inside an enormous, circular, thatched-roof hut. He followed after the rest of Eclipso's away team led by local environmental activist Aninha Floresta.

Raul Viana kept pace alongside. He reminded Augie of a circus ringmaster parading with a motley crew of clowns, elephants, jugglers, and gaudily dressed trapeze artists.

Augie and company lowered themselves cross-legged onto matted-down straw, as directed by Aninha. Scores of *Yanomami* men, women, and children stood nervously backing away from them.

Augie noticed one of the larger birds he'd ever seen, perched on bamboo near the center of the thatched-roof ceiling. He recognized it from his years-ago journey to the Amazon searching for dinosaur fossils younger than sixty-five-million years.

The beautifully blue hyacinth macaw had a bright yellow pigment ring round each eye. Soon as Stephen took his seat, this magnificently plumaged bird hopped from his perch, and spread his wings wide. Then with majestic slowness, he flapped his wings on a spiraling descent to the ground beside Aninha.

Next thing anyone knew, setting off gasps from the *Yanomamis* as much as by any of the newcomers, the local shaman stood beside Aninha. He dropped his arms to rest, thereby folding up immense wings attached to them. Not actual wings; rather, they were comprised of stitched-together feathers from what Augie guesstimated had to have been a good dozen hyacinth macaws.

The macaw itself was nowhere to be seen.

Augie suspected a sleight-of-body magic trick. For a change, he empathized with Stephen's skeptical reaction. He kept his mouth shut nevertheless; no sense risking an insult to the locals before he had a better handle on circumstances.

"Prepare to be even more amazed," brazenly warned Raul while the shaman strutted about like a rooster, so Augie and others thought.

The shaman's bobbing head keyed him in on each search team member like she or he might be a delectable seed or fruit worth pecking at.

"That is," Raul went on, "when one of you is spirited away tonight for boiling the flesh off your bones, that they might be ground down to a fine powder for garnishing their soup! There's your noble savage for you!"

"Ironic coming from a guy who wanders these settlements regularly, with impunity, to recruit more people for destroying their way of life!" bellowed Aninha.

The shaman had no inclination to show he understood the back-and-forth between Aninha and Raul. Instead, he waved a feathered arm towards Ali, Fred, and Kevin, and stated in his native *Yanomami* that Aninha translated, "These three have not been born yet. But the rainbow gods brought them here from after they will be born, to help clear this planet's lungs of toxic materials."

"That's truly the case," Ali laughed in astonishment at how accurately the shaman described his, Kevin, and Fred's circumstances. They were there in 1982 from the future, having not been born until the late 2030s. Extraterrestrials encouraged and boosted their time travel to bit-by-bit rid the past of "toxic materials" also known as weapons of war. And said extraterrestrials claimed to have dreamed themselves to Earth on a peculiar rainbow seen to have arrived from well outside the solar system.

"There's that tapir poop about the planet's lungs again!" vented Raul. "What's really ironic, Ms. Earth Mother Aninha, is that for these 'visions,' your birdman inhales enough nicotine and *yokana* dust from his three-foot-long pipe to blanket this entire *shabono* in a poisonous hallucinogenic fog, if it wasn't crapping up his lungs instead!"

"Why wasn't I told of those three men's origin previously, Irene?" Aninha asked Irene. They had a history together from Irene quizzing Aninha for the cryptozoological folklore book.

"I wasn't sure how long they'd still be with us. Any moment, they could go poof! before our very eyes, on return to their present."

"Aninha is your name?" asked Stephen.

"Aninha Floresta," Aninha swelled her voluminous chest to say, lending her a proud chicken's demeanor, Augie felt. "Never forget that I am of the people of this land!"

"Yes, of course. But just for the record, some of us, or at least this one of us," Stephen pointed at himself when his fellow explorers gave him a leave-me-out-of-this regard, "saw no sense sharing their incredible claims with you while there is not sufficient evidence to bolster them."

The shaman flapped his arms, then strutted onto a thick bamboo pole left flat on the ground. He curled his toes around it for his perch, and cawed like that still-missing hyacinth macaw.

But if you really believe you are a bird, sir, you're probably ready to believe anything.

"Um," ummed starship engineer Kevin Smith hesitantly, "how do I respectfully address, um, him?" He nodded towards the perched shaman.

"*Macawoyano*; he's the bird-enspirited shaman of this *Yanomami* settlement," Aninha nodded approvingly of Kevin's inquiry.

"*Macawoyano*," Kevin bowed his head the shaman's direction while remaining cross-legged on the straw ground cover, "were I one of you, hearing what we have to say for ourselves, I would have thought us well beyond crazy." He paused for Aninha to translate. "Among other matters," he went on finally, "we have mentioned a shuttle pod to our mother ship, and the possibility we might suddenly vanish into thin air." Another translation pause. "So, don't know how you did it. But like my friend Ali here indicated, you described our circumstances with impressive accuracy." Translation. "Yes, we travelled here from eighty years into the future. Although, um, maybe you track time in other, um, units." Pause for more translation from Aninha into the *Yanomami* tongue. But Kevin would have umm-ed to a grinding halt in any event, noticing an ant the size of a cockroach on Artificial Intelligence Entity Charly's right arm.

All of Kevin's fellow travelers had donned long-sleeve white cotton shirts as well as full-length pants, to deny such creatures the opportunity to crawl across their own bare skin. In addition, Sherman had sprayed their clothes with his latest, less-putrid version of nasty critter repellant.

But Sherman skimped on such details for Charly.

Anyhow, Kevin debated himself. Should he explain Charly wouldn't care, or be bothered the least bit more, were the ant a rattlesnake with its venom-oozing fangs dug deep into his latex skin? Or should he just keep talking about what the shaman said regarding him, Fred, and Ali?

The latter course won out; *might as well complete our host's understanding of one surreal thing before I move on to the next surreal thing.* "About that rainbow you mentioned, there are these extraterrestrials, other-world beings named the Nuah Cherpels, um..." Kevin had to "um" again, greatly unsettled by the *Macawoyano* nodding his head as in, *Of course, I know all about the Nuah Cherpels.*

"I am sorry to interrupt you, esteemed time traveler," said Aninha before Kevin could resume, "but you over there," she pointed.

Click...whirr... "You can call me Charly."

"That ant on your arm..."

Keeping the rest of himself perfectly still in addition to his trespassed arm, Charlie craned his head to look where directed.

"Do not move your arm until the creature leaves of its own volition."

Click...whirr... "Okay; I was going to keep that arm unmoved in any event, unless required to deal with evidence of non-avian dinosaur survival to the present day."

"We call that a bullet ant; its bite is so painful, feels like you've been shot."

Click...whirr... "If by 'bite' you mean penetrating the skin, according to my sensors it has already done so, three times."

"Three times?!" Aninha rose from her squat beside Augie to exclaim. "You feel no pain?!"

Click...whirr... "I didn't want to interrupt Kevin Smith's explanation of why he's here, so I wouldn't hurt his feelings."

"That wasn't going to hurt my feelings, buddy."

Click...whirr... "Not Buddy. Charly. Oh, I get it. Buddy as in 'good friend.'"

"Letting us know that big-assed ant is hurting you, that's a whole lot more important! Jesus Six-legged Christ!"

Click...whirr... "Jesus was never reported to have had six..." Click...whirr... "Oh, right. So yes, the three bites hurt a lot, a whole lot." Click...whirr... "Ouch." Charly plucked the ant off his latex arm, and gave it a good close look, concluding, "Nothing helpful here that I can detect for finding a living non-avian dinosaur." Then he stiffly left the *shabono*, presumably to release the bullet ant somewhere it wouldn't bother anyone.

"Before Charly returns, well I should have explained this earlier," said Sherman, pausing for Aninha's translation. "Charly is an Artificial Intelligence Entity, a very smart robot if you will. Hopefully, he can help us in our quest he alluded to, for a still-living dinosaur." Translation pause. "To smooth his association with you people, I developed an empathy program for him. But seems to still have a few bugs in it, not of the stinging variety. Ah, there you are."

Click...whirr... "If you are referring to me, then yes, here I am," confirmed Charly on his return.

"Charly, if you're not actually experiencing any pain from the bullet ant bites, there's no need to say, 'Ouch.'"

Click...whirr... "But my sensors did detect it tearing into my skin," Charly managed to say without, where Augie was concerned, sounding the least bit defensive. Click...whirr... "Detecting damage to me is defined as hurt, and hurt requires an expression, a public notice. According to my empathy logarithms, there were several options available. I went with 'ouch,' but could also have gone with..."...click...whirr..."...'shit,' 'help,' or 'AAA!!!' among others."

"Do you prefer your skin torn or not torn, Charly?" Irene couldn't help mischievously asking.

Click...whirr... "I prefer whichever skin condition would give us more data regarding our dinosaur quest. But since neither condition..." Click...whirr... "Okay, the better my condition, the better I can search for a living non-avian dinosaur. I prefer no torn skin. And since my database suggests that complaining about my ant bites will achieve faster repair than if I say nothing..."...click...whirr... "OUCH!"

"Charly, if you're really not feeling any pain, there's no need to complain. Tears in your latex skin will not compromise any of your data-gathering functions. I'll patch it up later, regardless."

"Okay, so no 'ouch'?"

With an impatient huff, the *Macawoyano* pointed from Charly to Sherman and then from his thumb to himself. And as Aninha translated, he said, "Charly is to that explorer what my fingernail is to me! Nothing more!"

"A good thing that's the case," Irene whispered out the corner of her mouth to Scott seated beside her. "Or his feelings would be really hurt."

"You think Sherman cares that much?" Laura couldn't help asking.

Before either Aninha or the macaw-infused shaman could react to Laura's snark, Sergeant Fred Frankly abruptly burst out, "So Charly, for entertainment purposes, how about one of us saws off your f-ing head?"

Click...whirr... "Don't do that."

"Why the hell not?"

Click...whirr... "Because I would expect an especially big 'ouch.' And more importantly, it might inhibit my functioning in search of a surviving non-avian dinosaur."

"But sawing off your head might make me very happy."

Click...whirr... "That's not nice. And..." ...click...whirr... "aren't there other things you could do that would make you very happy, without having to cut off my head?"

"Like what?"

Click...whirr... "Playing a card game?"

"Unless I miss my guess, don't think anyone here brought along a deck of cards, or in the case of our *Yanomami* hosts, even has a deck of cards to bring. And sawing your head off would be so much more fun anyway."

Click...whirr... "Then how about inserting your penis in someone's vagina? I assume your penis is still attached..."

Click…whirr… while Charly swiveled his head from side to side. "…and I believe there are plenty of vaginas present here to choose from." Click…whirr… "Sorry, just realized how rude that is. Okay, go ahead with sawing off my head." Click…whirr… "Would you like me to help?"

"Shut yourself down please, Charly," Sherman said while half-patting Charly on the back, half-feeling for the "off" switch.

Click…whirr… "But shouldn't I help Kevin decapitate me first?"

Click! With that successful disabling by Sherman, Charly slumped forward where he sat cross-legged.

Aninha promptly translated what the *Macawoyano* said next, something to do with his remark before the artificial intelligence entity so elaborately interrupted him. As Kevin expected, but not the *Yanomami* shaman's exact wording. To wit, "Let us hear more about your dream time explorations, time traveler."

"Yes, that," Kevin resumed. "The Nuah Cherpels, from a distant solar system, have been aiding us in very targeted journeys to the past. We confiscate weapons before they can be used for war, and leave artifacts in their place for more peaceful endeavors."

"Animal spirits around the world rejoice in your mission. The planet's lungs are far less clogged by pollution than they otherwise would have been!" Aninha translated the shaman clearly exulting. But then on a note of irritated puzzlement he continued, staring down Kevin with bright yellow pigment round his eyes as with the hyacinth macaw, "So why are you here? We are not wielding anything more destructive than hunting tools. We certainly have nothing that approaches the end-of-world potential of your society's nuclear weapons you haven't yet finished confiscating. Though you've successfully kept any from actually being detonated, aside from a few underground tests."

"No, instead of that, *Macawoyano*, you're killing job opportunities with your anti-progress obstacles to clearing underbrush for better farming," grumbled Raul.

The *Macawoyano* stared long and hard into Raul's eyes before abruptly spreading wide his feathered arms, and screeching, "Caw! Caw!" which jolted even fellow *Yanomamis* accustomed to his behavior.

"By 'clearing underbrush,' he means burning down jungle that has thrived here for millions of years. And could include certain plants and frogs found nowhere else. Meaning their permanent extinction in exchange for transient benefit," Aninha explained to the guests. "And by 'better farming,' he means bunching together pigs and cows in uncomfortably large numbers, producing poisonous amounts of methane. And then sending their meat elsewhere, fueling soon-to-be epidemics of heart disease and obesity. And those 'job opportunities' here, raising crowds of animals in a haze of toxic fumes? They actually represent huge losses of time for gathering nuts and fruit that keep the *Yanomami* diet healthy. For what? For money that is meaningless to the *Yanomami*? Unless they use it to buy the very foods that will raise their blood pressure and shorten their life expectancy?"

"Maybe they could purchase golf clubs? At huge discounts?" aspiring golf-course developer Alistair Frump suggested. He cringed while doing so, though, fearing what might be thrown in his face, from a variety of possible directions.

"Look, our time traveling friends are waiting to be spirited back to the future," Augie jumped in before Raul could respond to Aninha. "They accompany us to keep a low profile, away from certain folks not very pleased, to put it mildly, with their anti-war interventions." Translation pause.

"Aninha already knows our purpose here, from past conversations with one of our expedition's principal financiers. We search for living, non-avian dinosaurs. And on a subsidiary note, someone who might have perished nearby…" Augie trailed off. Aninha's subtle yet emphatic head shake reminded him that in *Yanomami* culture, one steered clear of ever saying names of the dearly departed. "Anyway," he resumed, changing course, "from what certain, um, locals claim to have observed-," Augie saw no sense in any further specifying that at least one of those locals was a gold prospector, "-we are very interested in exploring the possibility your periodic tremors are connected in some way to the object of our quest."

"So that's what this is about!" Raul blew up. He noticed that while the *Macawoyano* nodded to Aninha's translation as though to say, *About what I expected*, several of his kin reared back and opened their eyes extra-wide. Obviously, they were by turns astonished and terrified. "Somehow, you tree-aroused perverts set off explosives every nineteen days to scare off the miners and development surveyors! And now to keep them away, and scare off anyone else as well who might be interested in real progress, you're planting ridiculous rumors of prehistoric monsters!"

"Actually," said Aninha, "I have late news for our dinosaur-seeking adventurers. In to me from Belém, not too far northeast of here. They had a significant ground tremor followed by at least two reports of a large creature with a reptilian tail scaling a high-rise condo. Am not clear what us tree-humpers have to gain, staging a dinosaur roaming through there."

"Late news has come to you exclusively!" scoffed Raul. "How f-ing convenient! Why don't you rummage around inside your voluminous asshole to see what other choice turds you can hurl at us like a howler monkey?!"

Talking about yourself again? Aninha refrained from saying.

No holding back the *Macawoyano*, though.   He surprised his guests by suddenly blurting out in albeit halting English, "To better, um, understand those tremors of every nineteen days, you, um, have to go back to what you named, um, the end of the dinosaur age. But which has a different, um, significance for us."

I hope it's something purely geological, or erosion-related, Stephen thought of saying.   However, the rainforest humidity beat down on him as unrelentingly as a feeling of helplessness over challenging the *Macawoyano* over anything.   After all, the *Macawoyano* believed himself possessed by a bird spirit. Stephen settled with taking a deep, hydrating swig of guava juice from his canteen bottle, then holding his head in hand to stave off another headache.

Laura Gómez seated beside Stephen continued taking copious notes.

Beyond disgusted, Raul crossed his arms as in, *None of what follows has any bearing.*

"We all do agree," the *Macawoyano* proceeded, back in his *Yanomami* tongue, "a mountainous asteroid hit the Earth. But us *Yanomami* believe an evil spirit hurled it here. And so, the *xapieri*, the good spirits surrounding us, directed our *Omama*, our supreme creator, underground for protection. There, She was nurtured by a river far greater than the Amazon that flows across the surface. At times, gold miners have accidentally cut into it when they wound the Earth Mother."

"I've heard from geologists," Aninha interrupted to footnote the *Macawoyano*'s remarks, "that in one particular mine, at certain depths they found downward-flowing ground water shift to running horizontal. If they discover this at other mines spaced far apart, that could confirm an underground river mightier than the Amazon."

"Expected of course," nodded the bird shaman. "So anyway, whether animals or people, we are all interchangeable. In fact, my macaw spirit has an origin close to yours, I sense," he said nodding Augie's direction.

Not the Houdini Chicken connection! Augie couldn't help wondering.

"All these spirits," the shaman went on, "all of us," he waved a feathered arm leaving nobody out, "we can thank the great underground river for sustaining the *Omama* until it was safe to re-emerge from her, back to the surface. That would include, of course, any of your dinosaurs not content to subsume themselves in birds or other later-evolved animal spirits.

"And now, with the advent of the recent tremors, I have taken numerous *yokana* journeys…"

"He's smoked a local hallucinogen into mental oblivion, in other words," Raul offered as his bitterly snarky translation.

The *Macawoyano* slowly turned his head Raul's direction, keeping the rest of his abundantly feathered body perfectly still. Augie was reminded of an owl he'd once seen at the zoo.

Provoking numerous gasps, even from fellow *Yanomamis*, the shaman then appeared to rotate his head the entire way around, returning to level a severe stare at Raul.

Augie suspected he somehow rotated his body along with it, to facilitate the illusion.

Stephen lamented how realistic the 360-degree head turn appeared, more than he puzzled over just how that stunt was accomplished. Same as Augie, he assumed the shaman couldn't have actually done what it looked like he did, an impossibility even for an owl.

"I am sorry for your deprivation," the *Macawoyano* said finally to Raul. And he looked off into space, continuing, "On those spirit journeys, the *xapieri* have told me the great *Omama*, always nurtured by Mother River, grows restless from another anticipated threat. Not necessarily another fiery mountainous rock hurled at Earth by an evil spirit. But some other bad thing, definitely."

That's vague enough for you to declare any destructive phenomenon from the skies, even just a particularly nasty thunderstorm, was what you predicted. Stephen stifled himself from saying this.

"What I cannot tell you is how the disturbed *Omama* might manifest Herself," the *Macawoyano* continued. "As the behemoth snake whose writhing carved the meandering riverbed for our nearby tributary? Or as mother of more recent dinosaurs? Or as some other animal spirit? Recent reports of a hill-sized reptilian head rearing out of our swamps…"

"It's easy to see how one might conclude a meandering river bed was the product of a snake with a body the thickness of a truck," conceded Stephen, no longer able to keep quiet. "But any slightest variation in water flow causes erosion to increase along one side of the riverbank while silt is deposited on the other side. That process eventually leads to significant meanders, no creature involvement required."

The macaw shaman turned his head Stephen's direction like he might spin it all the way around again, or repeat that illusion. But instead, he said, back to his halting yet impressively eloquent English, "No doubt that is how most river beds formed. But you are the baby who, um, chews on everything. You, um, mistakenly assume everything is edible since you have, um, discovered how to use your mouth. Caw! Caw!" he concluded, flapping his arms like wings again.

"Let's say at least a few non-avian dinosaurs did survive the asteroid impact sixty-five million years ago. The same as several other reptiles, plus amphibians," said Scott. "Maybe their hibernation ability for long stretches is the reason why. So, isn't it possible that locally, a particular dinosaur has just emerged from an especially long slumber? And the reportedly large reptilian head rising out of the ground nocturnally, and gulping down an ostrich-type dino, well that's like a mama gator protectively carrying baby gators in her mouth? Plus, her partial emergence made the pickup truck flip on its side?"

"Always hate when that happens," deadpanned Stephen.

"Oh," Raul nodded knowingly, "now I get it! You're here to bolster those monster rumors! Make certain the developers who were scared off by them remain scared off!"

"Au contraire!" stepped in Alistair. "We want to entice a different sort of development that works with nature rather than fighting against her! We're talking about bringing a very special golf course to this neck of the Amazon basin! That is, assuming we can confirm the survival here of non-avian dinosaurs. But must confess, I thought those reported tremors might pose an issue. However, what if we can treat them like Old Faithful in Yellowstone National Park? What if we can establish where each time there's a rumble, an elephant-sized subterranean dinosaur head emerges like a cuckoo from a cuckoo clock? Imagine teeing off beside THAT!"

"Wait," this time it was Raul rather than Stephen with hand to head, like he was dealing with a bad headache. "So, in place of raising cattle, there would be people here from around the world with too much wealth to know what to do with themselves. And they would roll little balls into holes in the ground, while hoping along the way to see a living dinosaur?!"

"Exactly! But you're leaving out the part where they spread that wealth around! In addition to no buildup of those toxic cattle fumes! And just maybe, some locals wind up on the world golf tour, spreading the word about your good spirits, *Macawoyano*," Alistair bowed at the shaman. "It's a win-win-win-win!"

"Jesus Mushroom-smoking Christ," Fred muttered to himself. "Deliver me back home to the ephemeral dragons and other crazy with which am already well familiar, like yesterday!"

"Time-space conundrums being what they truly are," Ali seated beside him whispered, "yesterday might not be altogether impossible."

"Okay, I'm not exactly clear when you're expecting your next tremor," Laura looked up from her copious notes to address the shaman. "Eight days from now?"

"Caw! Caw!"

"I'll take that as a 'yes.' Well, from what I'm hearing, sounds like there's a best bet for experiencing this monster snake or overgrown, slowly reawakening subterranean dinosaur. And that would be staking out the general area where it was last seen, starting a week from now."

"Yes, by all means, we should initiate our next stakeout no later than a day before the next anticipated tremor," said Sherman Peabody, his chin as usual squished firmly into his neck. "I've been reading about *Namazu* of Japanese legend. There seems to have been a chicken-egg, which-came-first aspect perhaps relevant to our present-day search."

"That's the giant catfish the Japanese believed caused earthquakes," Irene clarified. "Wrote about that in my *Crossroads* book."

"Of course, we know that no catfish could be giant enough to cause an earthquake," Stephen jumped in. "The same as it's impossible for a dinosaur to have ever been as big as has been suggested."

"Although, consider the tonnage of certain sauropod dinosaurs that lived in Argentina, and were over a hundred feet long," Scott pushed back. "If they ever left the swamps to wander on dry land, and we think they most certainly did, their footsteps could have caused a rumble or two. And if a herd of them ever stampeded...look out!"

"Brontosaurus doesn't mean 'thunder lizard' for nothing," added Augie.

"I'm impressed, *Doctor* MacDonald," said Irene. "When it comes to bringing to bear precise knowledge of what we're looking for, you're obviously more than just a pretty face."

"Wonder if one of those Argentinian dinosaurs could also have made people blush like the 'Doctor' is doing?" Laura whispered to Irene.

Irene made a weird noise as she squelched a giggle, and her own visage flushed visibly.

"About the catfish, or *Namazu*," Sherman patiently picked up where he left off, as though there'd been no interruption at all. "It might well be true that no such fish could ever grow large enough to account for even the smallest of Japan's many quakes. Curiously, though, seismologists have documented that as for the behavior of catfish of most any size, they tend to become more agitated in the days and hours before major quakes. Not consistently enough, or in large enough numbers to be a reliable indicator, but far more often than random chance would suggest."

"Of course," agreed Stephen. "Those fish probably react to micro-tremors prior to the major ones."

"In other words, if there is some non-monster cause of your local tremors," hopped in Augie, "something to do with underlying fault lines, perhaps…"

"Here! Here!" Stephen cheered on Augie.

"What I was going to say, Stephen," Augie couldn't help bristling, "was maybe the tremors disturb a remnant surviving dinosaur, or one of those school-bus-sized Titanoboa snakes. It's awakened from hibernation just long enough to feast on some hapless lizard before returning to sleep."

"No! No!" Stephen opposite of cheered.

"Who knows?" chimed in Irene, ignoring Stephen. "In order to flee the wakened monster's maw, could be some terrified iguana rises up on its hind legs to make a faster run for it. Then the surprised observer mistakes it for a small theropod dinosaur."

"And when your mistaken observer sees the caiman or other crocodilian in hot pursuit, he also misapprehends it is far larger than the reality. Especially…" Stephen turned to Laura, as the journalist of the group carefully compiling everything, to ask, "Wasn't the gold miner's sighting in the headlights of a pickup truck at dusk?"

"With his partner spilled from the overturned vehicle disappearing into the creature's mouth, yes."

"Or into a yawning abyss from the tremor, mistaken for a mouth," Stephen offered correctively.

"Or into a pile of steaming hot b.s.," vented Raul, "because he was paid off to make up that ridiculous story!"

"Paid off by whom?" Irene asked with her chin raised high.

"Paid off by communist anti-developers, using naïve radical tree-huggers from the U.S. as intermediaries!"

"So, they've got more money to play with than the mining companies and the cattle industry, huh?" Irene asked with her chin still held imperiously high. "What's your evidence?"

"I'm not going to share that with you dinosaur-hunting nut-jobs!"

"Uh huh."

"Something about the creature's sleeping habits, whether it's a caiman, or an extraordinarily proportioned subterranean-dwelling theropod, or monster snake," said Sherman, determined to make his point despite Raul's conspiracy theory detour. "We do know your typical crocodilian sleeps off its meal for as long as seventeen hours. And if he's feeling too sluggish from cool weather, he'll burrow into a mud flat, and hibernate there for months, let alone nineteen days. And I am correct in saying am I not, Dr. Matias, that you paleontologists suspect your typical theropod dinosaur, such as an Allosaur or a T-Rex, probably took weeks to sleep off a meal?"

"A most accurate assessment of our current understanding, Sherman," Augie Matias confirmed. "What's more, we can't be sure your garden variety meat-eating dinosaur didn't also burrow into the ground for that, even in tropical warmth. That way it could avoid a gang of velociraptors stripping him to the bone while he slept."

"Whether it manifests as a so-called Titanoboa or a dinosaur, the *Omama* underground spirit is the sole cause of the recent tremors. Its awakening is surely from sensing the approach of an evil force," insisted the Macawoyano.

"Ooo, so scary! Be very afraid!" Raul snarked, waving his hands about in faux panic.

"While we wait for the eve of the next tremors, something else I alluded to might be worth your while investigating," said Aninha. She steered a wide berth round the question of whether some enormous beast was producing the tremors with astonishingly consistent, every-nineteen-days regularity, or they were geologically sourced like Old Faithful in Yellowstone National Park. "Friends of mine in Belém, they report a creature with extraordinary camouflage capability appears to have climbed out of a sinkhole. What's more, it's apparently interacted with their hyacinth macaw that took up residence with them. Made a mess of their living room sofa in the process."

"And it looked reptilian?" Augie asked excitedly; he suspected that "extraordinary camouflage ability" explained why it was so difficult to get more than a fleeting glimpse of whatever quacked, and tore a hole in his pants near Papua, New Guinea, on the first leg of the dinosaur search.

"My friend insists it has a long, reptilian tail."

"The macaw spirit informs me it seeks union with the troubled *Omama* ground spirit over that way," announced the *Macawoyano*. He pointed eastward in what Augie surmised was the proximate direction of Belém.

"If we are going to Belém," said Stephen, "at least maybe we can find a restaurant with good local food."

"You mean, you don't plan to stuff yourself here on fried tree grubs?" snarked Irene, whole lotta snark going on. "You have to give them a try, not to seem rude."

"Um, yes, might I...?" In his usual unpresuming manner, Bernie Coleman hunched his shoulders to raise a tentative hand. Like he might have to dodge someone trying to wallop him for his impertinence.

"Please, Bernie, you know you can always feel free to jump in," Augie assured him.

"Yes, thanks so very much. Let's say our Belém side-trip doesn't completely fill up the many days left before our next dinosaur stakeout. The Venezuelan border is not all that far from here for our steam-powered drone, I should think. More specifically, the Kurupira plateau, there, is home to the stoa legend. At the plateau's base several years ago, one morning, could have sworn I saw an exceptionally large, lizard-like head poke out from amidst dense foliage.   A small horn above each eye was consistent with the fossilized skull of the theropod dinosaur, Carnotaurus.   If that subterranean river you spoke of, *Macawoyano*, extends all the way there…"

"Mr. Coleman, are you familiar with pareidolia?" asked Stephen. "This is an important phenomenon for the rest of you to consider, as well. I should have brought it up earlier."

"You're talking about a survival behavior that has us reading animal shapes into clouds, correct?" Bernie asked. "Kept our ancestors alert, so they didn't fail to spot the sabretooth cat stalking them at night."

"That is…correct," Stephen reluctantly admitted. He had hoped pareidolia would be something brand new for Bernie to reckon with.

"If I know where you're going with that, the answer is 'yes.' I can't be certain a combo of pareidolia with my wishful thinking didn't magically inflate a small iguana's head, like it was a full moon enlarged by an atmospheric inversion.   But I distinctly remember a full-sized cycad beside it for reference."

"Okay," said Stephen. *If that's what you want to believe.*

"Caw!   Caw!" cried the *Macawoyano*, flapping his abundantly feathered arms like they were wings, again.

Next thing anyone knew, a hyacinth macaw returned to the ceiling perch, with the shaman nowhere to be seen.

Oh, brother, Stephen moaned to himself, headache-y forehead in hand.

Chapter 8

"Oh, Augie, it's been so long, I did a happy dance when Liz told me she was invited to a sleepover tonight!"

"Wo, cowgirl; I'm feeling it too, believe me. But I can guarantee you this call is being monitored," cautioned Augie.

Meanwhile, the steam-powered, sports-field-sized drone, Cloud Nine, made its way eastward zipping through low-hanging overcast, bound for Belém, Brazil.

"That's right! Phooey! Eclipso is still trying to find out who tips off the hoaxers on wherever you guys go, isn't he?"

"And more importantly, my Queen Victoria, we don't want to make Bonsai Gator blush. Might throw off his reggae dancing."

"There's a good question for my students to investigate: Do alligators blush?"

"Might I jump in there, Augie?" asked Sherman. He just happened to be passing Augie's door the exact same moment Vicky's question burst from Augie's speaker phone.

Augie left his door open to relieve claustrophobia, as his room aboard Cloud Nine was the size of a cruise ship's economy-sized stateroom.

"If you're referring to the phone sex, Sherman, we've rather gone off that notion. Besides, a three-way was never in the cards to start with."

"Augustine Matias!" protested Vicky.

"I wouldn't know about that," said Sherman, for a rare moment lifting his chin off his neck and looking on quizzically. "But hopefully it's safer than sitting in a baby pool."

"Huh?" Vicky and Augie grunted in unison.

"Anyway, to reiterate: no. I'm referring to the question of whether alligators ever blush."

Well, if they don't, Augie thought to himself, *I suspect that even as we speak, my ears alone are ruling out any possibility I'm a gator in disguise!*

"Ah," meanwhile reacted Vicky over the speaker phone as in, *Thankfully, this is a most innocently interesting subject. And I will get to hear the legendarily eccentric Sherman Peabody expound upon it! Wow!*

"The short answer is: We're not sure. If alligators and other crocodilians *do* blush, it's not to any obvious extent. But that being said, chameleons are another matter entirely."

"Oh?" said Augie.

"Yes, indeed. At least where mature male chameleons are concerned," Sherman nodded his chin into his neck. "The presence of another male, or female, excites them, whether for rivalry or mating. Then they turn bright colors such as yellow. Of course, a biochemical purist might argue that's not real blushing, because it does not involve capillaries flooding the skin with blood. However, there is one behavior, a protective reflex response, that alligators do share with humans down to the fine details."

"And what might that be?"

"No 'might' about it, Dr. Matias," corrected Sherman, shaking his chin into his neck. "It most definitely is...the sneeze."

"Alligators sneeze," Augie spoke in wonderment.

"Captured by video on more than one occasion. Not a far stretch to speculate that given the proper conditions, dinosaurs sneezed...and still do, if they've survived."

"This would be super interesting for my students," remarked Vicky.

"Unlike flatus emissions, or farts as they're called in common parlance, reptilian sneezes are near impossible to tease out of a general wildlife recording. That's why I don't yet have a sneeze detector to accompany my flatus emission detector."

Sherman sounds apologetic, Augie marveled.

"One more thing before I go; you might have realized this already, Augie, on our short venture to and from the *Yanomami shabono*."

"Our harmful critter repellant!" Augie snapped his fingers. "I was going to comment how pleasant it smelled. Hints of lilac, even! But with everything else going on..."

"It still incorporates a mix of urines, enough to keep away ninety per cent of the animal kingdom. However, it's reformulated to pose less challenge to our own olfactory sensibilities."

"Splendid."

"Well, I better let you two get back to whatever you were discussing that you're off the notion of doing."

"Thanks for your input, Sherman," Augie ran outside his small room to say.

Sherman was already well down the hallway by the time he finished excusing himself from the paleontologist's presence.

"He sounds like a sweet guy," said Vicky. "Was he embarrassed by your kidding around?"

"Afraid so; could see it in his ears glowing red on his hasty retreat. Apparently, he and I display embarrassment the same way. Anyhoo, an issue has occurred to me regarding our next big dinosaur stakeout."

"Eclipso doesn't want my class eavesdropping anymore? In light of security concerns?"

"No problem there at all; he's happy to have his quest used for educational purposes. No, the problem is timing. Didn't think about this before."

"That's right!" exclaimed Vicky in dawning realization. "Due to the presumed nocturnal nature of any self-respecting non-avian dinosaur, the bulk of your searches take place at night!"

"Not an issue coordinating with your teaching schedule when we're halfway around the world, and night for us is daytime for you."

"But now that it's what, only an hour later where you are?"

"Exactly. And that's for Belém, to where we are returning temporarily. Our actual focus is further west, most likely in your exact same time zone."

"But are you saying, my Augie-Doggie, we won't be able to video eavesdrop on your Brazilian search?"

"Hopefully not; have developed a bit of a workaround. Got Eclipso's permission to transmit to you from each night patrol, the morning after. You can edit out all the boring, extraneous, waiting-for-a-pin-to-drop stuff. Just focus on the moments of pure excitement. With the understanding, of course, you're not to let any of it out of your hands. And naturally, when or if we film a Stegosaur preening for the cameras, the magnitude of that..."

"Eclipso might want the world premier to take place in a venue other than my classroom."

"Exactly!"

"With my new schedule, that will probably work better in any event. Assuming too-small enrollment numbers don't shut me down altogether."

"That part really sucks."

"For sure. Anyway, here's the deal: I used to have one set of students all day, running the gauntlet from math to reading. I scheduled my so-called 'integrated skills unit' for whenever you tried to sneak up on Mr. Iguanodon. But now, integrated skills will be my sole focus, as an elective. Two to six sessions a day, depending on enrollment. The bottom line is, I need to edit your transmissions in any event, to boil them down to what I can rerun multiple times."

"That's good," Augie sighed with relief. "But hmm, wonder what that means for this Friday?"

"Friday?" Vicky perked up.

"We actually are going to do a little daytime field work then. Think I told you about the tremors they've having here, spaced nineteen days apart, always towards midnight."

"You did."

"Well sometimes, they coincide with brief sightings of large reptiles, one ridiculously large. And after the most recent tremor, a deep furrow was left by something just outside the *Yanomami* village, beside an Amazon tributary. Such furrows are said to have shown up previously, with or without the tremor. But those have long since filled in with a slurry of jungle detritus, collapsing ground, and muddy flows from daily rainforest deluges. And this new furrow reportedly leads into an enormous burrow."

"Like alongside the Sangha River in Cameroon? A pattern, Augie?"

"We are excited about that, my Vicky Vixen."

"Hope you closed your door, Augie-licious. Nobody else needs to hear our pet names."

"Of course," Augie lied while trying to close his door gently enough to avoid making any sound his wife might hear over the phone. He couldn't believe how loud a click! the latch made. "Whoops; think someone out in the hall made a rude noise," he lied again.

"I didn't know doors could fart!"

"Okay, busted. Be that as it may," Augie bulldozed ahead, "after returning from Belém, we're going to conduct a rare daylight reconnoiter of the furrow. Including at least the first couple yards into its burrow I'm told is big enough for a giraffe to roam without bending over."

"Wowee zowee, Augie-Doggie, that timing couldn't be any better!"

"Great! How so?"

"Friday there's this get-to-know-your-teacher-before-the-first-real-school-day orientation event. It's a drop-in-whenever thing. And it's wide open for electives, so your burrow reconnoiter might lure additional kids away from other electives. Again, children shouldn't have to give up art, phys-ed, or music to follow a dinosaur search."

"I can imagine your arch nemesis, Diane, rubbing her hands together with glee while saying, 'Nya-ha-ha!'"

"Something like that. But what's this about a side trip to Belém?"

"Eclipso's point person here, who knew his wife before she vanished into a sinkhole or a monster's burrow, take your pick...Anyhoo, she's this prominent environmental and human rights activist named Aninha Floresta. She's boarded Cloud Nine to direct us to a hi-rise condo in Belém. A friend there believes he spotted something large and reptilian crawl out of a fresh sinkhole."

"Well wouldn't that be something! After all those expeditions to the middle of nowhere, you end up discovering a surviving dino right smack inside some big city!"

"Yeah, it won't be looking for love in all the wrong places, like that country song goes. It will be more a matter of having looked for living dinosaurs in all the wrong places."

What Augie didn't have the heart to tell Vicky about, he held in the palm of his hand. He pondered it while he continued talking with her, passing the time until Cloud Nine reached Belém. But it wasn't Vicky he feared hurting. It was the potential for sorrowful effect on Eclipso, assuming he eavesdropped their conversation.

The object of concern was a years-old photo Aninha entrusted to Augie, of her standing beside Eclipso's wife,

Agnes. The exterior of the *Yanomami* village-sized *shabono* showed in the background, the very same *shabono* Eclipso's search team just visited. Smiling *Yanomami* women sat cross-legged in the foreground, their lips and cheeks pierced by several small sticks.

Also clearly in evidence was Agnes's pretzel-thin physique, and her cheery disposition, hauntingly devoid of any sense of the cruel fate soon to have awaited her. But what struck Augie most was her brightly dyed bandana tied round her neck. It featured a bright-orange ceratopsian dinosaur standing amidst a lush, fern-splashed, equally bright-green backdrop. Augie wondered whether it was a gift from her husband, Eclipso, by his own admission as stick-in-the-mud stay-at-home as she was get-out-there-and-travel. Augie would have to share this photo with the team's incredibly generous benefactor, sooner or later. But when, exactly?

Chapter 9

Harriet Letterman returned to Cloud Nine's navigation bridge accompanied by Aninha Floresta. Aninha urged her forward with an arm draped protectively round her shoulders.

Harriet's husband, Harry, followed after them, hunched forward like he couldn't straighten his back after he stood up.

Augie was of the impression Aninha and Harriet could have been high priests, Harry their acolyte.

For sure, it was Harriet and Harry's first public appearance Augie could recall, that they weren't practically in each other's lap.

"I've been talking with my new friend here," announced Aninha, waving attention to Harriet like she was introducing her to Augie and company. "And have learned she'd really like to be more directly involved in your field work."

"That's right," nodded Harriet assertively. "I need to be my own check and balance for a change," she added.

Harry reacted with head bowed, a deeply furrowed forehead. He looked teary-eyed to Augie.

"You could join us at the condo in Belém," offered Scott. "A rather interesting situation is developing over there."

"But a condo isn't actually a field is it, Scott?" Harriet bristled. "Chairs, tables, television, floors, no plants aside from what they have in pots...not much different from aboard Cloud Nine, here. No, I want to explore a wilderness where there's a chance for adventure. Even if a Brachiosaurus doesn't poke his head out!" On Harriet concluding this explanation, she gave Alistair Frump unabashed dreamy eyes.

Poor Harry, Augie thought to himself. *He's scrunched his chin almost deeper into his neck than Sherman habitually does!*

"Well, here's something I brought up before without any takers," Bernie Coleman said, oddly emboldened by Harriet's firm resolve. "Say we have extra time after the condo visit, before your reconnoiter of ground that was transformed during the most recent tremor near the *shabono*. The Venezuelan border, where you find the Kurupira plateau, isn't really that far from there."

"Ah!" Cloud Nine navigator Samuel Longbottom let out as a petite exclamation. "Our Eclipso's powers of foresight must be powerful indeed. As we speak, by remote control he is directing the second habitable drone, Cloud Ten, to rendezvous with us in the skies over Belém. Once we reach Belém, I'll be watching for it on radar. But with our video monitor, we will need to scan the skies for a fluffy cumulus floating out of sync with other cumulus. Anyway, with our attention soon to be divided between the *Yanomami* region and Belém, Eclipso guessed we might require dual stakeout abilities. But adding a third location into the mix...well that cinches it!"

"Correct me if necessary, Bernie," said University of Maryland zoologist as well as cryptozoologist Dr. Roberta Quiñones. "Doesn't the creature of interest in the vicinity of that plateau, the stoa, bear striking similarities to a certain medium-sized theropod dinosaur named Carnotaurus? Which is to say, couldn't it be an aggressive meat-eater the size of a truck, if there's anything to it? Am not sure how safe you and Harriet would be there on your own."

"They'll be fine," scoffed Stephen. "That is, unless there's also risk of a man-eating unicorn showing its face. A spray from Sherman's all-purpose, new-and-improved dangerous critter repellant ought to more than suffice."

"But if it doesn't," inserted Alistair, to Harriet's wide-eyed delight, "allow me to be the knight in shining armor who leaps to your protection, m'lady." Alistair genuflected before Harriet, complete with a low, arm-sweeping bow. On dawning realization, though, he awkwardly pivoted on his bent knee to curry favor with Fred, Ali, and Kevin. "Can I put you time travelers in the 'yes' column? We could use backup, um, just in case Mr. Carnotaurus requires a wee bit of persuading to go off the notion of mauling us until our intestines spill out."

"Oh, c'mon now," Stephen scoffed once more.

"That's the kind of argument for which I'd like to have had along my trusty old AR-15, to do the persuading for me," said Sergeant Fred Frankly. "But I don't want to see you tree huggers, who we could deliver to a planet where the trees hug back, faint from the vapors. Rest assured: I would have taken great care to merely wound the dino critter in one leg. That could have been easily patched up afterwards. Anyway, my sidekicks and I will concoct a good-enough defense that's more than just running for our lives. However, there is a potential T-Rex-sized problem with leaning on us alone for 'backup.'" Fred employed finger quotation marks. "And I'd be less than honest if I didn't admit to pining away for it."

"Oh?" Alistair furrowed his brows in puzzlement.

"What if right smack middle of our genius-level effort to protect you from a dinosaur attack, the three of us are raptured out of here, back to 2064?"

"Well two things, really," Bernie did not hesitate to respond. "I should think the creature's perplexity over your suddenly vanishing would provide us sufficient time for the running-for-our-lives bit. Or at least a very good head start. But more importantly, perhaps, I should also think we humans are creatures with which our prospective Carnotaurus has little to no familiarity. Given reptiles' generally over-anxious, reclusive natures, our large-numbered presence in its presence could scare it off. Before we get a really good look at it, I mean. That would seem the bigger danger, if we don't keep hidden during our creature tracking."

"Assuming the dinosaur's lack of existence seventy million years after it went extinct hasn't already scared it off," drily remarked Stephen.

"Wait; all this noble sacrifice, dragging along time-travelling friends for insurance," Irene nodded towards Fred and company, "you're just scoping out another venue for Jurassic Links golf, aren't you, Mr. Frump?"

Alistair Frump held up his hands to admit, "Guilty as charged, Irene. Imagine if you will, Bernie, a tee box atop that plateau you called Kurupira, with the green so many hundreds of feet below. Think of the thrill watching your golf ball plummet all that way down! Then think of the amazing bonus thrill when your Carnotaurus sticks out its head from a cave in the cliff side, to wonder what the hell's going on!"

"I'm actually thinking about how nobody will ever see that ball again," gently chuckled Bernie. "After someone launches it off the top of Kurupira, falling that far, it's going to bury itself down deep. The ground round the plateau's base is generally very moist."

"You're talking about that game where people hit balls long distances before they try rolling them into little holes in the ground?" Aninha asked, wondrously appalled.

"They don't just try," corrected Alistair a teensy defensive. "They succeed, unless they pick up the ball in frustration and move on to the next hole before they've finished." Unnerved by Aninha crossing her arms and giving him a silently quizzical regard, he prattled on, "Actually, I left a bag full of toy golf clubs and golf balls aboard our cigarette boat. Biodegradable clubs and balls!   Was going to share them with the *Yanomami* children.   But when that blow dart standoff happened, decided it might not be the right time.   Look, here's the deal," Alistair laughed nervously.   "What I saw going on inside their *shabono*, people were busy painting each other's faces, tending their gardens, etcetera etcetera. Well, say they can accept my people working with stretches of rainforest along the tributary.   Not to cut everything down, heaven forbid! But rather to integrate a luxury golf course resort, where one never knows when a hippopotamus-sized head of a hibernating dinosaur might emerge to roar, 'Hey man, what's happenin'?!' or 'I dare you to use me for whack-a-mole!' If they can allow that, if they can even see themselves managing the resort, caddying for the golfers and such, just think of it!   The money that comes pouring in will set them up for life. They can paint faces, garden, and all the other et ceteras to their heart's content!"

"But they already do that now," observed Aninha, "without needing detour into any of those other activities you mentioned they might even dislike."

A frown flashed across Alistair's face as he persisted, "I should have also mentioned that who knows, some *Yanomamis* might want to become golfers themselves."

"To what good purpose?"

"Okay," testily said the would-be golf course architect, Aninha's challenge accepted. "I've noticed many of the boys pretend-fight with sticks. Their elders put them up to that, to prepare for battle in case there's a dispute with another village, correct?"

Aninha made a clipped, noncommittal nod.

"Well, imagine instead of beating swords into plowshares, as that Biblical saying goes, those sticks are replaced by golf clubs. Won't that be healthier, preparing to compete on a golf course rather than on a battlefield?"

Aninha kept her arms crossed.

But Alistair could tell he'd given her pause for thought.

"I'm still not clear how your proposed resort can integrate with the rainforest, and not destroy parts of it."

Alistair opened his arms wide to respond, "I'm sure my development team would welcome your input!"

"And maybe you could teach me how to swing a golf club?" eagerly jumped in Harriet.

Alistair arched one eyebrow, puzzled at Harriet's sudden interest in golf as much as he welcomed anyone's sudden interest in golf. Maybe not so surprisingly, though, he quickly regained his high-octane, upbeat mojo to say, "Who knows? Maybe we'll have time to spare on our stakeout of Kurupira."

"'Our stakeout,' yes," reacted Harriet dreamy-eyed.

"I might also be interested in swinging a golf club, dearie," inserted Harry, glowering with jealousy.

But there might be things I'm interested in doing you have no interest in, my handsome man. And vice versa, Harriet thought, while she couldn't bring herself to express that sentiment out loud, afraid of further hurting Harry's feelings.

"Maybe I should tag along on your sidebar operation as well," said Irene. "Especially on the off chance our time-traveling, history-tampering starship officers are suddenly raptured out of your presence during a Carnotaurus attack."

Augie noted a look of helpless distress briefly cloud Scott McDonald's visage. He resolved that the next chance he got to speak with Scott in private, he'd put in his two cents. Augie would advise him that if, as appeared, his fellow dinosaur searcher had a serious thing for Irene, he should let her know soon. That is, before someone else did. If it turned out she already had a significant other, better to find out ASAP rather than continuing to torture himself, especially if she was gay.

In any event, Scott's apparent ongoing misery wasn't the only simmering happenstance. Odd friction had clearly developed between Harriet and Harry after they'd been glued to the hip for so long. And Roberta continued to look troubled over some unmentioned thing.

Augie was left wondering, *Of course the time travelers' top priority has always been crystal clear. But are there other things my fellow recruits by Eclipso are searching for besides – dare I even think it? – "just" surviving non-avian dinosaurs?*

Chapter 10

Augie, Scott, Roberta, Laura, Sherman, and last but not least, the stiff-moving Charly filed after Aninha through the front foyer into Ron and Rosa's fifteenth floor condo.

Ron welcomed them, saying, "Wow, Aninha; looks like you've opted out of saving rainforests to conduct guided tours instead. Not that I'm unhappy our little love nest might have become literally so for Milton Nascimento."

"SQUAWK! Yours is no disgrace! SQUAWK!"

"But we didn't even have time to set up a gift shop for selling off our junk. Besides, I think lots of other locations in Belém would be of far more historical interest."

"Isn't your husband just the *coisa mais fofa* when he's trying to be funny, Rosa?" asked Aninha, up in Ron's face belligerently close, and pinching his cheeks painfully hard.

"He's the cutest thing, alright," nodded Rosa as she hurriedly gestured the guests to any seat on the rattan furniture. Aside of course from the sofa with the torn-up cushion. Moreover, she offered tall, ice-filled glasses of passionfruit juice. "He's so cute, I could just love him to bits...with a machete and a hedge trimmer."

Click...whirr... "I am not constructed for processing this fluid and ice mixture," explained Charly in full robotic mode, nevertheless receiving the drink into his latex skin hands. "Nor is it clear how this concoction will assist in our search for surviving non-avian dinosaurs."

"You'll have to excuse Charly," said Sherman, lifting the passionfruit juice glass from Charly's mechanical grasp. "He's an artificial intelligence entity we're hoping will help expedite our search."

"No apology necessary," happily responded Ron. "I didn't realize the tourist attraction was coming to us rather than the other way around."

"We really do appreciate your accommodating Ms. Floresta's request on such short notice," Augie hastened to explain. "And apologize for any inconvenience. This juice is deliciously refreshing, by the way."

"Great! No inconvenience at all!"

"Especially if you can explain what's happened to our sofa," added Rosa. "Could our Milton Nascimento have done all that himself? Why would he?"

"Wait," Ron held up a hand as in, *Hold it there a second*, "it's just sinking in; did I really hear your non-drinking mobile ironing board say something about a search for a living dinosaur?"

"That's what they're, what we're here for," Laura Gómez took the initiative to answer. "We've been granted unlimited resources to look worldwide. What we've learned so far basically comes down to two things. Thing one: If, and it's a very big 'if,' surviving dinosaurs of the non-bird variety are real, they seem inclined to burrow away like numerous other reptiles."

"Which would have conferred a distinct advantage for surviving that end-of-the-world asteroid that struck the Earth sixty-five-million years ago," added Augie.

"Correct," nodded Laura. "Thing two: They might have brought camouflage to an entirely new level, over tens of millions of additional years evolving."

"Which is what has us so interested in what you reported to Ms. Floresta here," excitedly leapt in Scott, "about seeing a giant reptilian tail one moment, gone the next."

"One of those sightings was up the side of a building in the direction of our condo. After that, we found this mess on our sofa. Our hyacinth macaw, Milton Nascimento, has been in a big bother ever since."

"SQUAWK!" squawked the bright-blue-shaded bird, ruffling his feathers in reaction to hearing his name mentioned again.

"That sofa cushion sure has been shredded. And I see odd bits of ribbon and leaves and twigs added," marveled Augie. He seized the moment to rise from his seat and edge near as he dared to where the macaw seemingly stood guard, perched atop the sofa's rattan backrest. Too near, and he feared provoking an attack by the bird, pecking at him with his formidable beak. The hooked part reminded Augie of a fossil Velociraptor claw. "Looks like a nest, doesn't it?"

"Not only that," said Ron. "Check closely. Am I crazy, or is that a depression left from an egg the size of an ostrich egg?"

"That's an 'and' not an 'or,'" snarked Rosa. But before Ron could process what she said, she'd sidled up beside him, arm round his waist to plant a big, affectionate kiss on his cheek and say, "That's okay; we can be crazy together."

"I see the depression," Scott said, followed by Milton Nascimento's most intense "SQUAWK!" yet, in case any of the humans entertained the idea of edging even one inch nearer to the presumed nest.

"If we could only collect a sample of the shredded cushion material to check for DNA," said Augie feeling the frustration. "But how strange; if the egg has hatched already, where are pieces of broken shell? And if it hasn't hatched yet, who or what stole it?"

"You're the first guests we've had since this happened, unless someone or something came in through the balcony," Ron insisted. "And yes, if you want to keep all your fingers, I recommend keeping your distance."

"Maybe with the egg gone, he'll soon lose interest," said Rosa.

"Did you guys ever have a good look at the egg?" asked Laura, busily taking notes.

"No," said Ron in a tone that clearly conveyed how surprised he still was by that reality. "We never even had a bad look at the egg, or any look at all."

"What we're assuming, of course," said Sherman,-

By "we" you mean your chin and yourself, Augie couldn't help thinking, for how typically Sherman scrunched his chin into his neck.

"-is that your avian dinosaur, essentially, was able to successfully mate with our dinosaur of the more prospectively prehistoric variety."

"And didn't care for the home your macaw prepared for the egg?" speculated Roberta.

"Maybe would have preferred something more French colonial? Sorry, people; without Irene here for the snark, I sensed this vacuum...," said Laura. She became red-faced thinking that had Irene heard her, she would have said, *That's okay; I'm sure Tom would have laughed*, referring to her boyfriend.

"And to think it crawled all the way up here," said Sherman, lost in wonderment as he ignored Laura's nonsense to stride out onto the balcony. "Goodness, that's quite the cacophony of wildlife noises carrying over from across that river."

"When the breeze blows anywhere from the west," confirmed Ron.

"Well presumably, then, your breeze carries other noises this direction, in addition to the more obvious chirps, buzzes, hoots, and whistles."

"Sherman is referring to dinosaur farts," explained Laura.

"Dinosaur farts?" Ron's eyes lit up to accompany his silly grin.

"That jungle past the- What's that? A junkyard beside a big garbage pit? The other side of your river?"

"Yeah, that's the Guamá River. And that pit is a sinkhole, formed only a few weeks ago. They were piling wrecked cars with an electromagnet."

"The rumble we felt when that sinkhole formed," added Rosa, "was like an earthquake."

"I don't know about the forest back behind it," continued Ron. "But if you're going to listen for, or sniff out, dinosaur farts, the sinkhole might not be the worst place to start," *though certainly one of the most crazy-assed things I've ever heard of doing!* Ron kept to himself as he went on aloud, "A landfill project there has been suspended temporarily. If the river seeps into the sinkhole, could be even worse pollution."

"Even worse pollution?" Augie repeated.

Aninha, who had remained standing the whole time with hands on hips, shook her head in helpless disgust.

"You don't want to be here when the breezes shift direction, coming more from the south. You'll get a whiff of the open landfill downriver that will leave you wishing for a dinosaur fart instead," said Ron.

"So why does checking out that sinkhole for dinosaur farts make even a little sense?" asked Laura.

"Within minutes of its formation, thought I caught a glimpse of a reptilian tail waving hello from the pit. Had to have been much larger than a caiman's tail for how big it appeared from this distance."

"Hmph," hmphed Augie, enthralled.

"At first, I assumed I drank too much moonshine *cachaça* from Rosa's cousin, and was hallucinating. But then we boarded the *trem da alegria* – the happy train – for a fun ride through the city at dusk. Spotted that same tail on what we thought was someone costumed as Katydiddly. That is, until he scaled the side of a market warehouse wall, headed towards our condo."

"Charly, why don't you come out here on the balcony with your flatus emission detector activated?" suggested Sherman. "See if we pick up any tell-tale signatures?"

Click...whirr... "Because I haven't been told to yet."

"Then come out here with your flatus emission detector activated," ordered Sherman, more patiently voiced than Augie could have done.

"'Flatus emission detector'?" Ron repeated, lit-up eyes and silly grin again.

Out on the balcony, Charly unzipped his pants, and the extremely sensitive microphone for the detector poked way out.

"A most unfortunate location for that particular measurement device, I know," apologized Sherman. "But given all the other devices with which Charly is outfitted, I simply ran out of room for any other location than his crotch."

Pffft!

Click...whirr... "Besides several insect flatus emissions from a distance away, I have detected a human flatus emission within a radius of fifteen feet," announced Charly in his robotically monotone voice. "Nothing helpful yet for confirming non-avian dinosaur survival."

"Impressive," laughed Ron.

Rosa gave Ron a severe, arched-eyebrow regard as she said in an admonishing voice, "Ronnn?!"

"Trust, but fart."

Slap!

"Hey," protested Ron, "that slap provides nothing useful for confirming non-avian dinosaur survival!"

"That noise you made provides zero help for *your* survival!" Rosa laughingly shouted as she chased Ron for a follow-up slap, wending her way around their guests variously standing and sitting.

"SQUAWK!"

Next thing anyone knew, Milton Nascimento was perched on Charly's obscenely located microphone, bent over trying to tear it apart with his beak.

Charly ran stiffly around the balcony, to no avail.

Frankenstein in a panic, Augie mused.

"You can stop fleeing the attack, Charly," said Sherman. "That macaw cannot damage your flatus emission detector."

Click...whirr... "Do I have other choices?" Charly asked in a monotone voice devoid of the usual intonation for denoting a question.

"I'll rephrase that: Stop running!" As Milton Nascimento kept biting at the tip of the microphone with his sharp, hooked beak, Sherman added, "You also might want to retract the flatus emission detector mike and zip up your pants."

Click...whirr... "I neither want nor don't want to do that, as neither choice offers data related to the search for surviving non-avian dinosaurs."

"Well let me rephrase that as well: Retract the flatus emission detector mike, and zip up your pants!"

Click...whirr... "Done."

"Done?" asked the normally unflappable Sherman, clearly becoming very flapped, indeed, since Charly hadn't yet begun to retract the mike.

Click...whirr... "I let you rephrase that. I did nothing to stop you from doing that."

"Yes, good!" huffed Sherman impatiently. "Now also retract the flatus emission detector mike! And zip up your pants!"

"SQUAWK!" squawked Milton Nascimento, the blue hyacinth macaw, at the mike as it retracted back inside Charlie's pants.

Far as Augie could tell, Milton Nascimento might as well have said, *Don't poke out of there, ever again! Stay put!*

"Maybe your pet bird mistook the microphone for a snake, and was defending the nest?" Augie speculated.

"A nest where both the egg and the mother are no longer there; not saying that's not possible," Roberta strained to add. "But how very unusual."

"I must apologize for Charly's behavior," said Sherman. "His semantic logarithms tend to interpret situations a bit too literally despite my further tinkering with them."

"I'd like to ask Charly something," said Ron.

"Be my guest," said Sherman, waving a hand towards his invention as in, *Have at it.*

"Charly, when you were running in circles after the macaw grabbed your mike, were you afraid?"

Click...whirr... "I am programmed to avoid damage. Damage appeared possible, so I ran."

"Are you chicken?" laughed Ron.

Click...whirr... "I am neither chicken, beef, fish, amphibian, or reptile. I am an artificial intelligence entity."

"So do you feel fear?"

Click...whirr... "Fear is part of my empathy program, which is switched off at this time."

"Please switch on his empathy program, I'm begging you," Ron addressed Sherman.

"You are so devilish, *minha querida!*" Rosa slapped her husband backside the head, while Augie noticed their macaw having resumed standing guard above the empty-looking nest.

"I didn't say I wasn't!" snarked Ron, crouching with arms raised over his head to fend off any further assaults from Rosa.

"I would be interested myself to hear how Charly interacts after the tweaks I've also made to his empathy program," said Sherman with his chin scrunched so far into his neck, as usual, Ron wanted to ask, *Are you talking to me, or your belly button?* "But I must warn you," Sherman added, "it might still become a bit embarrassing."

"That's what I'm hoping."

"Ron!" Slap!

Sherman went ahead and switched back on Charly's empathy program, heedless of Ron and Rosa's interaction. Then he said, "Okay, have at it."

"Great!" enthused Ron. "So, Charly, now do you feel fear?"

Click...whirr... "This is not a fearful situation."

"How about if I turn you off?" said Ron approaching Charly in a faux-threatening manner. "I paid close attention when he turned you on." Ron directed a forefinger at Sherman.

Click...whirr... "Please don't. If you turn me off, I will be of no use searching for surviving non-avian dinosaurs."

"But does my threat to turn you off make you genuinely afraid? Whether or not you can help us? Tell the truth."

Click...whirr... "No." Click...whirr... "But I can still empathize with you." Click...whirr... "I have a hobby, besides searching for surviving non-avian dinosaurs."

"Tell us more."

Click...whirr... "I like to build plastic models."

"Which type?"

As Ron asked this question, Augie could see and feel Aninha growing impatient; the conversation was getting them nowhere, beyond its possible entertainment value. Her arms crossed, she shifted her weight from right foot to left foot then back again, over and over. She could have been the hyacinth macaw, how that bird anxiously moved from side to side on his rattan sofa perch, guarding a nest that seemed to contain nothing more than a depression from an egg no longer there. An egg presumably hatched, or carried flying away.

Click...whirr... "My favorites are antique cars like the Model T."

"Why those?"

Click...whirr... "Because that's the choice my randomized selection made, so I can appear to empathize with people who have a hobby."

"But do you *really* like to build plastic car models?"

Click...whirr... "Are you suggesting I'm..." ...click...whirr... "bullshitting you? If so, I'm..." ...click...whirr... "...very hurt."

"*Meu Deus!*" Aninha finally erupted. "We know he's not really hurt at all! That's just the way he's programmed to react to an accusation of dishonesty! And it gets you nowhere in your search for surviving dinosaurs! I have great interest in that search! Its success could help protect the habitat those magnificent creatures claim as their home!"

Click...whirr... "The question of whether or not I feel actual 'hurt' doesn't get us any closer to finding surviving non-avian dinosaurs, Aninha. Since we agree on that, would you like..." ...click...whirr... "...me to insert my flatus emission detector microphone-"

Click! With one extended whirr, Charly suddenly slumped over again.

Sherman had raced to turn him off before he could complete his sentence.

"Aww," sighed Ron in mischievous disappointment. "Could you please turn him back on, at least in his non-empathetic mode?"

"Ron," said Rosa in an admonishing tone, anew.

"I can do that. But using my artificial intelligence entity for entertainment purposes is really beside the point. I say we best return to the *Yanomami* village, now, to prepare for our stakeout of that deep ditch left in the wake of their most recent tremor."

"But we should leave someone behind with you, Rosa and Ron, to help keep an eye on this situation with your macaw and his empty nest," advised Scott.

"I volunteer," said Roberta raising a hand. "While studying to become a zoology professor, spent two years managing an aviary for a major zoo."

"I volunteer Charly to join you," Ron smiled, his eyes still gleaming with mischief. "He won't be as boring. No offense, Professor."

"Ron!"

"No offense taken; I've been called worse things than boring!"

"I can't leave Charly here unattended by me," Sherman shook his chin into his neck.

"Just give us a list of what he needs, and directions for disabling him if he becomes too frisky," Ron practically begged.

"That's very kind of you to offer," responded Sherman.

"More like desperation!" Ron laughed.

"However, we need him for a special reconnoiter of a hole in the ground, possibly burrowed there by some monstrously proportioned creature."

"Well, I guess that settles it. Charly, I'm really going to miss you."

Click...whirr... "That's good that you are intent on missing me. I won't have to focus on avoiding any objects you hurl my general direction..." ...click...whirr... "...unless your aim is really poor..." ...click...whirr... "...or you're lying." Click...whirr... "Are you lying?"

Chapter 11

"That side of Kurupira is dramatically transformed from twenty years ago." Bernie pointed at the steeply elevated tabletop plateau displayed on the navigation room viewscreen. "I assure you it's far more than a mere matter of seeing the tepui from up here rather than at ground level, as I did back then."

By "up here," Bernie referred to being aboard Cloud Ten. Which steam-powered drone's operation Kevin Smith-Park found quite easy to handle, compared to flying the starship Smoke and Mirrors. That is, of course, once Samuel Longbottom trained him.

Kevin had just peeled Cloud Ten off a camouflaging course across an especially fluffy stratocumulus cloud layer, for descent towards the immense plateau.

A dense fog bank enshrouded the plateau's base, giving it the creepy appearance of floating mid-air. In the distance, crossing well over the Brazilian border into Venezuela, other dramatically steep and sharp-angled plateaus rose out of low-level clouds.

"Tepui?" spat out Sergeant Fred Frankly somewhat derisively. "What, that's a name the locals give these flat-assed mountains?"

"'House of the gods,' yes, that's the translation," softly responded Bernie, well used to Fred's crassness.

"Truly easy to see why they believe that," remarked Ali Magabu, Fred and Kevin's fellow time traveler. "Bernie, didn't one of these tepuis inspire Sir Arthur Conan Doyle's fiction version of a dinosaur search entitled *The Lost World*?"

"Roraima, that wedge-shaped formation out there along the far horizon." Bernie pointed at the view-screen again.

"Hundreds of millions of years ago, this entire region was a vast sea, depositing sandstone on a granite under-girding. Then over millions more years, that sandstone was eroded, at times accelerated by magma intrusions. The eventual result were these isolated, flat-topped mountains much as you see in Monument Valley in the American Southwest. Coincidentally, not long after the mass dinosaur extinctions, such erosion fully separated the tepuis from one another."

"You know what I'm thinking?" asked Alistair, his eyes lit up like they usually were.

"That you can't hit a golf ball far enough to make the carry from one tepui over the valley to the next tepui?" snarked Irene.

"Close!" laughed Alistair, though an arched-eyebrow regard of Irene flashed across his face. "No, I'm thinking a golf course for each tepui! Lost World Links! And Bernie, it will be okay if your resident dino..."

"The stoa."

"Right. Suppose the stoa is more on the meat-eating side of things, as you suspect. No reason caddies can't be armed with special tranquilizer guns. I'm already imagining the write-up in the brochures: 'Your Lost World caddies will not only give you good reads on your putts. When the opportunity affords, they'll photograph your group standing astride the T-Rex-type dinosaur they safely put to sleep for your protection, while you lift your favorite golf clubs triumphantly high!'"

"As I've pointed out before, there's a big problem with that," warned Stephen in his authoritative-sounding deep voice. "The asteroid that caused the mass die-off you mentioned, Bernie, happened only a few thousand miles north of here. As harsh as conditions became the other side of the planet in New Guinea, they had to have gotten completely un-survivable here."

"And yet the rainforests below are teaming with plants and animals, including quite a few reptiles," pointed out Irene. *We've had this argument before.*

"Small reptiles," amended Stephen.

"And we know there were some dinosaurs no larger than a chicken!"

"This is true," Stephen conceded. "Although, doesn't the chicken itself come under the heading of a surviving avian dinosaur?"

"We do know that even back in the dinosaur age, partial sandstone erosion and fracturing of every tepui had already honeycombed them with vast cavern networks," said Bernie. "It is not a far stretch to believe that when the asteroid hit, the resultant fire storms, windstorms, etc. chased several dinosaurs inside those caverns. Denied their main food sources, the plant eaters would have died off while the meat eaters such as the Carnotaurus picked their bones clean. Once things settled down enough outside the caverns... Oh, I am definitely seeing a big difference from last time."

Bernie Coleman strode right up before the panoramic view-screen, close enough to touch it. Which he did, running his fingers across where the Kurupira tepui appeared dramatically transformed. "My, my," he sighed, overwhelmed, and still running his fingers across the screen, as though he could touch Kurupira directly. "I know what's changed. A slice of the plateau has collapsed partway, like a glacier calving. Look closely." Bernie tapped his forefinger insistently on one small part of the screen.

"Truly amazing, if my eyes aren't deceiving me," said Ali, squinting at the screen to give a close look where Bernie indicated. "Appears to be a waterfall partially concealed by vegetation. Only... How can this be? Like the ebb and flow of the ocean, it regularly reverses direction, falling uphill as well as downhill!"

"Wait." Hand to head as though suffering an intense headache, Stephen held out his other hand in protest. "That has to be an optical illusion."

"See for yourself, Mr. Feldman." Ali waved towards the partially concealed waterfall on the view-screen.

"Okay, I see what you're talking about," admitted Stephen after a close look. "Maybe a pulsing magma flow deep below the surface is responsible. And for all we know, it's also incidentally responsible for those regularly spaced tremors. Knock off two birds with the same stone. But we still need the view from ground level, to rule out the optical illusion possibility. There's so little of the waterfall in sight between the foliage on the semi-collapsed cliff side."

"I'm going to bring this Cloud Ten contraption to a low hover, a few feet above ground to avoid entangling the landing gear in any foliage," announced Kevin.

"Might need to gather together our gifts for whichever locals claim they own this region," cautioned Alistair. Of course, he was focused on the toy golf equipment he always brought along for children.

"Or we might not," said Irene as Cloud Ten descended further, and the video feed revealed another expansive *shabono* similar to the one along the Amazon tributary. Only this *shabono* looked a shambles, what Irene would have likened to match sticks scattered about. "That settlement looks trampled down, and abandoned."

"Trampled down?" scoffed Stephen. "Again, let's see how things appear from close-up ground level."

"I want to be on the away team!" burst out Harriet. Holding up a compass, she added, "There's information we, I mean that the team needs to keep collecting. It might be nothing, but..."

"Well now you have us *really* intrigued, fair lady!" enthused Alistair.

Harriet blushed.

*

"Whether this *shabono* was trampled down, or collapsed from a tremor or storm, whoever resided here has clearly fled, truly," declared Ali.

Ali, Kevin, Alistair, Bernie, Irene, Stephen, and Harriet spent several minutes stepping about bunches of straw and bamboo that littered the bare muddy ground.

The fifteen-hundred-foot-tall tabletop mountain named Kurupira loomed in the background. Its partially collapsed section faced the former village. And its partially concealed waterfall sounded like the ebb and flow of surf.

"If this place wasn't trampled down," said Irene, having lifted one bamboo stick from among a host of others, "how were so many of these broken in the middle, like something stepped on them?"

"Before you rush to conclude an enormous dinosaur crushed this place underfoot," cautioned Stephen, "you-

"I think the idea would be that a creature or creatures stampeded through, collapsing the structure. Then they reversed course to trample what they brought down," Irene interrupted.

"Perhaps in an aimless panic from the calving of Kurupira," added Bernie.

"But I think you first need to consider the possibility a tremor caused this *shabono* to collapse. After that, a violent rainstorm swirled the bamboo sticks breaking against each other. You see these mud puddles, and bits of leaves and small branches off nearby trees? Maybe there were microburst winds."

As defensive as Stephen sounded to Irene, she had no idea what was really going through his head. On concluding his assessment, he nervously double-checked that Cloud Ten still hovered close by, from where he and the others climbed down a short drop-ladder only minutes earlier. In case there was some herd of creatures in the vicinity, not necessarily surviving dinosaurs (but who knows?), he wanted to make the fastest possible getaway. Moreover, he also found himself listening extra intently to the variety of bird calls. He hoped not to discern some unusually harsh screech, like a ramped-up eagle's cry, that might indicate a theropod, T-Rex-type dinosaur nearby.

"Well, see what we have here, people," said Irene, already down on her knees to take a closer look.

While everyone else crowded round, Bernie Coleman lost no time photographing the foot-long, three-toed track in the mud, half-filled by water.

"Before anyone rushes to a conclusion," cautioned Stephen as much for himself as anyone else, "years ago in the Himalayas, mountain climbers found large tracks in the snow, thought to have been from the Abominable Snowman. Turned out they were bear tracks enlarged by melting. Something similar might be going on here from that rainstorm. Might have been from a macaw or blue heron, for all we know."

"I'm not convinced any rainstorm could enlarge a blue heron track this much, without washing it away altogether," flatly stated Irene, crossing her arms and shaking her head.

"Okay, you're asking us to accept an absolutely incredible explanation for this single track before we've ruled out everything else," complained Stephen. Although, he anxiously jerked his head on hearing an especially loud, "CAW! CAW!"

"Again, I'm not necessarily concluding it was made by a dinosaur. Maybe there's some monstrously large caiman, though I would think such a creature walking on all four legs would have left more than just one imprint..."

"And a bird might have landed only long enough to leave this track before flying off," Stephen quickly added. "It's not as though birds have never been known to rest standing on one leg."

"Maybe Pteranodons did the same thing."

"Oh, c'mon, now!" scoffed Stephen for his umpteenth time, though still listening nervously for more of that especially loud cawing.

"Think I'd have to go with you on this one," said Fred to Stephen. "A collapsed shack plus one single three-clawed track do not a living dinosaur make. Especially in the wake of what was clearly a violent thunder bumper, and something obviously geological having caused a nearby epic mudslide. If you're really set on proving such a critter still exists, you'd be better off returning to Cameroon, check out the swamp where we lost our shuttle pod. Whatever rocked it about while we were cooped up inside, had to be bigger and more powerful than your typical elephant. And there's that one thick stump we glimpsed briefly through some muddy-assed water. If it wasn't a tree trunk, the only thing I think would fit the bill is the leg on one of those classic Brontosaurus types."

"Once we're sure we've eluded the hoaxers for good, I'd be all for giving Cameroon a second try," said Irene.

"In the meantime, are we agreed to camp out here a few days? See whether that periodic tremor our *Yanomami* friends have been experiencing also happens here?" gently asked Bernie. "During that time, of course, we could carefully scout the area for whatever made this track."

"Definitely," agreed Irene.

"Wouldn't it be safer to sleep aboard Cloud Ten when we're not poking around for unicorns?"

"CAW! CAW!"

Noticing Stephen's eyes bug out on hearing the cawing again, Irene couldn't help snarking, "Oh, I get it; Mr. Supreme Skeptic poo-poos any notions of prehistoric monsters romping about here, but that macaw's distant cries really have him spooked."

"So that's what that was," said Stephen, unable to hide his relief. "But that's not what I was worrying about!" he added uncontrollably defensively. "I know we have snakebite antidotes and the like at our disposal. However, I'd rather avoid those less-than-dinosaur-sized threats in the first place."

"Uh huh," grunted Irene, nonplussed.

"You did bring your golf clubs with you, Mr. Frump?" Harriet finally worked up the courage to sidle up beside Alistair Frump to ask, having returned her compass and notebook to her backpack.

"My dear young lady, you might as well ask whether I remembered to bring my toothbrush and toothpaste! I never travel anywhere without my golf clubs, plus plenty of extras for others to share! Nor will I! Why do you even ask?"

"Can you teach me how to hit a golf ball?"

"But of course! Why not?" Alistair enthused, though Irene noticed a hint of worry flash across his face as in, *There might be a good reason why not.*

"He's going to be my golf teacher, and I'm going to be his golf student," Harriet announced to Irene, blushing.

"Oh boy."

Turning back towards Alistair, Harriet asked, "Will you put your arms around me to teach me golf?"

Alistair darted his eyes all about, searching for an escape hatch as he responded, "Um, come again?" Met by Harriet's perplexed look, he added, "Can you explain what you mean exactly?"

"In a TV show, a woman asked a man to show her how to swing a golf club. He put his arms around her, and guided her to hit a golf ball."

"Oh!" Alistair laughed nervously. "That's not really necessary. What I do is ask someone to watch carefully as I swing a golf club, then simply imitate me."

"I'll learn better if you hold me in your arms." More blushing...

"Well, here's the thing. Uhh, I saw this movie where someone was going to teach someone how to, um, swing a tennis racket." Alistair figured he better change a detail, i.e. tennis racket instead of golf club, to make his fib sound more believable. "But- But when he wrapped his arms around her, he proceeded to strangle her."

"Oh, no!"

"Oh, yes," Alistair nodded, putting extra oomph into lying. "He was a serial killer. Well, ever since watching that film, have had such nightmares! I've not been able to teach golf swings that way, ever again. Besides, I know you're smart enough to learn by observation."

"Nobody has ever called me smart that way before," said Harriet, giving Alistair a lovesick, bespectacled gaze. "Not even Harry. But people sure have called me stupid many times."

"Well, it's true," insisted Alistair, his heart going out to her, well aware of her Down syndrome and wondering how people could be so cruel...and blinded to reality by their prejudices. "I mean, the smart part."

"I know what you mean," Harriet giggled. "I also know you would never strangle me! And that I would learn golf better if you hold me in your arms."

"Here's an idea: I teach Harry how to swing a golf club, then he holds you in *his* arms to show you how it's done. I did hear him say he was also interested in golf."

"That was just to please me, and I don't want him doing that," Harriet bristled. "I want him to find what he enjoys, that might not be what I enjoy."

"Well, we'll figure out something," Alistair concluded, walking away from Harriet towards Bernie, like he needed to discuss something with him. But on the way, he gripped his own neck, sticking out his tongue like he was being strangled...

...prompting Bernie to ask, "Do I need to rescue you from yourself?"

Chapter 12

Flying in his helicopter, Raul Viana couldn't help a small twinge of conscience, no matter the previous times he'd seen the abandoned mining community of *Colina Pelada* (Naked Hill) from overhead. He kept reminding himself that enough unearthed gold would really benefit the natives in the long run. It would be good even for those he considered stuck in the Stone Age past, the *Yanomamis*. Who he also considered shamelessly exploited by young, heads-up-their-spoiled-asses know-it-all environmental fanatics. Made no difference, ultimately, that this stretch of land had been turned so barren, looked like something akin to anthills, seen from any altitude. Could have been a lot worse, could have been *Serra Pelada* (Naked Mountain) further west. *Serra Pelada*'s barren starkness not only sprawled epic distances. Untold thousands of mud-covered gold miners labored there, lending the effect of an actual giant ant infestation.

At least the cattle fields will be green after forest clearing, Raul rationalized. *But God damn it! Those accursed, nineteen-day tremors! Why did they have to be linked to some cachaça-fueled monster dinosaur hallucination?! Bad enough how that's scared off everyone from mining; think most of them went west to the human anthill. But can't even bribe any teenaged Yanomamis to resume transforming the land. Or allow us to bring in laborers from outside, and not threaten them with blow darts! Crap! Might have to wipe out their whole community to make way for progress. Relocation would be more humane, if only those f-ers would accept what's good for them and everyone else!*

Raul did appreciate that the hovel where mysterious developers said they would meet him was located where promised. Also as promised, the painting on its corrugated roof featured a blue macaw munching on a cashew.

The two young men inside were both of string bean physique and swarthy, five-o'clock-shadowed complexion. To greet Raul, they rose from a simple table made of dark Brazilian oak.

Raul stormed inside, flanked by two bodyguards while the helicopter's propellor blades could be heard slowing to a stop.

"Aaron Silva here."

"And I'm Paulo Santos."

Both men reached for a handshake, but Raul would have none of it. "Why haven't I heard of either one of you clowns before, if you're really in the mining business?" Raul lost no time asking in a challenging tone.

"Cuts both ways, *senhor*," fired back Paulo. "Before we did a little homework, *we'd* never heard of *you!*"

"What my partner means to say," said Aaron, grabbing Paulo's arm in a cautioning *cool it*, "is that this is such a big country, it's easy for people in related projects to be unfamiliar with one another. Even more so in our case. We work behind the scenes for mining interests who prefer not to have any known connection with us."

"Plausible deniability, which I'm guessing is also your game, Raul," added Paulo, still prickly.

"You're from where in Brazil originally?" Aaron and Paulo's stilted Portuguese was not lost on Raul, however accurate and distinctly enunciated.

Aaron and Paulo exchanged looks as in, *We really need to tell him the truth.* Like that wasn't part of the plan in any event.

"My name is Aaron," Aaron admitted. "But it's Aaron Levy, and he's Paul Smith."

"We're from Philadelphia, in the United States," said Paul. "But the rest of what we told you..."

...*is a complete lie*, the mischievous part of Aaron had to stifle himself from also confessing.

"Okay, so what is this about, exactly?" Raul asked while motioning his guards to stand at ease. Not that he trusted his two new acquaintances any further than he could throw them. Yet he figured he might as well hear them out since they were obviously there to talk business.

"For the past few months, we've been conducting sub-surface dynamiting. At nineteen-day intervals, under stealth of night to avoid dealing with the locals," explained Raul.

"You're the ones responsible for those accursed tremors!" Raul shouted angrily, still motioning his guards to take it easy.

"Along the tributary a good distance from here," Paul reacted with faux defensiveness.

"Enough gold to go around for everyone, *claro que sim*?" Aaron asked rhetorically. "But on recent aerial reconnaissance, we noticed this camp looked completely abandoned. We wondered whether the riches here were already exhausted, or- we wanted to make sure the tremors from our dynamiting weren't causing cave-ins, or any other issue."

"Either way," went on Paul, "we also learned you ran into the usual probs with the locals when you wanted to clear underbrush for cattle grazing. Believe me, we can offer you a win-win."

"That won't be a problem much longer," Raul shook his head. "Put another way, a hundred or so *Yanomamis* suddenly vanishing won't be exactly missed. We're spreading the word that they decided to abandon their *shabono*, to start over again somewhere further away from civilization. It's in their nomadic nature. As long as we, uh, dispose of them discreetly - and the mining area provides lots of opportunities for that - nobody will know. Unless you want to join them, you'll promise right here and now that you won't know, either."

"Of course we promise, if it comes to that," said Aaron with labored nonchalance. "But why decimate a potential labor source, and possibly call down the Brazilian central government on you? For all your talk about dealing with the locals 'discreetly,' you know you have environmental fanatics like Aninha snooping around. If-"

"Stop right there, whatever your name really is." Raul held up a cautioning hand. "Let's back up to why our mining was abandoned in the first place. Those tremors your underground explosions have been causing? By themselves, they might have proven merely unsettling. But churned together with heavy drinking and local legends...it's sinking in how much you f-ers need to offer, to make up for what's happened. And get me off the idea I should 'discreetly' dispose of you two as well! Like immediately! Before you can disappear back to where I'd never heard of you in the first place!"

When Raul's guards raised their weapons in Aaron and Paul's direction this time, he didn't motion for them to stand down.

"You don't want to do that," Paul couldn't help bristling, as per his temperament. But before he could go any further, Aaron waved him off. And he drew from inner, meditative resources to calmly ask, "Could you elaborate on that local legend stuff?" As though he wasn't already well-versed in far more than Raul would have ever known. "Then we'll elaborate on how we plan to make it up to you."

With a sigh evidencing much weary frustration, Raul motioned for his guards to stand down again. "A rumor spread like wildfire that during one of those tremors, a pickup truck was overturned by a dinosaur. It emerged from below ground, supposedly, large enough to be Godzilla's twin brother. Every last miner was spooked into fearing those tremors are the subterranean movements of some ridiculously large monster. They've fled to join the human ant colonies in *Serra Pelada*, since the tremors from your explosives don't reach all the way there. You see, myths already ran rampant about train-sized snakes, and the *mapinguari*, some monster ape or prehistoric monster ground sloth.

"Incidentally, before you try talking your way out of your execution, why so long between those underground explosives?"

"To keep the *Yanomami* from discovering our presence," started in Paul on an explanation he and Aaron had long since formulated, taking credit for a phenomenon over which they actually had no control. "We had to spread them apart to allow adequate time for setting up each detonation under stealth of night."

"And carefully assess the results after each detonation, not to mention clear away any signs of our presence," added Aaron. "But I really want to get back to talking you out of our execution."

"The dirt floor is yours," said Raul. He took a seat on one of several tree-stump chairs strewn about the hovel.

"We've put the word out to young *Yanomami* men, to meet at a deep furrow running alongside their local Amazon tributary, this coming Friday afternoon."

"We've learned that's when a group of crazies from the United States will be there, searching for evidence of surviving dinosaurs," went on Paul seamlessly from Aaron's exposition. "They're persuaded some huge beast or a herd of them might be responsible for the furrow, feeding into *Yanomami* superstition."

"Haven't told them about our underground blasting," continued Aaron.

"So anyway," said Paul, seizing the explanatory reigns again, "it goes without saying that no dinosaurs or monster snakes are going to show up. But the American crazies should notice pyrite, otherwise known as fools' gold, mixed in abundantly with the rock and dirt in the furrow."

"The *Yanomamis* should also notice the yellow sparkles, right away," suggested Aaron.

"What, you're going to plant fake nuggets?" asked Raul in a not-altogether-dubious tone.

"It's already in the washout from tributary leaks caused by the explosives," explained Aaron. He trusted Raul and his gang had not done any snooping around there that would have told him otherwise. That what these two Americans were dishing out was pure bunk. "The *Yanomamis* would have discovered it already, if they weren't so afraid of what might crawl out of the cavernous hole the furrow leads into."

"If they're so scared of some imaginary beast, how are you going to convince them to tag along with the crazies to see that glitter in the first place? And if it's only fools' gold, and not the real thing, why should I care?"

"Like I said, the fools' gold is washout from the explosives," said Paul, sounding too testy for Aaron. So, Aaron beat him to the next punch, effectively interrupting him to go on, "Our preliminary tests have already turned up nuggets of the real thing. That will take extra work to tap into; it's not simply lying out there. No, the pyrite will act as the lure. But how we're going to get the *Yanomamis* to spy on the dinosaur hunters in the first place, that's where you come in."

"By now," Paul jumped back in, "your miners who joined the ant colony in *Serra Pelada*, many of them should be disenchanted. They ought to welcome word from you they'll have better chances of striking it big in our new mine, as well as returning to work your older one."

"You tell them you'll truck them. Better yet, that *our* people will truck them back here to see the proof it's underground explosives, not burrowing monsters, causing those tremors," Aaron continued in the partners' verbal relay race.

"Think of it," said Paul, at long last adopting Aaron's upbeat tone. "When the *Yanos* notice the truckloads of miners returning, that's when you tell them those tremors were from mining explosives, not monster snakes. And by the by, that f-er who claimed he saw a dinosaur, who started this whole panic in the first place: Didn't he conveniently vanish after rumored to have made off with a gold nugget that could set him up for life?"

"He's not the only one who claimed to have seen something. I'm sure they were all roaring drunk at the time. They were the only ones roaring, not some dinosaur *maldito*," angrily spat out Raul. "But again, from what you tell me, it's your detonations causing those tremors that nurtured their hallucinating such crap in the first place. They're going to have to hear it from *you* that there's not Godzilla to worry about. Anything I say, they know I'd like to reopen *Colina Pelada* any damn way I can. But why bring in the *Yanos* at all?"

"Their elders are blocking the land clearing needed for cattle ranching, true?" pointedly asked Paul, careful not to refer to it as deforestation.

His partner was a little more careless.

"During deforestation, they could stumble across nuggets that worked their way into the topsoil," Aaron speculated. "If they can be convinced of that..." As always, he framed matters more diplomatically than Paul.

However, Aaron's use of the term, deforestation, that Paul avoided, did give Raul momentary pause for thought.

Deforestation was a word more often used by environmental activists like Aninha Floresta.

"The younger generation of *Yanomamis* are more interested in progress than their literally stuck-in-the-mud elders," Aaron forced himself to say with a relish he definitely didn't feel in the least.

Paul gave him a glance that expressed what he would verbalize to him later, namely, *This is an incredibly dangerous game we're playing.*

"But if we can shut down the rape of the rainforest in this region at the same time...Well let me put it another way," Aaron argued with Paul later, after Raul let them go. "Say we do succeed in warding off Eclipso's crew. What value will that have, if our primeval creature still has its habitat devastated to the point it goes extinct? I know you fear I'm becoming a little too greedy. However..."

Chapter 13

"Adriana understands you're here to help," Aninha translated Adriana Sousa for Augie and company.

Aninha and Adriana stood outside Adriana's tin-roofed shack on a barren hill overlooking a lush, rainforest valley, in the rapidly darkening dusk found close to the equator.

"But she can't see herself climbing that ladder onto your cloud plane, even strapped in. She hopes you understand what the fear might do to her unborn child."

Augie saw Adriana gently massage her swollen belly clothed in a simply designed yet bright palm-frond-green dress.

"Of course we understand, please convey that to her," Augie assured Aninha.

Via walkie-talkie, Scott told Samuel Longbottom to retract Cloud Nine's ladder, and lift the steam-powered drone to the altitude of a few puffy cumulus clouds hanging practically still in the dark velvet firmament. Blending in there, it would be less unnervingly noticeable to Adriana.

"She welcomes us inside her home for passionfruit juice," Aninha translated after extending Augie's assurances to Adriana.

On filing through the low, narrow doorway into Adriana's home, Augie, Scott, Sherman, and Laura noticed a kitchen along one wall, and a twin-sized four-poster bed along another wall. Opposite the bed, an especially lumpy-looking sofa sat up against a third wall. Cushion-less rattan chairs were scattered about, and a wooden crucifix hung nailed to the wall beside the doorway.

"Sebastião isn't here?" Aninha asked Adriana in Portuguese while Scott, Augie, and Sherman crowded together on the sofa at Adriana's behest.

Laura carefully took a seat on one of the rattan chairs, half-expecting it to collapse.

"No, he is not here!" Adriana erupted tearfully, in Portuguese of course, as in *Isn't that obvious?!*

"What do you think happened to him?"

"He happened to himself!" angrily grieved Sebastião's wife while she nevertheless got busy serving her guests. She pulled a bottle of passionfruit juice from a Styrofoam cooler Augie saw had a big block of ice inside, worn smooth from melting.

"*Ah não, caro*, what does that mean?"

Finished pouring the drinks, Adriana took a deep breath to calm herself.

Laura rose to offer her the seat she'd taken. But as Aninha translated, she politely demurred, quietly saying, "I have already sat too much today." She went on, "The last time I saw him, he claimed he had a new plan for a better life for us, including for our child on the way." She patted her belly. "That was a week ago, and still nothing. Aninha told me you were anxious to speak to him about his dinosaur encounter." Adriana turned toward the three guys crowding the sofa while Aninha continued translating, "I am very sorry he is not here for you."

"No, that's okay," Augie shook his head, his heart going out to Adriana. "Any idea where he is? Maybe we could help find him?"

"Oh, I have an idea, alright," Adriana nodded emphatically, her emotions getting the best of her again. "Before he went into town each day, he gave me a lot of lip service I was supposed to believe, about seeking redemption looking for new work."

While continuing translations for Adriana, Aninha wrapped a protective, comforting arm round her shoulders.

"Long hours away, and he always returned in clean condition, as in not having worked the ground. He always said, 'Nothing yet, but please be patient.' This is what I think happened. He and his buddy, Cal, whose body was never found after that night, they unearthed a big gold nugget. They were taking it somewhere when the earthquake overturned Cal's truck, and a monster ate Cal. Before Sebastião crawled home to me, very upset, I believe he hid the gold, to go back for it later."

"I have to interrupt you there, *caro*," firmly yet gently said Aninha, breaking off from translating. "What evidence do you have about the gold?"

"In the days after Cal's truck overturned, I heard that the police were all over it and the surrounding area. In addition to Cal, they searched for gold nuggets. But they found nothing."

"That doesn't prove there were any nuggets to begin with," Aninha couldn't help pointing out.

Adriana reared back from the local activist's expansive embrace to look her right in the eye as she said, "I know when my husband is not sharing something. And the only things from *Colina Pelada* he would have not to share are gold nuggets."

"Did the police ever question him?" Laura asked hot on the heels of Aninha's translation.

"Of course," Adriana replied as in, *Wasn't that obvious?* "He and everyone he knew confirmed that he and Cal were very good friends, too good friends for murder."

"So, you believe Sebastião hid away gold nuggets? And then?" asked Aninha.

"Then I think- It is not that Sebastião is not well intentioned. But I can feel the temptation devils seized him, as they have in the past. From cashing in the nuggets, he spent money on gambling, cachaça, and other women. Then he was too ashamed to face me, and fled. Or was murdered for some unpaid debt. I'll never know!" she suddenly wailed into Aninha's shoulder, her own shoulders heaving with grief.

"That's...I'm sure we all feel horrible about that," reacted Augie, his heart going out to Adriana again.

Augie's fellow explorers nodded their ready assent to his including them, where feeling horrible was concerned.

"We could offer you and your expected child a new life, a less stressful life..."

Adriana calmed down to shake her head "No" as abruptly as she had sobbed into Aninha's shoulder. "I have good relatives and friends nearby who are my family. I could never leave them. The only thing keeping them away at the moment is your cloud plane over my home. Soon, though, they will knock on the door to see that I'm okay. But you make a nice offer; obrigado."

Just then, a brownish, scaly lizard about four inches long, a tegu skink, unwittingly ran out in the middle of the cement floor. It was on the trail of a lone, reddish-brown golden-haired ant, itself a good inch long. Suddenly realizing it had an unwanted audience of mysterious monsters, it halted its pursuit to look nervously up and around, tilting its head from side to side.

After their experiences with Bonsai Gator, Augie and friends half-expected the lizard to stand erect on its hind legs, cross its forelegs, and give them a remonstrative head shake. Rather than that, though, with a faint rustle it fled underneath the sofa as quickly as it showed up in the first place. Another reminder, where Augie was concerned, of how incredibly shy and reclusive reptiles could be, excepting of course the inimitable Bonsai Gator.

"What Sebastião reported seeing, any chance you or someone else could lead us to the location?" Scott inquired delicately.

"I'm sorry he isn't here to lead you there himself. But you can't miss it," went Aninha's translation. "The police have blocked off the road for repairs."

"Wow," whistled Scott. "Whatever it was did that much damage?!"

"After what he described, I was convinced he drank way too much. But he arrived home earlier than usual, said he hitched a ride. And there was no alcohol on his breath."

"Any further details about what he saw that he might not have shared with anyone else?" asked Sherman, his chin as usual tucked double-chinning into his neck like he was busy with something there. "Unique noises or smells, for example?"

Before Aninha could translate for Adriana, the chorus of chirps, trills, howls, and caws from outside Adriana's shack seemed to suddenly intensify, like someone had turned up the volume. And an odd mix of carnation-like scents with pungent feral odors permeated her home, easily masking leftover cooking smells.

Nevertheless, once Aninha did translate, Adriana nodded understanding, and answered, "He said the smaller dinosaur, not the monster head, reminded him a little of an iguana. But it was much larger than any iguana he'd ever seen before, and ran on its hind legs. And, there were feathers down its back."

"Feathers down its back?" Scott repeated excitedly.

"Yes. He said they rose like porcupine quills! To be honest, I am not sure what he saw, but he was never so terrified before."

"If Stephen were present, he would have reminded us it is not unknown for smaller reptiles to stand on their hind legs for a brief run," said Sherman.

Or dance to a reggae-fied Beatles tune, in Bonsai Gator's case, Augie told himself. *Not with feathers, though.*

"Since the night of the monster," said Adriana, "one of my friends said her home did something very strange. One evening, it moved several yards, very slowly, like a snail was carrying it on its back."

"It moved," Laura repeated, incredulous.

"Well maybe we could check that out, and the accident scene; we have two days before the next anticipated tremor," suggested Scott.

Suddenly, a sparsely clothed, bare-chested man burst through the door, shouting, "Aninha *caro!*" Spinning about, taking in the many other people crowded there, he said in very stilted English, "I sorry for interrupt." Nevertheless, back to Portuguese he went on, "I just got off the village phone with a brother. He said Raul held a meeting with many young brothers that included some of his miners, and didn't include the *Macawoyano.* He promised an experience that will change their lives, if they stake out the new monster snake furrow this coming Friday, late afternoon."

"That's when we plan to be there, scouting it out in advance of the next tremor," Augie reminded Aninha after she translated.

Before Aninha could react, Laura's walkie-talkie erupted with a burst of static, followed by Harry from back aboard Cloud Nine saying, "This is Harry Letterman, over."

"We hear you, Harry. This is Laura, and no need to say 'over.' Tell us what you've got."

"I roll with the circumstance, so I *will* tell you what I've got. Harriet just reported to me, and I can hear in her voice that she really misses me. Isn't that great?"

"We are happy for you, Harry," enthused Laura, trying to empathize despite her impatience. "But what did Harriet say that was important enough to contact us?"

"That's right! She *did* think it was important to contact you!"

Laura let enough time elapse for Harry to have gone on. But with him remaining quiet, she finally followed up, ever mindful of his special needs despite his high intelligence, "What was Harriet's message?"

"Yes, that, sorry. She's not here to be my balance. But I wrote it down like she advised."

"Okay, let's hear it," Laura followed up immediately, to forestall another awkward silence, maybe.

"Sergeant Fred Frankly reports receipt of a message from the starship Smoke and Mirrors."

"Remember the time travelers?" Augie asked Aninha, addressing her bug-eyed, quizzical reaction.

"The starship is currently inside a wormhole," Harry went on reading from his written-down communique, as heard over Laura's walkie-talkie. "It's entrained by the gravitational pull of a donut-shaped vehicle, fifty miles in diameter, of likely extraterrestrial origin. Starship Captain Helena Taylor expects both spacecraft to exit the wormhole somewhere close to Earth in seven to eight months, our time. But a lot shorter for them due to relativity. That is when the captain hopes to retrieve Sergeant Frankly, Officer Magabu, and Officer Smith. In the meantime, though, she has a special request that Sergeant Frankly thought Sherman Peabody might be able to oblige."

That last part got Sherman's chin off his neck, glancing towards Laura's walkie-talkie.

"An Officer Leung has been trying to establish communication with whoever might be aboard the donut-shaped vehicle of likely extraterrestrial origin. But in exchange for pictograph transmissions, he has only received a recording of odd yet familiar noises. Here's a snippet."

What issued next from Laura's walkie-talkie were said noises.

"Good God!" exclaimed Scott. "That sounds like a parade of farts!"

"I wanted to activate Charly's built-in flatus emission detector," said Harry. "With Sherman not here, however, I was afraid I might mess up something."

"A wise decision, Mr. Letterman," Sherman nodded his chin into his neck.

"We better return aboard Cloud Nine to take care of this pronto," Augie told Aninha as he and fellow explorers rose to their feet.

Laura said to Harry, "We'll be right up."

"But please assure Adriana," Augie was careful to add, "once we deal with the extraterrestrial communication, we will devote the next couple days to searching for her husband."

"I wonder whether he would have gone to that other, much larger gold-prospecting region further south, where many fellow miners apparently fled," Laura wondered.

Chapter 14

"Sergeant Frankly, how did your starship captain send a message outside a wormhole to you?" Augie Matias asked from back aboard Cloud Nine.

Cloud Nine was still hovering above Adriana Sousa's humble abode.

The sergeant was still camped out with his fellow time travelers and members of Eclipso's expedition in the shadow of the plateau, Kurupira, the Brazil side of the Brazil-Venezuela border.

While talking, Augie saw on the navigation room's panoramic view-screen that Adriana's neighbors were variously giving her hugs and pointing skywards. He assumed they were ogling Cloud Nine's passable imitation of a night-time cumulus cloud in a sky crowded with them, the full moon lending them all a luminous silver lining.

"Our know-it-all applied-physics genius, Buddy Leung, resorted to some old-fashioned spaceflight technology. He improvised a hydrogen engine strapped to one of our firefly donuts, using up fully half the fuel the Smoke and Mirrors carried for such an emergency."

"Firefly donut?"

"Oh, yeah, have to bring you up to light-speed on all our futuristic gizmos that even have me still f-n' amazed," Fred cussed casually, his norm. On the television-screen-sized video phone, he was cast in silhouette by the hanging lantern behind him, inside a large tent pitched beside Kurupira.

Kevin Smith-Park hovered Cloud Ten nearby, to keep a watchful overhead view for any marauding beasts, or people returning to the trampled-down *shabono*.

"The firefly donut is this donut-shaped gizmo," Fred went on, "the size of a medicine ball. It helps maintain communication between planets and spaceships as much as fifty light-years apart, without too much f-n' lag time."

"They're also sent wayyyyyyy ahead of starships, to give truly ample advance warning of hazardous space debris," added Ali Magabu.

"And they're usually launched from a starship well out of reach of any significant gravitational pull," resumed Fred. "But this time, too-close proximity to such f-n' pull was unavoidable. The captain reports there's this fifty-mile-diameter alien vessel. She speculates it might harbor a whole spacefaring ecosystem community, possibly from a planet facing some doomsday crisis. Any f-n' how, its gravity shed is so strong, the firefly's usual photon propulsion system can't cope. To escape the alien vessel's pull, they had to jury-rig an old-fashioned hydrogen rocket boost. Once that boost carried the firefly donut far enough distant from the ET Noah's Ark, the mirror array magic – that's a story for later – kicked in. Our hi-tech donut was finally able to exit the wormhole, for transmitting to us. When it delivers our two cents' worth back to the Smoke and Mirrors, it will remain far enough away from her not to rejoin her entrained for heading heaven-knows-where."

"It appears truly likely that both the extraterrestrial vessel and our starship will emerge from the wormhole very close to Earth, as best our Officer Buddy Leung can calculate," Ali added.

"Okay, phew," phewed Augie back on Cloud Nine.

"Now about what we'd appreciate *your* two cents on…"

"Excuse me, Sergeant, before we get to that," interrupted Augie.

"Yeah, shoot."

"Thanks. If I understand this gravity stuff correctly, why doesn't your starship captain use conventional rocket boost power for your starship as with that firefly donut thingie? To free the Smoke and Mirrors, is it? from the immense extraterrestrial spaceship's gravitational grasp?"

"Officer Leung figured that even if one hundred per cent of- Put it this way: They needed fully half their available hydrogen fuel simply to provide amply thrust to the freakin' firefly donut. The Smoke and Mirrors starship is three times the size of one of your f-n' drone clouds. Ergo, there's not nearly enough hydrogen, not even close, for the necessary oomph."

"That sucks."

"Sucks long and hard, don't have to tell me. But now, something we'd like to pick your brain about, especially Sherman Peabody with his artificial intelligence sidekick. Our folks recorded these peculiar noises transmitted from that f-n' immense ET vessel."

"Charly is programmed to rapidly identify numerous different sounds aside from flatus emissions," acknowledged Sherman, his attention drawn to the video phone before Augie could call him over. "That's in addition to linguistic processing, provided there are sufficient cognate-related clues."

"F-n' wonderful," swore Fred. "But I'm not sure you'll need- Well just have Charly listen for itself, himself."

"Are you with us now, Charly?" asked Sherman after switching him back on.

Charly's head stiffly performed a full, three-hundred-sixty-degree rotation, before click...whirr... "I see I am with an 'us' that includes you, Sherman Peabody, plus Augustine Matias, Scott MacDonald, Samuel Longbottom, and Laura Gómez."

"F-n' fantastic," swore Fred again. "So, listen to this."

Pfft! Pfft! Pfft! Pfffffft-spllfff... Bum! Bum!

There seemed to Augie three different noises. There were what he could only describe as staccato farts, or flatus emissions as Sherman's more polite term for them went. Those were interspersed with lengthier, fainter but somehow more massive farts, perhaps heard from behind a barrier. Lastly, also interspersed were irregular poundings, like someone or something trying to break through...

Click...whirr... Click-click...whirrrrrr... "I will have the readout for you shortly," Charly plainly stated in his robotic monotone voice.

To Augie's relief, Charly's microphone for the built-in flatus emission detector retracted back behind his pants zipper before Fred could notice on the video phone.

"However, I can already report that results from my flatus emission detector do indicate possible saurian involvement," Charly went on. "There are two classes of emission, actually."   Click...whirr...   "One bears resemblance to typical mammalian output, while the other leans the more reptilian direction." Click...whirr... "While the mammalian source is more diminutive, the reptilian source is on a larger scale."

"So, we're talkin' possible dinosaurs from space? Give me a f-n' break!" Sergeant Frankly cursed as usual.

Click...whirr...click...whirr... Ticker tape suddenly spilled from Charly's mouth, which Sherman hastened to spool in his hands before it could fall to the floor.

"We shouldn't jump to any premature conclusions," cautioned Sherman as he unspooled the ticker tape inches at a time, to carefully pore over them. "However, this confirms my general first impression. Hmm...never expected anything quite like this. But it is a big universe out there."

"Care to share?" Laura intruded delicately.

"Yeah, like I haven't already experienced more than enough crazy, ever since signing aboard the Smoke and Mirrors!" less delicately vented Fred on the videophone from hundreds of miles away.

"Oh, why yes, of course," Sherman's head jerked his chin off his neck like he'd just been roused from dozing off. "The one set of sounds, unmistakably they fit the profile of a large reptilian creature, possibly dinosaurian if our mystery readout from Cameroon is evidence in that regard. But I find the second set of emissions even more intriguing. Mammalian-type flatus emissions from something no larger than a Scottish terrier, for sure, but in rhythmic patterns that remind me of Morse Code."

"Damn!" vented Fred. "Here we are, stuck wondering whether there's some underground monster capable of causing earthquakes. And meanwhile, the people we depend on to get us back home to the future are being drawn through a wormhole by a spaceship whose operators, whatever they have to say, literally blow it out their asses! F- me! And what if said spaceship is out of control, once it leaves the wormhole close to Earth? It could come crashing into our planet, the starship along with it!"

"Unlikely to sustain a velocity that would make it any kind of apocalyptic- No, scratch that," Ali shook his head inside the tent pitched beside Kurupira. "Say its propulsion system performs similar to our starship's. It could be approaching Earth at speeds far in excess of what made a certain asteroid, much smaller, such a threat sixty-five million years ago. Although- Well something truly hopeful occurs to me," Ali perked up, realizing. "There's nothing in our history, from well ahead in 2064, that suggests such a large object got anywhere near Earth back here in the early 1980s."

"Of course, we're on an alternate history line now with our time travel intervention," weighed in Officer Kevin Smith-Park, manning the controls of Cloud Ten in hover above Kurupira. "Hopefully entraining the S&M has done nothing to alter the alien space vessel's trajectory that dramatically."

"Excuse me, Sherman," said Scott aboard Cloud Nine, the original steam-powered spaciously appointed drone, presently situated well south of Cloud Ten. "This will sound like trivial pursuit, I'm sure, compared to that scary stuff our time traveling friends are discussing that I can't even deal with. But- It's a bit awkward saying this in front of Charly…"

Click…whirr… "That's quite alright," Charly reacted after having stood completely motionless since the last time he spoke. "My empathy program is switched to the 'off' position. I won't be pretending to have my feelings hurt."

"Oh, well that's good, I guess."

Click…whirr… "Your remarks do not amplify on the latest evidence of possible non-avian dinosaur survival."

Scott found himself fully satisfied that not only did he worry needlessly over Charly. Giving that artificial intelligence entity any further attention at that time would prove irritatingly unproductive. Therefore, he turned Sherman Peabody's way to say, "In short, Sherman, why does your flatus emission detector's readout emerge from Charly's mouth?"

"Building such a complex machine, you see, involved resorting to certain admittedly bizarre-looking economies."

"Understood. But why the mouth?"

"Dr. MacDonald, you saw where I had to install the flatus emission detector mike. Regarding the mouth, I'm sure you can imagine, um, shall we say a less elegant orifice from where the readout could have emerged?"

Chapter 15

When Augie unexpectedly broke through an abundance of bushes, ferns and other plants along the Amazon tributary, he lost balance, and nearly plunged head first into the enormous furrow produced by an unknown force. Only Laura and Scott's quick reflexes saved him, grabbing his arms at the last possible moment.

Brazil nut trees towered a hundred feet above everything else. Amidst them, camu camu berry bushes, passionflower vines, water reeds and numerous ferns blocked the furrow from view, any distance away. And over the short couple of weeks since it first appeared, a dense, slippery carpet of moss and lichen had covered the furrow's steep sides.

Liana vines snaked down into the furrow made ever more mysterious by a cavernously sized burrow at one end. Plus, there was a second, smaller burrow into the far side of where the expedition approached.

Long before reaching the intended stakeout location, Eclipso's search team climbed down the rope ladder from Cloud Nine into a large clearing not far from the impressively large *Yanomami* communal *shabono*. That's where journalist Laura Gómez couldn't help commenting, "Is it just me, or is this entire region distinctly more fragrant than where we snooped about Cameroon and New Britain Island?"

Click...whirr... "I am not equipped to address the matter of fragrances," said Charly set on whisper mode by Sherman. "More specifically..."...click...whirr..."Laura, I contain no data relative to your odor level in Cameroon and New Britain Island as compared to here. Nor do I have such data for where you snooped about Cameroon and New Britain Island as compared to here."

Click!

"I've just switched Charly to mobility mode only, for the time being," announced Sherman. "But I'm pleased you noticed the added fragrance."

"Really?"

"Might well be that this neck of the Amazon is indeed more fragrant than what we've experienced before, especially with all those tree-clinging orchids and passionflower vines. But I dare say no small part of what your olfactory organs are detecting originates from my new pest repellant formula. I've been able to incorporate more flower-based scents that not only stave off certain nuisance creatures. They also effectively mask the, shall we say, more offensive odors still required to keep us safe from venomous snakes and the like."

"But I don't recall your spraying us with anything this time before we left Cloud Nine," Laura pointed out. *I had kind-of hoped you'd forgotten, despite the danger wandering tropical forests without it.*

"That's the other thing, Ms. Gómez. I managed to treat everyone's clothes with my new concoction before they were last removed in bulk from the Cloud Nine clothes drier."

The long-awaited advance stakeout was finally getting underway, of the notably deep furrow beside an Amazon River tributary not far from a *Yanomami* community. A new tremor was expected there that evening, as had been happening every nineteen days in recent months.

Prior to said stakeout, the dinosaur searchers delivered on their promise to Adriana Souza. They sought her husband far and wide, albeit to no avail.

As well, they revisited where the husband's buddy, Cal, had his pickup truck overturn. Adriana's husband claimed to have seen his buddy, plus an ostrich-sized dinosaur, swallowed whole there, by a behemoth reptilian head that rose out of the ground.

Snooping about the accident scene brought to light nothing really that helpful. Nevertheless, mounds of overturned soil and road macadam had required a makeshift gravel road detour around them. They were tantalizingly suggestive of something immense and subterranean having indeed caused a major upheaval.

Subsequent interviews at *Colina Pelada's* small mining town turned up no sightings of Sebastião since the day before the pickup truck accident. Zero accounts of him or anyone else having torn through there, dropping wads of cash for drinks, gambling, and prostitutes.

Suppose Cal did carry a sack full of gold nuggets aboard his pickup truck. There was no evidence of where it went.

Of course, as Adriana continued to suspect, her husband could have made off with the loot to one of the big cities. Maybe he intended to gamble it into an even bigger fortune, then share that happy news with her. But he lost the bulk of it, bad luck at poker leading him to waste the rest on booze and brothels.

Visiting the still-active larger mining area, *Serra Pelada*, proved even more worthless, if only for the deadly danger experienced there. Augie and company uncovered a Brazilian oil company keeping a close eye on the gold prospectors. Were one of those prospectors to stumble upon an oil reserve, said company would dive in like a vulture, thereby avoiding lots of exploration costs.

Long story short, a rumor circulated that Augie's gang intended to hog in on the oil company's game. Lawyers would split anticipated oil profits between themselves, the dinosaur hunters, and the prospectors, cutting out the oil company completely.

In short order, Augie and company found themselves fleeing hired goons through rainforest jungle, looking for a clearing where Cloud Nine could rope-ladder them back to safety. One of the goons actually fired his pistol at them, albeit not so much to kill as to scare them off.

That's when Charly, the artificial intelligence entity, driven by his purpose-infused program, suddenly not only came to a full stop. He stood to his full height, and turned to face the pursuers.

Ping! Ping! Ping! Bullets bounced harmlessly off Charly's titanium-underlaid latex facial and neck skin. Click...whirr... "I have confirmed that the objects impacting me are not fecal pellets fired from the anus of a surviving non-avian dinosaur."

Ping!

"No; they are bullets fired from a non-anus source, such as a pistol. This readout should provide confirmation."

Charly opened his mouth like he was about to vomit, so it appeared to one of the armed goons. Instead, a two-foot-long ticker tape spilled out. That scared the bad guys into a hasty retreat while Charly tore off the paper from inside his mouth, and held it forward in offer to any takers.

"You probably saved our lives, Charly," Laura returned beside him to say appreciatively. "Thank you!"

Click...Whirr... "You're welcome."

*

"The only concern I have with my new pest repellant formulation," went on Sherman Peabody, crouched amidst thick rainforest foliage, "happily seems less of a worry with each passing moment. Namely, that any one or more of us might develop sneeze-inducing allergies. Lots of luck, sneaking up on a surviving non-avian dinosaur if you have a bad case of the ah-choos."

Just then, Augie, Scott, and Laura heard a very faint noise, conceivably the very teensiest and shortest of sneezes. None of them were at all sure it wasn't a product of their over-active imaginations, though. The power of suggestion after Sherman's remarks. They kept quiet about it, remained crouched beside Sherman and Charly surrounded by flowering shrubs and numerous passionflowers.

"Now what?" Scott asked impatiently. "Aninha says the developers intent on raping this wilderness for riches and cash-cow cattle plan on bringing gold prospectors and *Yanomami* youth here tonight. Do we assume they won't actually arrive until after sunset? Give us enough time to reconnoiter that furrow and its burrows? Then in hiding watch them watching for a washout of gold gleaming in the moonlight?"

"Okay, I didn't say anything the first time," burst out Augie. "But it's happened again. Could have sworn I heard a sneeze. A very little sneeze, but a sneeze nonetheless."

*

"Ah, ahhhh...CHOO!!" went new fourth-grade student Brantley Gilmore in Vicky Copplestone's back-to-school orientation session at Green Pastures Elementary School in Rockville, Maryland, three days before the official first day of the 1982-1983 school year. He was among the handful of students enraptured by the lush tropical setting displayed on Ms. Copplestone's television. A video camera affixed to her husband Augie's headband had transported them to an Amazonian rainforest thousands of miles away.

"Hey you guys!" shouted Brantley at the television. As though Laura, Scott, and Sherman, bent down amidst an abundance of violet-accented passionflowers in full bloom, could actually hear him!

Fellow classmates variously giggled and sighed.

*

"Thought I heard it too!" Laura whispered urgently. "Could some *Yanomamis* or gold prospectors have arrived already, in hiding?"

*

"Over here!" Brantley stood out of his chair, waving at the TV screen. "We're not hiding at all!"

"Ms. Copplestone, think I've found the flowers they're sitting next to," said student Erin to Vicky, holding a book open before her. "They're passionflowers, yes?"

"Aren't those beautiful?" enthused Vicky. "Maybe you can read us more about them."

*

"Not necessarily a human sneeze," suggested Sherman. "We're not the only creatures who develop allergies. It might be a snake."

"A snake can sneeze, seriously?" said Laura, giving Sherman a dubious regard.

"Oh, I don't think a snake expresses any sort of attitude when sneezing, whether serious, comical, boastful, or something else," Sherman shook his head. "Any more than you would employ one of your own sneezes to say, for example, 'This is not something to be laughed at.' Or am I *seriously* mistaken? Anyway, without question, snakes can, and do, sneeze, though that's not something they are particularly known for."

Your belly button has learned a lot from you over the years, hasn't it? Augie mischievously wanted to ask Sherman, the way Sherman continued scrunching his chin into his neck to speak.

*

"Did you hear that?" Brantley asked fellow students, flushing tomato red with his amusement. "He said snakes can sneeze. And they might have just heard one!"

"Hello again, students, parents and teachers, from Dr. Klondike," principal Marsha Klondike's voice burst from the intercom above the chalkboard at the front of Vicky Copplestone's classroom. "It's time, students, for you to change rooms as indicated on your individual schedules. Don't forget that high school volunteers wearing the Green Pastures badge can help you to your next location."

"Awwww!!" rose a collective moan, like Vicky remembered making herself back when she was a kid. That is, whenever her mom or dad called her indoors for supper from romping around on a summer's early evening.

"Come on, Erin," said Erin's mom. "Your other special, art, is next. You don't want to miss that, I'm sure."

"But you see what I'm doing, Mom?" protested Erin, holding a paper in her face. "This is a passion flower sketch I want to finish. And I also want to see if they come across a dinosaur near that- I think Ms. Copplestone's husband called it a tri-bu-tar-y," Erin carefully sounded out the word.

"Yes, tributary, that's correct; very good!" remarked Vicky.

"You can finish your sketch at home. And I'm sure your art teacher will want to see what you've done so far." Erin's mom held back on what she really wanted to say, for fear of making an even bigger scene with her daughter. Soon as they got home, she intended to call the school, have her daughter removed from what struck her as a blasphemously insane instructional program. *They might as well be trying to convince my daughter the Earth is flat! For sure, Erin doesn't need that awful Copplestone woman putting thoughts in her head of sneezing snakes, and dinosaurs still romping about South America!*

"Hey, what's going on in here?" asked Winston Robertson. He poked his head through the classroom door to see why he heard so many students complaining they didn't want to leave yet.

"Ms. Copplestone's husband is staking out a tributary in the Amazon rainforest. He's searching for a living, breathing dinosaur!" Erin gestured ecstatically at Winston, blowing off her mom's imploration to leave.

"And they think they might have heard a snake sneeze!" flushed-face Brantley giggled his way through adding.

"I've gotta check this out!" Winston announced. He headed for the nearest empty seat.

"Hey buddy," said his father, "you have art class now, remember?"

"Ms. Copplestone has drawing paper, colored pencils, crayons, everything I need to work on this passion flower sketch" Erin noted for Winston's benefit. And then, "You see where those explorers are crouching down?" Erin pointed at the television, again ignoring her mother, who sternly said, "Erin Camilla Taylor, we must leave this minute!"

"They're in the Amazon?"

"That's video *live* from the Amazon!" confirmed Erin for Winston.

"Please, Winston, let's not make a fuss..."

"Let's not *you* make a fuss, Daddy-o!" Winston cut off his father while clutching at the underneath of his chair. He made clear that if "Daddy-o" tried removing him forcibly from Vicky's classroom, the chair would go with him.

"But I thought art was your favorite-"

"I can do all the art I want at home," Winston cut off his father again. "And you heard 'Erin Camilla Taylor.' I can draw in here if I need to."

"But you should really meet with the new art teacher before-"

"Well maybe I want to change my elective to Ms. Copplestone!"

*

"What else might that sneeze have been from, if it's not someone who arrived over there earlier than expected?" Laura quizzed Sherman.

Laura still crouched alongside fellow explorers, amidst passionflowers bordering the steep drop-off into the enormous burrow. And she was note-taking at a furious pace. "Do any insects sneeze, for example?"

"Insects actually respirate through pinholes in their exoskeleton carapace. They don't possess nostrils, per se, and therefore don't sneeze."

"But dinosaurs probably did sneeze if snakes sneeze," concluded Laura. "Any chance, then, that a sneeze detector might help us find our quarry, in addition to your flatus emission detector?"

"A curious thing about sneezes," said Sherman, making eye contact with one of the buttons down the front of his long-sleeve canvas-sack safari shirt, if he was making any eye contact at all. "Suppose I played you a recording of a snake's sneeze. Apart from its petiteness, you would be hard-pressed to discern any difference from a comparably short and soft human sneeze."

Click...whirr... "So, sneeze analysis is worthless for detecting the presence of a surviving, non-avian dinosaur," concluded Charly. Click...whirr... "Therefore, it is a waste of time even talking about it, and that makes me feel..." ...click...whirr... "...mad..." ...click...whirr... "...and frustrated."

"I'm trying out a modified, toned-down empathy program with him," Sherman whispered.

"Really?" Laura asked the artificial intelligence entity in a dubious tone. "You *really* feel mad and frustrated?"

The challenge was on!

Click...whirr... "Not really." Click...whirr... "But it fits."

"Okay people," whispered Scott, straining not to raise his voice given the genuine frustration *he* was feeling. "Are we just going to keep crouching down here? In case those two small sneezes we might have heard came from the extra-early arrival of our expected company? Then wait who knows how long for that tremor to go off again like it has been doing every nineteen days? Or is anyone still with me about getting our clothes a little dirtier? Into the furrow for a daytime look-around of the thresholds to those two large burrows?"

Click...whirr... "If that provides us evidence related to survival of non-avian dinosaurs, I am all for it."

"But we don't know those sneezes were not from the prospectors or the *Yanomamis*," Laura whispered back urgently again. "If any of them carry blow darts like before, they might pick us off to keep us away from their damned gold! I say we wait a few more minutes, at least. Make sure it wasn't one of them we heard sneezing."

*

"No! Don't wait!" complained Winston watching from Vicky Copplestone's classroom thousands of miles away. "Explore that furrow! Do it now!"

"Listen! Like this!" giggled Brantley, so red in the face that Vicky had to remind herself there was no need to worry. His head wouldn't actually explode.   "Click...whirr..." Brantley went on, making stiff robotic arm, shoulder, and head motions, "Do it!   Click...whirr... Do it now! Click...whirr..."

By this time, there were twenty-four students in Vicky's classroom. Apart from Winston, they included six who should have already left for their next orientation section, five who were supposed to take their place, and an even dozen who, like Winston, simply didn't want to leave after dipping their heads in. All of them joined Brantley by rising to their feet and stiffly, robotically saying, "Click...whirr... Do it! Click...whirr... Do it now!"

"SLAM!"

Oh-oh thought Vicky.

A door slammed shut was succeeded by a distinct Click! Click! Click!

"Can I have your attention, robot people, please?" Vicky pleadingly raised her voice to not quite an out-and-out shout.

Winston and company giggled at being called robot people, but they did quiet down.

"Click...whirr... Thank you, fellow zombie-bots," Vicky said making her own stiff-arm gestures to scattered applause and more giggles. She went on, "I believe Ms. Mueller is about to enter, so please be on your best behavior."

Knock! Knock!

The children rushed to their seats. Their accompanying parents remained standing. And without even waiting for Vicky to answer the door, curriculum leader Diane Mueller stormed stomping inside.

"What exactly is going on here, Ms. Copplestone?" Diane asked in the harshest tone she could muster.

Vicky imagined Diane's pursed lips was the expression on her own face, those few times she sucked on an especially tart lemon.

Children's hands went up, respectfully quietly.

"Yes, Erin?"

"I've been learning all about passionflowers," Erin explained, holding up her half-completed colored-pencil sketch. "I didn't know they are so pretty, and grow a fruit that people use to make a drink after the bloom withers. Now I hope to try passion fruit juice."

"I think that can be easily arranged, especially since I'm also curious. I'm Erin's mother," Donna offered as an excuse for breaking in without asking permission to speak.

"I've tried it; good stuff," said Vicky pleasantly if also nervously. Nevertheless, she fearlessly proceeded, recognizing another raised hand, "Winston?"

"I've been learning about artificial intelligence. There's this artificial intelligence robot that looks like a real dude.

He's helping Ms. Copplestone's husband and his friends search for dinosaurs in the Amazon rain forest, in South America." Winston gestured towards the television, which at that point displayed one, moss-covered side of the deeply carved furrow. "But he's a little out of it on anything other than searching for dinosaurs."

"Certainly does seem that way, doesn't it?" pleasantly chuckled Vicky. "Brantley?"

"I've learned that people aren't the only ones who sneeze! I didn't know snakes can sneeze!" Brantley couldn't help giggling. His face turned beet-red yet again.

"Are all of you supposed to be in this classroom?" Diane asked severely, wanting to shut down the hilarity resulting from Brantley's remarks, politeness be damned. "Weren't some of you supposed to move to your next orientation session? And aren't some of you... Winston, are you supposed to be here at all? I don't recall seeing you registered for Ms. Copplestone's special."

"As Winston's father, if I might," weighed in Mr. Robertson, "my understanding was that no student was required to attend school today. This was supposed to be a bonus getting-to-know-you session under relaxed, informal circumstances."

"Well, to a certain extent..."

"What's the harm in my Winston and other students checking out classes they aren't necessarily registered for, to satisfy their curiosity?"

Rather than respond, Diane Mueller made a show of checking her wristwatch. Then she hurried out of Vicky's classroom, leaving another slammed door in her wake.

Brantley rose from his chair, and moving robotically, said in robotic monotone, "Click...whirr...the operation was a success," drawing laughter and applause, even from parents.

"Okay, everyone, let's quiet down and listen closely," advised Vicky Copplestone, reluctant to smugly join in the hilarity, as satisfying as she found the rebuff of Mueller by Winston's father. "We don't want to miss anything important."

*

Growing impatient sitting crouched for so long, Laura poked her head up from amidst the passionflower vines. That's when she could have sworn she caught out the corner of her eye no less than three heads ducking back up into the rainforest canopy.

The rainforest canopy hung draped across a number of Brazil nut trees, the opposite side of the deep furrow from where the Eclipso team kept indecisive vigil.

"I think we're under surveillance already," Laura whispered to Augie beside her. "Pretty sure I spotted three dudes, probably Yanomami, peek down out of the aerial forest."

"Really?" With that, Augie poked *his* head up. He was just in time to spot a few heads poke up from varied shrubbery across the furrow from him, directly underneath the aforementioned rainforest canopy or aerial forest, as Laura put it. They turned every which way until they spotted him, sending them ducked down out of sight the same time as Augie.

"I spotted a couple also," Augie whispered loud enough for everyone in his group to hear, not just Laura. He trusted the rainforest critter din to drown out his voice for anyone further away. "But they rose out of the ground cover."

"I don't want to be left out," said Scott, popping up his own head to have a look-see. He caught the canopy snoopers and ground cover snoopers noticing each other simultaneously, then ducking back up and down into hiding.

"This is ridiculous," Scott remarked, ducking back down out of sight, himself. "It's like whack-a-mole out there, minus the mole whacker."

Click...whirr... "I don't understand why you devote so much time to the subject of who you can spot who might be watching us. It appears to have zero bearing on the issue of surviving non-avian dinosaurs," weighed in Charly.

"Sh!" Laura Gómez curtly shushed the artificial intelligence entity, forefinger firmly to her lips. "Careful," she went on whispering. "We need to make sure whatever noises we make blend in with the rainforest creature racket."

Charly's flatus emission detector mike poked out of his pants again, pursuant to which the rainforest din of insects, frogs, birds, and the occasional howler monkey grew exponentially louder.

To Augie, it was as though someone suddenly turned the amplifier volume way up...until he realized it emanated from Charly crouched beside him.

"What the hell are you doing *now*?" Laura asked Charly in a furious whisper.

The magnified rainforest din cut off as abruptly as it started, long enough for Charly to click...whirr... "I'm making noises to 'blend in with the rainforest creature racket.'" Then it resumed, louder than ever.

"Charly, I think what Ms. Gómez meant about blending in was to whisper softly enough for your voice to become lost in the general plethora of rainforest noises. Which is to say, for anyone not down here beside us," patiently whispered Sherman. "Not to imitate it."

Click...whirr... "I understand," responded Charly, his rainforest din cut off for good. Click...whirr... "I'm sorry."

No, you're not sorry at all, Laura thought to herself with more than a little exasperation. *That's simply a logical conclusion from your empathy logarithm.* But ensuing events set this matter aside for her, in a hurry.

A young *Yanomami* gentleman had ducked down out of the rainforest canopy, puzzled over the rainforest din having inexplicably intensified and softened not once, but twice. Thusly distracted, his own powerful sneeze caused him to lose hold of a liana vine, and fall from his perch. He landed on a gold prospector below with a distinct thump.

Two screams followed.

Whereupon several gun barrels popped out of the ground cover shrubbery, the opposite side of the deep furrow from where the dinosaur search team squatted hidden. They were aimed at the rainforest canopy.

Several blow dart straws poked down out of said canopy, aimed at the shrubbery below.

"*Basta!* Enough!" shouted Aninha Floresta in both Portuguese and English. She emerged from rainforest cover behind Augie's crew, attired in what reminded Augie of the Hawai'ian muumuu dress, the same bright blue of the hyacinth macaw. Her imperious strut likewise reminded Augie of Rosa and Ron's macaw, Milton Nascimento, strutting atop their rattan sofa, guarding a seemingly empty nest shredded into one sofa cushion. After a fluent translation into the *Yanomami Xiriana* tongue, she went on, "This is ridiculous! If you shoot and blow-dart each other, there will be none of you left alive! Come out in the open! Now! Everyone! And state your ambition!"

Click...whirr... "We are searching for a surviving non-avian dinosaur." Click...whirr... "If diplomacy is required to abet our mission, we could sing, dance, and share food with you." Click...whirr... "But I will have to watch while you eat, as my machinery is not equipped to process food." Click...whirr... "In addition, the insertion of-"

Click!

Charly slumped forward, hunched over. Sherman Peabody had raced to switch him off before he could finish what Sherman feared would be a reprise of an earlier remark found generally offensive.

"I thought you modified his empathy program to be less, um, extreme," Laura remarked delicately.

"Indeed, I did," nodded Sherman. "It is vexing how despite that, he keeps defaulting to mention of, uh, a certain sexual matter."

"Our robotic, um, person is still having difficulties maintaining proper conversation," Augie went on, pausing for Aninha to translate along the way. "But he did describe our ambition correctly. All we are here for is to gather evidence that dinosaurs might have survived to the present day, or recent times." (pause for Aninha's translation) "Of course, we want to respect *Yanomami* norms, and avoid disrupting the rainforest ecology..." (another pause) "To be perfectly honest, though, the evidence already gathered is so paltry, I doubt we will succeed, at least in this particular rainforest region. Truck-sized snakes or overgrown lizards, such as a horse-sized iguana, seem more likely than a dinosaur on the loose."

"So, what is it exactly you plan to do now, besides watching and waiting, *senhor*?" asked Raul Viana in a challenging, wanna-fight-about-it? tone. He emerged standing amidst bunches of huge ferns.

Augie mused that Raul might as well have been Moses parting the Red Sea, the way he pushed aside the ferns to step forward, close to the precipice of the very deep furrow.

"We will watch and wait after sunset," Augie finally answered. "We want to see whether the ground trembles again, like it has been doing at nightfall every nineteen days for the past couple of months, reportedly. And will that chase some prehistoric creature out of those two burrows down there? We don't know. But assuming approval by our *Yanomami* friends, we would like to enter this furrow, and carefully explore the thresholds to those two burrows while there's still daylight. Tracks, spoor, maybe even a broken-off claw..."

"Okay," said Raul. He didn't even wait for Aninha's translation of Augie's final remarks, while the prospectors and *Yanomamis* put away their respective weapons, albeit with slow reluctance. "You dinosaur hunters-"

"We prefer the term, 'searchers,' to 'hunters,'" corrected Sherman, his point-of-order finger raised. "Indeed, we are determined to protect, not harm any relic prehistoric survivors we might come across."

"Dinosaur searchers," Raul closed his eyes and nodded as in *Whatever*. "Well, here is something you need to know: Around the same time that you expect your impossibility to be flushed out into the open, we expect drainage down there to flush out gold flecks evidencing a much bigger stash! We have it on good authority that those tremors go off every nineteen days due to underground exploratory detonations, not Godzilla's ovulation cycle or anything like that."

"And why isn't the *Macawoyano* here?" asked Aninha. Her chest swelled noticeably with her expansive inhale. Like she could draw out a truthful response that way, Augie found himself thinking.

The young *Yanomami* men still hanging down from the rainforest canopy, plus the one fallen to the ground, looked shame-faced in the wake of Aninha's *Xiriana* translation.

"Oh, I understand," Aninha nodded at them knowingly. "You were certain the *Macawoyano* wouldn't approve, so you've kept this from him."

"You see how they've painted themselves?!?!" bristled Raul defensively. "They'll keep the traditions alive! But they also understand the need for progress, to get out ahead of progress so it doesn't steamroll over them!"

Aninha nodded knowingly again, and smiled bitterly. "Their painted visages will make an excellent tourist attraction when they turn this place into a Disneyworld theme park!"

"Listen!" cried out Augie holding up his hand as in, *This is getting too out of hand*, "Any gold we find down there, that's all yours! We have no interest in that!"

"Better be true," said Raul. "Because we will be keeping an eye on you; anything you pick up down in there, we need to inspect it. We need to make sure it's only iguana poop you'd like to believe was deposited by a dinosaur, and not a gold nugget!"

"Fair enough!" said Scott MacDonald, supportive of Augie's effort to turn down the emotional heat, at least. The physical heat combined with pea soup humidity had Eclipso's crew frequently reaching for chilled water from Sherman's dry-ice contraption.

"Don't think we have more than an hour of full daylight left, guys," Laura advised Scott and friends. "If we're going to do our advance reconnoiter..."

"And trust someone won't pick us off like the proverbial fish in a barrel," said Scott worriedly. His fear of circumstances had finally gotten the best of him.

"I fret over possible danger as much as anyone, Scott," started in Sherman Peabody.

"And remember, he's the guy who keeps recalculating the odds of being struck by a meteorite," Augie reminded Scott encouragingly.

"Yes, that's true," acknowledged Sherman, nodding his chin into his neck as usual. "But as I was starting to say, I am by nature most notably averse to risk. Of all people, I would be the first to pull the plug on my own descent into such an astonishingly deep furrow. Especially a furrow characterized by the spooky cavernous entrance one end, and a somewhat smaller but no-less-hauntingly mysterious burrow on one side. That is, if I genuinely reckoned some untoward danger lay in wait down there. But I am supremely confident my latest, less-odoriferously-offensive pest repellant keeps us safe from all manner of insects, arachnids, poisonous frogs and the like. And furthermore, that any relic, monstrous prehistoric reptile for whom either or both of those subterranean entrances serves as its lair is very probably still asleep, this time of the day. *And*, let's suppose it is awake already, set on a daylight prowl. We must also suppose an exceptionally reclusive nature, like most every other reptile I know anything about. All the noise we've been making out here, various whisperings included, have probably set it on edge. Yes, it might well be ready to take a bite out of anyone who ventures close enough to poke at it, provoke it. But otherwise, I suspect it wants to hold back, wait for our quieting down to suggest we've departed."

"Unless it hasn't eaten in days, weeks maybe," countered Scott, "and is so hungry, that easily supersedes that reclusive nature. It's ready to rumble, right now, woe be for any animal in its path."

"But don't forget, it might be as effectively offended by my new repellant formulation as a creature one-tenth its size."

"Yeah, what about its size, Sherman?" said Scott. "What if there's some snake or burrowing dinosaur here so ginormous, it *is* what produced this furrow? And makes the ground quake every time hunger wakes it to go hunting? Say, every nineteen days?"

"Please tell us, Aninha," Sherman looked towards the large, colorfully attired woman of domineering presence. "Those tremors have been a relatively new phenomenon?

Not to date having posed any special danger to the local *Yanomami* settlement?"

Aninha crossed her arms for her severe regard of Sherman as she responded, "No special danger to the local *Yanomamis*, true...for now. But as you already know, one gold prospector reported his companion prospector disappeared into the maw of some reptilian beast raising its elephant-sized head out of the ground. And isn't it true that to the far northeast, at the Venezuelan border, part of your expedition found an abandoned *Yanomami shabono* in shambles? Possibly trampled underfoot?"

Just then, Augie saw a small, bright-green snake raise its tiny head above some nameless shrub, and sneeze a most petite "Ah-choo!" before quickly sinking back out of sight.

"Yes, I have to concede everything you say is correct," said Sherman, his chin seeming to Augie scrunched ever deeper into his chin. "If I am being completely honest, my impassioned curiosity over what we might discover is overriding my usual excessive caution."

Another petite sneeze originated from where neither Augie nor anyone else had their attention focused. It punctuated the conclusion of Sherman's unexpectedly frank admission, while Aninha nodded approvingly.

"Okay, you *bobos* keep clucking away like so many chickens headed for slaughter. The sun will set before you have time to explore down in there for dinosaur shit or whatever!" spat out Raul. "You better get on with it! But don't try pretending your dinosaur poops gold bricks! Like the goose who laid the golden egg! And don't worry about any blow darts! We see just one of those blow dart straws poke out of the canopy," Raul pointed overhead, "my men will make it rain dead *Yanomamis!*"

For someone complaining about our "clucking away" too much, you're doing quite a bit of the buk-buk-buk-buk-

buk! yourself, Augie didn't dare do any more than quietly think to himself.

As if Raul's remarks weren't enough, before Scott could say, *Okay, well let's get going, then*, Aninha added, "A spokesman for these young *Yanomami* men has just reassured me. If they see even one gun barrel re-emerge into view, all of Raul's gold prospectors will immediately find themselves stung by needles dipped in the most venomous frog toxin found anywhere in Brazil."

"That gives me a warm fuzzy feeling, caballeros," said Laura. "Shall we have at it before they destroy each other over our security?"

"I will re-activate Charly to lead the way," announced Sherman. He pressed a few buttons on the artificial intelligence entity, then snapped shut the compartment on its back. "Better that his latex skin receive a poisonous wound from some critter not repelled by my latest olfactory concoction. Than one of us, that is."

Click...whirr... "Scanning for..." ...click...whirr... "...evidence of surviving non-avian dinosaurs..." Click...whirr... "Whoops!"

"'Whoops'?" Augie whispered to Laura.

Losing traction on his descent into the deep, moss-covered furrow, Charly quickly lost balance. Then, he did a reprieve of what he did to board Samuel Longbottom's Turok Tours bus. He rolled himself into a ball, much like a frightened hedgehog or armadillo, and rolled the rest of the way down.

"I'd guess that 'Whoops!' is a programmed reaction from what Sherman terms his toned-down empathy function."

"I say, are you okay there, Charly?" Sherman asked his creation with genuine, non-logarithmic concern.

Charlie uncurled tentatively slowly. He ended up awkwardly standing on his head without using his hands for balance, as instead they were busily checking various parts of his body. Click...whirr... "All my systems are operating within acceptable parameters. I find no significant tears in the latex exterior, merely shallow scratches..." Click...whirr... "I think that's the operational definition of 'okay,' to answer your question." Click...whirr... "What's more, I was able to retract my flatus emission detector mike before it could have been snapped off." With that, Charly curled his legs back behind himself with mechanically stiff motions, despite thereby demonstrating a flexibility found usually only in Olympic gymnasts. Once his boots were firmly planted behind him, he resumed his mechanically stiff motions, and slowly brought himself back to fully upright.

Click...whirr... "Be careful on your way down."

"Why thank you, Charly," said Sherman as he went on hands and knees to slowly crawl backwards into the furrow.

Click...whirr... "You're welcome..." ...click...whirr... "...even though that provides no useful data regarding the possible survival of non-avian dinosaurs."

Augie noticed more snake sneezes, including from another he saw poke its head out from amidst a passion fruit vine. Plus, one spider monkey in the rainforest canopy overhead went, "He-he-he-ah-choo!"

By the time the explorers carefully climbed down into the immense furrow, the snake and spider monkey sneezes had multiplied. There was a steady drizzle of them, presumably from allergies to Sherman's new, improved, less-stinky pest repellant. Augie and Scott wished it would subside so they could confirm they were hearing a sporadic rustle echoing from the smaller burrow. Sounded like something moving about inside there, something massive.

"Must say," remarked Laura, stepping slowly about the spongy, moss-covered ground, "the stench down here reminds me of certain unpleasant odors inside the gorilla house at the National Zoo in Washington, D.C. Maybe not quite as pungent in this open air, but still…"

"I'm thinking more the smell inside their reptile house," said Augie.

"Yeah, maybe with notes of bouquet de feces mixed in for the worst wine, ever," snarked Laura. "Okay, what are we looking for here exactly, short of being stampeded by a herd of Triceratops?"

"That is a significant question," affirmed Sherman. He joined Charly bending over then crouching down to inspect the furrow's mossy floor more closely. "Obviously, any foot tracks left here are concealed by this impressively fast-growing moss. And daily rainforest downpours would have washed them away in any event."

"What I'm thinking," said Scott, joining the crouch-down, "is that we look for broken-off teeth, bits of shed skin, hard scales…"

"Those are the sorts of things alligators often leave in their wake, to the tune of hundreds of lost teeth in a lifetime. Why not lost dinosaur teeth as well?" Sherman nodded while already inspecting something. He tossed it aside on realizing it was an empty scarab beetle shell. "Yes, that makes perfect sense, indeed."

Augie and Laura were about to join the crouch-down themselves, when they both thought they heard the opening "Ah" from an aborted sneeze. They looked around warily.

As close as that sounded, must have been from a member of our weapon-wielding audience, Augie concluded. *The acoustics out here…*

"Ahhh…"

That "Ah" was loud enough, with a bit of a reverberating echo, to lift Sherman and Scott's heads to join Laura and Augie in their anxious look-around.

Out the corner of his eye, Augie noticed miner and *Yanomami* heads popped back out of hiding, turning this way and that. *They must have heard that too!*

Charly had no reaction to the aborted sneeze at all, appearing lost in analysis of something he picked off the mossy ground. He shook it about, then let it go.

"Ahhhh…"

"I say, Charly," said Sherman, in another rare lift of his chin off his neck to give his artificial intelligence creation a direct look, "what was that in your hand?"

"…ahhhh…"

Charly inspected both his latex-covered appendages before replying, click…whirr… "Nothing, unless you're referring to the assortment of electronically operated gears and hydraulic devices literally inside my hands, rather than-"

"No, no, no!" Sherman shook his head impatiently.

"…AHhhhh…."

"I'm referring to the slender filament you just released from your grasp after picking it up!"

Click…whirr… "That turned out to be a long hair with coarseness comparable to grizzly bear fur, rather than a feather quill possibly shed by the type of surviving non-avian dinosaur from which birds might have evolved. In other words, totally irrelevant to our search."

"…AHHHHhhhh…"

"Very well, Charly," said Sherman. "But at least please tell me that's you, pretending to hold back a sneeze there's no need for you to produce in the first place."

"…AAHHHHH…"

Click…whirr… "Okay, that's me pretending to hold back a sneeze there's no need for me to produce in the first place."

"Really?!?"

"…AAAAHHHHHHH…"

Click...whirr... "Not really, but you pleaded for me to tell you that."

"...AAAAAAHHHHHHHHHHH CHOOOOO!!! Chooo! Chooo! Chooo!" the monstrous sneeze echoed and re-echoed from deep inside the smaller burrow along one side of the furrow. A rush of fetid air accompanied it, even more pungent than what already stunk up the furrow.

Eclipso's expedition team scrambled as far away from there as they could get without climbing out altogether...

...which meant they ended up huddling fearfully close together, on the threshold of the much larger, forbiddingly dark-looking tunnel at the end of the furrow closest to where Augie knew the local Amazon tributary ran.

What everyone heard next echoed from the tunnel out of where the monster sneeze echoed. And overwhelmed the steady din of snake and howling monkey sneezes presumed caused by Sherman's less-offensive pest repellant. They were scrambling noises, growing louder and louder. They reminded Augie of the racket squirrels made in the attic of his parent's old house a decade ago, only amplified dramatically.

As the scrambling racket came closer and closer to the burrow's entrance, they were accompanied by intense huffs and puffs. Those huffs and puffs were of such regularity, under other circumstances Augie might have thought them emanating from an approaching steam locomotive.

Next thing anyone knew, all the noises came to an ominously quiet halt.

A squirrel-like head Augie thought the size of a Tyrannosaurus Rex skull poked tentatively out of the darkness. It loomed some ten to fifteen feet above the mossy ground, he guesstimated.

Turning this way and that, the large head protruded a long, fleshy tongue, probing the air. And the furry beast's nostrils were in a commotion like an anxious rabbit's sniffing for danger.

That's when Charly went into full action mode, too abruptly fast for Sherman to switch him off. With stiffly straight legs hardly bending at the knees, the artificial intelligence entity stormed at the monstrous beast of still-unknown but, where Augie and Scott were concerned, suspected identity. Charly also stiffly raised his arms, hardly bending at the elbows. He flailed them about wildly while emitting at maximum volume a recording from his vast hard-drive library, of an angrily trunk-trumpeting elephant.

That's when Sherman recalled he did have a remote control whereby he could disable Charly up to a thousand feet away. It also dawned on him that the volumes of info programmed into his creation must have included how best to ward off a wild animal attack. *He's trying to appear larger and more threatening than he actually is!*

Charly suddenly stopped moving, and he slumped forward, remaining on his feet. But Sherman was too late shutting him down.

The relic Megatherium, a giant ground sloth supposedly gone extinct over ten thousand years earlier, was beyond pissed. Scrambling out of shelter into full view, it reared up on hind legs to a towering height Augie believed to be well over twenty feet, and let out an angry guttural roar short-circuited by its loudest sneeze, yet.

Augie and company remained cowering in the shadows of the much larger burrow than the one the giant ground sloth emerged from. Thankfully for them, however, said sloth showed no interest in them. Rather, it was set on getting as far away from slumped-over Charly as possible. Returning down on all fours, it made a mad dash up the side of the steep furrow. Ferociously, its unusually long claws scraped away the moss, leaving bare, muddy clay in its wake...

...on the side where Raul's gold prospectors were keeping watch.

Land developer Raul shouted urgently, "When I say 'Fire!'-"

"NO!!" shrieked Aninha so loudly, she drowned him out, and scared the prospectors into standing down on the verge of brandishing their pistols and rifles. "Anyone who shoots at the *mapinguari* is a dead man! Out of its way! And look above you!"

The panicked prospectors cleared a path for the noisily scrambling monster sloth, its huffs and puffs interrupted by yet another incredibly loud sneeze. But a few did spare a glimpse above their heads. They spotted blow-dart straws protruding again from the rainforest canopy, aimed directly at them rather than at the locally named *mapinguari*.

Meanwhile, Augie was struck by how much the *mapinguari's* mad scramble reminded him of a groundhog seen while golfing with his wife, Vicky. As it hurried across the fairway, from one hole in the ground to another, fat jiggled like Jello under its furry pelt. Similarly, the sloth's boulder-sized mounds of fat rippled under its coat of yellowish-brown fur.

The "officially" named Megatherium finally climbed completely out of the furrow, drenching terrified gold prospectors with fetid, stringy mucus from its latest thunderous sneeze.

Aninha, perched halfway up a coconut palm, said in Portuguese the same as earlier, addressing Raul and his men, "I've just saved your lives! Had you shot that magnificent *mapinguari*, his relatives would have hunted you down until they disemboweled every last one of you! To stay safe, you would have needed to journey a thousand miles away! At least!"

By the time Aninha finished making what Augie found to be an astonishing claim, the monster sloth had scurried off into the rainforest, completely out of sight. Only scant evidence remained, of its ever having been there: a fetidly musky odor, the receding noise from it crashing through the woods, and claw marks in bared clay along the side of the furrow where it scrambled out. And lastly, Augie suspected it left behind another stray hair or two like the one Charly dismissed as not useful for finding a surviving dinosaur.

"Wow! Just wow!" Laura Gómez neatly summed up the experience. She still trembled from shock in the shadow of the far larger burrow's threshold. "You guys don't suppose Eclipso would settle with a relic monster sloth as an adequate consolation prize, in lieu of a surviving non-avian dinosaur?"

"I'd be the first to admit the discovery of something like a living Megatherium was far more likely than a living Iguanodon or some such," conceded Augie. "And it's certainly a momentous zoological discovery in its own right. But no, I don't believe it will be enough for Eclipso." ...or Bonsai Gator.

"Do you suppose the camcorders mounted on our head bandanas will confirm our observations?" asked Scott of nobody in particular.

"I wouldn't be so sure of that," Sherman shook his chin into his neck. "That hair Charly analyzed might yield an intriguing DNA fragment or two. But between our mad scramble, and cowering in this burrow entrance..."

"Well Harry and Sam back aboard Cloud Nine should be able to tell us soon enough," said Augie. "I bet they're reviewing the footage as we speak, before they check in with us. And I suspect my Vicky's open-house class, before school officially opens for the new semester, is having all kinds of fun with our close encounter."

"Oh, yeah, that's right," said Laura in dawning realization mode. "Your spouse has been turning your cryptozoological adventures into her lesson plans. Must be so much educational fun for her students!" she enthused, even while batting away a bird-sized damselfly that unwittingly got in her face. "Although the fallout from our encounter with a presumed-extinct monster mammal might bring her more media attention than she-" Laura went silent, suddenly swerving around to face Scott. "I'm feeling very conflicted here," she said in genuine puzzlement. "Part of me wants to say, 'Please don't say you were breathing down my neck.' But the other part would prefer-"

"I felt it as well," said Scott.

"Likewise," said Augie.

"Seems to come in spurts from deep inside this burrow," added Sherman, raising his chin off his neck as he reactivated Charly. "Consistent with what one would expect from the exhalations of an extraordinarily large beast. There you go, Charly," he said, his artificial intelligence entity having stepped ahead of him, further into the burrow. "Only, no more flailing your arms and making loud noises to scare off whatever's in there. That worked with our relic Megatherium. However, am not at all confident this other monster won't feel cornered-"

CRASH!!

The sharp thunderbolt coincided with a blinding flash of light at the cavernously vast burrow entrance. This drew Augie's attention to just how dark it had gotten outside, well in advance of the expected sunset.

Of course, it dawned on Augie, *we haven't had our daily rainforest downpour yet, yikes! If it floods this furrow, it might also flood out whatever's exhaling so noticeably from deep inside!*

That's as far as Augie's thoughts got. Déjà vu overwhelmed him, with the first big drops of rain falling outside the burrow entrance, and splashing on the mossy floor like so many bursting water balloons. Retreating into a hole in the ground from stormy darkness outside: *How can this feel so familiar?*

"I know we want to follow Charly and Sherman farther inside!" Scott shouted to be heard above the thundershower din.

CRASH!

"But we could be trapped if this place floods!"

"SHERMAN!!" Augie was already shouting into the burrow darkness where Sherman and his robotic creation had both just vanished from view, flashlights directed there notwithstanding. *Unbelievable how reckless Sherman has become with his own personal safety!*

"AHH..."

Oh-oh. Augie could hardly wrap his head around how much louder this new, threatening sneeze seemed than the Megatherium's prelude to its own full ah-choo. "WE GOTTA GET OUT OF HERE!! NOW!!!" he screamed, chiming in with Scott's urgent call that already had Laura stumbling and slipping across the rain-soaked, soggy ground well outside the enormous burrow entrance.

Laura headed for the same side of the furrow the monster sloth had clawed down to bare clay, hoping the miners would toss her a rope. Or that the unusually low-hanging cloud on rapid approach might be Cloud Nine to the rescue.

"AAHHHHH-AHhh-ahhh..." echoed from the burrow, succeeded by another blinding lightning flash and sharp crackle of thunder as Augie and Scott followed after the *Puffington Post* journalist.

That's when Augie realized he was up to his ankles in flash-flood rain water impeding his progress.

Was some of that water flowing out from the cavernously large burrow?

Augie found himself paralyzed, frozen still. He felt conflicted between continuing his retreat, and turning back around to attempt a foolishly heroic, doomed-to-failure rescue of Sherman and Charly, but mostly Sherman.

"AAAHHHHHHHHH-
CHHOOOOOOOOOOOOOOOOOOO!!!!!!!"

Whatever rush of musky fetid air Augie experienced from the monster sloth's sneeze was a faint scent compared to the hurricane-force blast that hit him from the much larger burrow. It would have literally blown him off his feet weren't he up to his knees in flowing water. And thank goodness for the thundershower-cleansed air! Without its diluting effect, Augie could have passed out from the extra-foul stink carried on the sneeze of the hidden, presumably incredibly monstrous creature.

Not so diluted was the accompanying furnace-like heat that where Augie was concerned, might just as well have originated from a fire-breathing dragon.

Meanwhile, poor Laura kept slipping, helpless to climb the stripped-bare side of the furrow. And the shower stormed too heavily to see whether Cloud Nine hovered amidst the extra-low storm clouds overhead.

Next thing Augie knew, a new noise cut through all the rest, thankfully very different from what he would have expected of some Godzilla-sized beast sloshing towards the burrow exit. The recurring splash had Augie imagining bathtub water turned off then on again, over and over.

Sherman emerged from the gaping burrow darkness, his head dwarfed by the airbag that engulfed the rest of him. Where Augie was concerned, he could have been a mouse poking its snout out of a ginormous beach ball.

The spherically inflated airbag bounced repeatedly across the deepening water, presumably propelled by the force of the monster sneeze. Each bounce produced the intermittent splashes Augie heard.

Moreover, Charly followed right after the airbag-engulfed Sherman, in a most peculiar state. His arms and legs formed the sides of a boat. He looked part-human, part-canoe. And the tumult of foam bubbling up from behind him suggested a propeller out his rear end, speeding him forward. *A repurposed fart?*

CRRACKLE-SPLASH!! At first, Augie took this deafening splitting sound to be another close lightning strike. But as an equally loud splash ensued, Augie realized one of the towering mahogany trees toppled over into the water that rapidly filled the furrow. He figured there was major breakage near the base of its trunk, possibly due to a direct hit from one of the two big lightning strikes.

So distracted had Augie become, he only just then realized a strip of cloth got caught in the corner of his left spectacle, perhaps blown there by the monstrous sneeze. On quick glance after he pulled it free, he noticed a faded design of fanciful little Styracosaurs with their spiked frills, strangely familiar. But that was all. He had to focus on the threat of being dragged underwater by the deepening, accelerating water flow, already well up over his waist.

"I say!" shouted Sherman louder than Augie had ever heard him before. "Everyone, grab the handles encircling my airbag!"

No sooner did the expedition's outside-the-box brainstormer say this than Augie identified the handles. He reached out to grab hold accordingly, screaming, "Got it, Sherman! Thanks! Laura?!?! Scott?!?!"

"Got it!" responded Laura.

"Same!" added Scott.

But Augie was already too distracted by a mind-blowing glimpse of something back deep inside the burrow where only minutes ago, they'd taken shelter from the panicking monster sloth. Or was it his wild imagination? Hallucinating feverishly amidst the stormy tumult, thanks to a lightning flash? Or Sherman's flashlight left behind when his protective airbag turned him into a human beach ball?

Sherman's inflated airbag swung Augie round and round in raging water that filled the furrow up closer and closer to spilling out on the rainforest floor. Nevertheless, he could have sworn he spotted two glowing eyes looking out at him from deep within the cavernous burrow.

One of Brazil's legendary behemoth snakes? The size of a school bus? Augie had to wonder. *Or a burrowing dinosaur that would easily have to be, by far, the largest that ever existed?* Either way, Augie could no longer spot it, the next time Sherman's airbag swirled him into another opportunity to peer inside the burrow.

Then not coincidentally, perhaps, Augie heard a tremendous SPLASH! It issued from back well behind the burrow, where Augie could picture the tributary ran. A deafening sucking sound ensued. *Tons of water down a drain the size of a swimming pool?*

"I SAY, CHARLY!!" shouted Sherman with all his might, to be heard above the collective din of the torrential shower, water sloshing over the sides of the furrow so that onlooking gold prospectors and Raul had to back away, and that sucked-down-the-drain racket still issuing from the nearby Amazon tributary. "Could you glom onto one of my airbag's handles, and motorboat us over to that fallen tree trunk?! To climb our way out of here?!?!"

"I could!!" Charly shouted in response, the customary click and whir from his speech processor drowned out by the aforementioned tumult.

"THEN PLEASE DO THAT IMMEDIATELY!!!" Sherman screamed, beyond frustrated over Charly failing to act yet. Charly's artificial intelligence algorithms distinguished all-too-literally between the ability to do something, and actually doing it.

"I am following your command immediately, even though it provides no useful data regarding the survival of non-avian dinosaurs!" announced Charly, again his clicks and whirs lost in the water-drenched din. His repurposed anus powered him over beside the human beach ball desperately clung to on all sides by Scott, Laura, and Augie.

To his ever-more-fearful distress, Augie felt something large and sharp-edged bump against one of his legs, unseeable down through the froth and murk of the turgid water. Soon thereafter, it bobbed up beside him before sinking back out of sight again.

It looked like a fragment of shell from an egg that would have had to have been the size of an elephant, or larger. No sooner was that Augie's perception, though, than he heard *Yanomamis* in the rainforest canopy shout urgently in their native tongue, and point. The tone made clear they were giving a warning such as *Look out!*

Sure enough, certainly warranting the *Yanomami* agitation, and not far from where Charly was motoring the human beach ball towards the fallen tree trunk, a long, narrow crest rose taller and taller out of the turbulent water.

Augie was reminded of a shark fin rising from glassy smooth seas in a nature documentary and certain shark-attack horror films. Or how a submarine periscope surfaced in documentaries about the mysterious disappearance of weapons worldwide that had probably averted at least one world war.

Only, the crest was different from either a shark fin or a submarine periscope. It continued to plow ominously against the flow of deep water raging through the burrowed-out furrow filled to overflowing. It looked very familiar to Augie. But he only realized what it was supposed to be when the rest started to emerge.

The slanted crest sat atop the skull of a supposedly long-extinct flying reptile: Pteranodon! Far larger than any previously unearthed fossil!

Not that Augie could get a very good look for more than seconds at a time. Rain still came down in buckets. And murky water kept sloshing against Augie's face, a struggle to keep from going up his nose.

On the other hand, Charly as a robotic motorboat canoe made adequate progress, dragging Sherman aka human beachball close to the toppled-over tree trunk. Laura was able to grab a branch while keeping a death grip on one of the handholds encircling Sherman's boulder-sized airbag.

Augie Matias did see one of the apparent over-sized Pteranodon's eye sockets long enough to marvel at its terrifying pitch-black darkness, even given the rain shower gloom.

At least it doesn't seem to have noticed us here, Augie reckoned relievedly. Immediately thereafter, he spotted something on the far northeastern horizon, from where sunset was rapidly approaching, albeit sunset lost in thunderstorm overcast. A pinpoint of flickering light moved slowly between palm trees. How unsettling, that it reminded him of those mysterious lights he and fellow expeditioners noticed in night-time skies on their prior dinosaur searches in New Guinea and Africa! *A second behemoth Pteranodon, maybe?*

Whatever, Augie couldn't continue tracking the mystery light with what was happening perilously closer to him.

The supposed Pteranodon's entire classic head had fully emerged on an impressively long, dragon-like neck from the swirling, eddying, overflowing furrow water. A long crest slanted backwards, and a pelican-like beak slanted down forward, carpets of moss and sheets of water falling away from both.

Augie figured the creature must have been hibernating, buried just beneath the moss at the bottom of the furrow.

He wondered how such a beast could launch itself airborne with its wings still underwater. But he didn't need to wonder long.

On a splashy WHOOSH!, an unexpectedly distended-looking belly, fat as a humpback whale if far more spherical, abruptly bobbed to the surface. From it unfurled two, wide, grayish, bat-like wings. Augie reckoned they were at least the size of the wings on a 747 jet. With majestic slowness, they flapped strongly enough to send water spraying off them every direction.

Augie heard screams from young *Yanomami* men and middle-aged gold prospectors alike, fleeing as fast as their limbs would take them.

Augie did find himself wondering at the monstrous flying reptile not striking a pose for its wings to dry off, much as he'd seen a bird called the anhinga do after emerging from a canal swim in Florida.

Regardless, its full liftoff had him awestruck breathless. The apparent creature's skyward climb left strong breezes in its wake...as the rope ladder dropped from the rapidly descending cloud generated by Cloud Nine's steam power.

"We will chase that thing, soon as we have you folks safely back on board!" Augie heard Cloud Nine navigator Samuel Longbottom shout in his earpiece far more loudly than he was used to from that usually mild-mannered fellow, always sporting a cardigan sweater of one, comfy-muted color or another.

"Drop it or die, Mr. Dinosaur Hunter!" Augie unexpectedly heard from Raul when the rope ladder had him halfway out of the water towards the low-hovering cloud generated by the steam-powered drone.

Raul was aiming a pistol at Augie from the far side of the water-engorged furrow.

"Drop what?! This?!" Augie held up away from him the bit of cloth printed with the faded Styracosaurus design that looked so oddly familiar to him.

"The gold nugget! Exactly!"

"Say what?! This isn't a gold nugget! It's an old cloth strip!" But then Augie realized the soaking-wet material glistened in the returning bit of late afternoon sun, and must have given the appearance...

"I need to confirm that! Drop it before I drop *you!*"

Regretfully, Augie did as ordered.

The cloth fluttered in the persisting breeze from the presumed relic prehistoric monster flying off, like it could have been a butterfly.

Quickly realizing no gold nugget would have fallen like that, would have just dropped straight down, Raul let out an expletive deleted while he tucked away his gun.

As the cloth was lost in swirling, murky waters, Augie finally remembered where he'd seen the dinosaur design before, not that long ago as it turned out: on Agnes's scarf tied sportingly round her neck, in the photo Aninha shared of standing beside her, Eclipso's long-vanished wife, who had been on a dinosaur search herself.

What, so that creepy thing with a hurricane sneeze from the burrow, it blew out a lone remaining fragment of her bandana? Stuck up one of its nostrils all this time?? Seriously?!?!?

Chapter 16

"Sunset is fast approaching, Harriet. We need to knock this off soon," aspiring golf-course developer Alistair Frump advised a legendary compiler of purported dinosaur sightings, Harriet Letterman.

Tabletop mountain Kurupira looming silently in the background, Alistair gave Harriet her golf lesson on bare ground beside the *Yanomami shabono* reduced to abandoned, trampled-down ruins. He flat-out refused to take her in his arms for guiding through a proper golf-club swing, as she had urged. Nevertheless, she showed unflagging determination to send a golf ball airborne. The result being endless worm-burners rolling across red-clay dirt dotted by matted-down broadleaf weeds.

After every so many attempts, Alistair interrupted Harriet to advise one tweak or another. Or he modeled perfectly launched iron shots that Stephen raced to retrieve before they might be lost to sight – and any hope of retrieval – going underneath the *shabono* ruins.

"As we know, Bernie speculates a Carnotaurus, a meat-eating dino, might be on the prowl here," Alistair went on presently, about why he needed to suspend Harriet's golf lesson. "We don't want to be sitting ducks for its nocturnal foraging, once night falls."

"We also want to avoid being impaled on a unicorn horn," deadpanned Stephen Feldman.

Irene McDowell, Bernie Coleman, and Sergeant Fred Frankly were part of the audience, standing in forest canopy shadows cast by several thin-trunked, wiry-branched shade trees.

Frankly's time-travel companions, starship officers Ali Magabu and Kevin Smith-Park, kept watch from aboard the steam-powered drone, Cloud Ten.

Cloud Ten hovered as just another of several puffy cumulus clouds turned reds and purples by encroaching sunset.

"I did it!" suddenly exulted Harriet. She raised a seven iron heavenwards, like it was the sword of some conquering hero, Fred imagined.

Harriet had finally launched a golf ball sky high, on a perfect arc, albeit dwarfed by the brooding majesty of Kurupira.

In the rapidly advancing sunset, Irene's attention couldn't help being drawn to Kurupira's cliffside wound, where the dino-search team had espied a rush of water mysteriously ebbing and flowing like respiratory inhale-exhale. It looked forebodingly, impenetrably dark.

When the golf ball finally landed just in front of the shabono ruins, Stephen couldn't react fast enough to prevent what happened next. With one big bounce, the ball leapt with seeming wild abandon, Bernie mused, into the thick of the ruins. Lost permanently, Alistair feared.

Or not.

A distinct rustle ensued from deep beneath the haphazard pile of palm fronds and various lengths of hollow reeds and cane stalks. Then Alistair barely had time to enthuse, "I say, Harriet, that was a smashing good hit!" before the golf ball shot out from the ruins, rolling along the ground at such speed as to take everyone by lost-for-words surprise.

But surprise was about to turn to disbelief.

There was a new, more insistent rustle from beneath the shabono ruins. It was the sort of rustle that reminded Bernie Coleman of two squirrels chasing each other across a blanket of fallen leaves in late autumn. A gray-haired agouti, like an oversized guinea pig, scurried out, its coarse hairs standing in alarm like porcupine quills.

That's when one pile of trampled-down *shabono* ruins seemingly exploded, spraying palm fronds, reeds, and cane stalks every which way.

CRASH!!

The approaching thunderstorm had been lost to the search team's attention, including the attention of Ali and Kevin back aboard Cloud Ten. They became too focused on Harriet's golf lesson, and then on the aftermath of her one solid golf shot. Nevertheless, in the flash of lightning after the crash of thunder, Bernie and Irene could have sworn they saw one, giant, three-toed track magically appear in the red clay mud.

During a subsequent lightning flash, a distinct chomp! was accompanied by the agouti magically vanishing from sight.

The suggestion to Alistair that some invisible beastie ate the entire poor frightened creature in one big gulp sent him racing to hug Harriet. On the way, he slipped and fell from the first pelting raindrops having already further softened the red clay. He wound up grabbing Harriet round her ankles, which left her thinking, *What a chicken! My Harry wouldn't act this scared!*

Chapter 17

"You're right, Rosa; who knew an electric violin harmonizing with a string synthesizer could sound so beautiful?" rhapsodized Dr. Roberta Quiñones out on the balcony of Rosa and Ron's fifteenth-floor condo overlooking the Guamá River in Belém, Brazil. "And all the percussion does add quite the folk music element."

"That's a samba rhythm!" helpfully added Ron after sipping from his passion fruit mango smoothie, also prepared for Roberta. "Yep, beautiful stuff," he raised his glass to toast the music playing from a small boombox set atop a night stand left out on the balcony.

"The name of the group couldn't be more beautiful: Sacred Heart of the Earth, isn't it?"

"Sagrado Coraçao da Terra," Rosa nodded.

"The name sounds even lovelier in Portuguese," Roberta rhapsodized some more. She also marveled at the setting sun providing a fiery orange backdrop for sinuous, towering palms that lined the far horizon, the other side of the Guamá.

Roberta also kept an eye on Rosa and Ron's shredded-apart rattan sofa cushion. This, on the chance their hyacinth macaw who made himself at home there several months ago, Milton Nascimento, might have nested for an amorous encounter with the unknown reptile Ron thought he spotted.

Originally, when Roberta proposed keeping the loving couple company, she feared considerable awkwardness could soon set in. If nothing else developed, or a second macaw showed up for a more conventional avian tryst, her hours waiting there could prove for naught. Meantime, how long could she keep up her interaction with these exceptionally nice and generous people before, like a fish left uncooked for too long, her presence started to really stink?

Happily, such worry turned out to be needless; the couple clearly enjoyed telling Roberta about their freelance translation work, as well as sharing local food, drink, and music with her. And Roberta certainly enjoyed being on the receiving end of all that. Moreover, Ron especially was utterly enthralled by Roberta's biological detective work. She recounted discovering a seagoing whale ancestor thought extinct for millions of years. Albeit on the edge of extinction, it still frequented where the Amazon emptied into the Atlantic Ocean.

Roberta did worry, though, how things were going for the contingent who camped out with Bernie Coleman at the base of an ancient tabletop mountain, including three purported time travelers.

And there was the other contingent, intent on exploring or at least keeping an eye on an enormous furrow beside a Yanomami community. The furrow might have been produced by anything from an eight-wheeler-truck-sized snake to their hoped-for relic surviving non-avian dinosaur. Or even a monstrous armadillo-type creature, the Glyptodont, also assumed to have long since gone extinct. That is, unless Stephen was correct about some freakishly dramatic erosion event.

Anyway, no word from either contingent since they left Roberta alone with Rosa and Ron. Did that mean those situations were turning out as uneventful as her own? At least for the time being? Until the anticipated recurrence of that mighty tremor felt from the *Yanomami* village all the way to Belém, every nineteen days?

Or on the other hand, was too much happening near the *Yanomami* village and at the base of Kurupira for her fellow explorers to share yet? Would her time have been much better spent helping one of those two contingents? Rather than keeping an eye on what would turn out to have been nothing more than Rosa and Ron's macaw having ripped apart their sofa for lack of anything else better to do? Or at best, for nesting with another macaw? And as for some overgrown lizard crawling out of a landfill-produced sinkhole across the river, then camouflaging itself as someone in a superhero costume aboard the so-called *trem da alegria*, the happy train: Was that merely a fanciful hallucination?

"SQUAWK!!

Te quero más

Te quero ser alma

SQUAWK!!"

"Here we go, maybe," Ron bubbled with excitement, a wild look in his eyes as he leapt to his feet from the balcony rattan chair and turned off his record player.

Before Rosa, Ron, and Roberta got anywhere near returning back inside, they could see the hyacinth macaw, Milton Nascimento, in a manically fluttering fuss about the shredded sofa cushion. He continued to squawk, and kept repeating the lyrics from one of his namesake's songs, "Anima," about wanting to see a loved one's spirit.

The three people crossing the threshold from the balcony back into the living room sent Milton Nascimento flapping his wings in their faces. *Don't come any closer to our nest!*

Standing on tippytoe from a distance, Roberta tried as best she could to snatch glimpses at what the bird's agitated behavior had her more convinced than ever was meant to be a nest. What she thought she saw, she needed to compare notes with her kind hosts to assure she wasn't losing it.

"Is it me, or is a depression in that nest moving from side to side, like something invisible there is rolling about?"

"You're not moving from side to side, so it must be an invisible large egg," Ron laughed. "Yeah, I'm seeing that too. Have to wonder whether that's from air turbulence created by Milton Nascimento's flapping wings."

That's what I'm sure Stephen would argue, reckoned Roberta.

"Maybe he's angry and frustrated, our poor Milton Nascimento," said Rosa sympathetically, "because a sweetie pie hasn't showed up yet to lay an egg?"

"In other words, he's begging for trouble," snarked Ron.

"Don't listen to him, Milton Nascimento! He's being cruel!"

"SQUAWK!!"

Just then, Ron waved his hands furiously as in, *Stop whatever you're doing!* He alternated that with pointing urgently towards the sofa cushion turned nest.

At first, Roberta found the blue-feathered macaw's squawky flapping-about too distracting to focus on the sofa. But...

Oh my God! Oh my God! Roberta blinked and rubbed her eyes multiple times to make sure she wasn't imagining things. In the nest, actually inches above its surface of chaotically entwined threads, a tangerine-orange beak was poking its way out of *What, an invisible egg?!* Very soon, the rest of its small, reptilian head floated there, body-less, looking every which way with evident perplexity.

Damn! Got too uncomfortably sweaty warm from the tropical heat, even with a fan blowing! Otherwise, I wouldn't have left my bandana with the camcorder attached in the other room beside the cashew tree! On this appalling realization, Roberta thought she heard a small yet harsh chirp issue from the sofa cushion nest. She ran for the half-open door to the guest bedroom, to both grab her camcorder and use her phone. *Did I really notice a small horn above each eye? Like on the head of the theropod dinosaur, Carnotaurus? That Bernie Coleman believes is a candidate for the identity of the stoa he's got Stephen, Harriet, Irene, and Alistair checking out near the Venezuelan border? To see if it makes an appearance there during the next tremor on that nineteen-day cycle?*

"Samuel? Irene? Augie? Anyone?!?!" Roberta anxiously called into her special phone linked by satellite to the other expedition groups.

"This is Samuel Longbottom," Samuel calmly, matter-of-factly answered. "Dr. Quiñones, is that you in urgent mode?"

"We have a developing situation here," Roberta Quiñones tried to report without screaming hysterically into her wallet-sized phone specially engineered by Sherman Peabody. "I kept waiting for an egg to be laid in that ripped-open sofa cushion when it was there all the time, invisible."

"Invisible?!" Samuel repeated not so matter-of-factly.

"What's hatched so far appears to be floating in mid-air. And the head bears no small resemblance-"

"Don't mean to cut you off, Dr.! We are in the midst of a situation I dare say rather overshadows yours!"

The same time Samuel interrupted Roberta, she could hear Augie in the background shouting, "Think I've got our view wired through for Eclipso, wow! That silhouette against the orange sky!"

"But is a Pteranodon going to be good enough for him?" Roberta overheard Scott wondering aloud.

"Did I hear Scott say 'Pteranodon'?" Roberta asked.

"The size of a commercial jet," confirmed Samuel, his matter-of-fact self nevertheless back fully in control. "We've been giving chase ever since she hauled herself out of floodwaters near the *Yanomami* village about an hour ago. And talk about eggs, there were bits of what appeared to be immense shell fragments left floating there."

"You've arranged for Eclipso to receive a good look at what you're chasing? Even though technically it's not really a dinosaur?"

"Of course! The silhouette against early dusk is really quite stunning! Especially her distended belly that has us wondering whether she's close to giving live birth."

"Even though you said she left egg shells in her wake, like she just hatched out?"

"Makes no sense, does it?"

Next thing Roberta knew, she was hearing in Samuel's background a reggae version of the guitar passage concluding the Beatles song, "I Want You (She's So Heavy)," repeated multiple times.

"Let me guess," said Roberta. "On split-screen you're seeing that monster Pteranodon in one half, and Bonsai Gator dancing up a storm in the other half."

"Our inimitable little reptilian fellow appears to be in more of a rapturous swoon than dancing, per se," corrected Samuel.

"Oh? Does that mean Eclipso will be satisfied with confirmation of a still-extant Pteranodon in lieu of an actual dinosaur?"

"Heavens no!" Roberta could hear Eclipso answering in no uncertain terms, seated well behind the rapturously swooning Bonsai Gator. Clearly, he heard Roberta on Samuel's end of the phone line, despite the contagiously tuneful racket of reggae Beatles. "Bonsai Gator is simply expressing, the only way he knows how, his happy anticipation of that long-awaited unarguable proof of non-avian dinosaur survival to the present day! We have a giant ground sloth formerly thought extinct, roused from its slumber! An oversized Pteranodon leading Dr. Matias's team heaven-knows-where! Plus, the latest fearsome event reported from the base of Kurupira! Not to mention your own call-in regarding something most extraordinary hatching from a most ingenuously cloaked egg, Dr. Quiñones! Considering all those many marvels, can the object of our quest be far from our grasp?"

"What's that happening at Kurupira?" asked Roberta.

"I don't know how you're going to manage your Jurassic Links Golf, cowering like this at the mere glimpse of a relatively small theropod dinosaur gobbling up an agouti," Roberta then heard Bernie Coleman addressing Alistair Frump, obviously.

"Yes, that three-toed track isn't *that* big," Alistair tearfully conceded while, what Roberta could not see on her phone, still clinging to Bernie's legs, down below his knees. Harriet had long since shaken him away from that fear-driven hug of her ankles. "But how do we know it doesn't have an oversized mouth that could also swallow one of us whole? Huh? How do we know that eating that poor agouti wasn't the same for it as popping a chocolate-covered raisin?"

"For the record, I don't endorse any of the remarks my illustrious colleagues here have just made," broke in the righteously deep voice of the ever-skeptical Stephen Feldman. "And I'd like to be aboard Cloud Nine with you, Mr. Longbottom, to discover what you're really following. You might think it's a Pteranodon, but that can't possibly be."

"Okay, Officer Smith, why don't you lower the rope ladder from Cloud Ten? Let's see whether Stephen can make the climb out of there, without disappearing - chomp! - into someone's mouth," Roberta could hear Irene in Bernie's background proposing with her usual snark.

"Gladly."

"SQUAWK!! Disgrace! Disgrace! SQUAWK!!"

"Dr. Quiñones?! You need to come out here pronto!" shouted Ron from the living room.

"Listen, guys, good luck. I'll fill you in soon as I can," said Roberta racing from the guest room back to the living room. "But one of the two 'Clouds' should hurry back here to Belém!"

Roberta's not-so-subtle plea fell on deaf ears on account of dramatic new developments both near Kurupira and seen from aboard Cloud Nine. Everyone she addressed neglected any further communication, paralyzed with amazement by what they were witnessing.

At the base of Kurupira, Irene, Bernie, Harriet, Fred, and Alistair huddled together underneath a tree canopy. They feared having Kevin airlift them out of there yet. Whatever made the agouti vanish with a distinct chomp! might leap at one of them, vulnerably exposed on the rope ladder. Maybe disembowel one of them, eat their entrails or something.

Nevertheless, Stephen shook his head disdainfully, and stood out away from the rapidly growing sunset shadows, all but saying, *Come and get me!*

Only wee tiny bits of remaining sunset peeked through dissipating clouds from the thunderstorm (which incidentally washed away the three-toed track that formed as from a ghost dinosaur). Sporadic flashes of receding lightning persisted, though. And one of those flashes highlighted the aforementioned open wound in the side of the plateau, where running water remained exposed.

Irene couldn't help feeling the mysterious ebb and flow there was as from some impossibly large subterranean monster's inhales and exhales.

Anyway, the lightning flash did nothing for Alistair, as he still cowered with his face buried in the cuffs of one of Bernie's khaki pant legs. But it highlighted the cliffside wound just long enough for Bernie, Irene, and Harriet to spot a grizzly-bear-sized creature that looked like a Carnotaurus, complete with a small horn over each eye. The creature looked back at them from the edge of the cliffside wound, where a section of the plateau had calved like from a melting glacier. One of its cheeks was puffed out, reminding all three observers of a squirrel with its cheeks packed full of acorns, scampering to bury them for coming winter. The agouti?

The dinosaur searchers were uncertain exactly what happened next. The apparent dinosaur seemed to melt away, leaving behind a curious palm tree that looked about to fall over into the rushing water exposed by the cliff face wound.

Did the creature exercise an extraordinary camouflage power? And did that power have something to do with a foot track seeming to make itself beside the *shabono* ruins? They could only guess...

...which wasn't the case with the supposed Pteranodon that Augie and company pursued in Cloud Nine. They hung far enough back, hopefully, not to scare it into one of its own unique disappearing acts.

Didn't matter, though. And left Bonsai Gator slumping his front legs limply forward, as dispirited as he was emotionally drained.

"Aydiomio!" exclaimed Laura Gómez in rare use of her Puerto Rican Spanish. "Our prehistoric amigo is coming unglued!"

"Literally coming unglued," nodded Augie with that sinking, here-we-go-again feeling, all too frequent on these dinosaur searches.

At first, Augie could discount the small flecks that sprinkled from the supposed real-life dragon's leathery wing-tips on each down-flap, highlighted by the orange dusk backdrop. He uncomfortably insisted to himself that the Pteranodon must finally be shaking off dirt, caked on from the silty flood waters of the long, deep furrow. But then the monstrous entity's overlong finger bone digits to which the wings were attached fell away.

The batlike wings themselves could no longer continue their majestically slow flapping. Rather, they were left wavering uselessly, like flags roiled by a breeze. That is, until they also fell away, leaving the head and bulbously swollen body still somehow maintaining altitude, wingless. Which is when the head itself gave the appearance to Augie of having been jettisoned like the used-up booster stage for a rocket launch.

Immediately thereafter, the reptilian tail, hind legs, neck, and whatever else also fell away. All that remained was the belly that had had Scott and Augie wondering whether a live birth was imminent. It lifted sailing heavenward like the helium balloon Augie concluded it doubtless had to be. And a firefly-like blinking light zipped off from it so fast, he had to wonder whether that was his imagination.

Chapter 18

"Nooooo!!!" rose the collective cry in Vicky's classroom, from students and parents alike. Their shock and disappointment was as one over the presumed real-life Pteranodon disintegrating against an orange dusk backdrop. They watched on a television screen as it happened thousands of miles distant, near the Brazil-Venezuela border.

A moment earlier, Vicky opened her door in response to a firm knock she was expecting, ever since secretary Bobbie Boland gave the heads up.

"Man, this is a tough crowd you've got here," said the teenaged delivery guy as he handed over three boxes of pizza. "I'm more used to cheers than protests when I arrive."

"Nooooo!!!!" the collective cry rose again, but this time devolving into laughter.

"I'm happy as a hyena to see those boxes of pizza!" said Winston risen to his feet. Then pointing at the television, he explained, "What we are moaning about, we thought we saw a real live flying reptile the size of a jet plane! Soaring across Brazil! From the dinosaur age! Not extinct like your typical Tyrannosaurus Rex!"

"Yeah, that's right," chimed in Brantley, whiny from his letdown. "But it fell apart like it must have been a giant mechanical toy!"

"It had a helium balloon belly that flew off into space!" added Erin, by then more awed than disappointed.

The way the pizza delivery guy shifted his head back while his shoulders remained still, Vicky was reminded of how chickens bob their heads. *Augie's weird stuff with Houdini Chicken in Cameroon, maybe we were all chickens in our past lives!* Anyhow, he remarked, "Wow! Well, hope you people find a real live flying reptile!"

Before anyone in the class could thank the delivery guy, his exit was eclipsed by curriculum specialist Diane Mueller storming in on her clicking high-heel shoes. She raged, "What's going on here, Ms. Copplestone?! Orientation ended hours ago!" Abruptly shifting gears, in her polite voice that Vicky still found simmering with impatience, she focused on the parents to say, "Our teachers need every last minute to finish preparing for your children's first real day of class on Monday. Because of that, we do everything possible to protect their planning time."

"Oh, Ms. Copplestone," Winston's father did a doubletake. "I had no idea, and here you even ordered pizza for us. At least let-"

"My treat, I insist, and no worries about my prep time," Vicky interrupted. "Had to come here this weekend anyway, to tie up loose ends."

"This is still taking advantage of you, Ms. Copplestone," commented Diane, her polite voice increasingly on edge.

Vicky mused that Diane's tone would have served just as well for saying, instead, *I'd like to wring your neck!*

Winston's father was having none of it. He got right up in Diane's face to say, "You see, Ms. Mueller, neither the children nor us parents could tear ourselves away from eavesdropping on Ms. Copplestone's husband's bold expedition in search of prehistoric beasts. Which apparently has already confirmed the survival of a giant ground sloth from thousands of years ago! Something most newsworthy, I should think! And her kindness indulging our overstay, even offering us pizza, well I would expect you to celebrate this behavior on an educator's part."

While hearty applause broke out, Diane nodded her head in reluctant acknowledgment with her eyes shut tight.

Vicky raced to say, "We have plain, veggie and pepperoni, since you're here pretty late yourself, Ms. Mueller. And I do appreciate you looking out for me."

"So, they're all waiting to see a living, breathing dinosaur on that TV screen, are they, Ms. Copplestone?" asked Diane, ignoring Vicky's invite to indulge a slice of pizza.

Like this is something brand spanking new I'm doing, rather than a continuation from my summer remedial group?

"Actually, Ms. Mueller," Winston's father again, "what we waited so long to see has turned out to be something of a hoax. We're all quite disappointed, aren't we, children?"

Now it was Diane Mueller's turn to bob her head like a puzzled chicken, Vicky thought.

Erin's mom weighed in, "I believe this experience has actually turned into a good cautionary lesson. About how you shouldn't become too carried away by some fantastical claim, or fantastical-looking event, until you are absolutely positive somebody isn't tricking you."

"My mom's right," a chastened Erin nodded slowly. "We have to be very careful something that looks amazing isn't phony."

"An invaluable lesson I'm sure the children want to thank Ms. Copplestone for," said Winston's dad as in, *C'mon, let's hear it!*

"Thank you, Ms. Copplestone," several young voices harmonized.

"Well look at the time," said Diane, checking her wristwatch that wasn't there. Too late realizing that, she made a show of pointing at the clock above the chalkboard in front of Vicky's classroom. Anything to avoid direct eye contact with anyone, before click-click-click rushing out the door.

What extraordinary irony, Vicky couldn't help marveling. *Augie and his crew keep getting stymied, every time they believe they're on the verge of proving a dinosaur, or in the case of the Pteranodon another sort of prehistoric reptile, has survived to the modern day. Meanwhile, Diane keeps getting stymied every time she believes she's on the verge of ridding me from the classroom!*

Chapter 19

When Roberta heeded Ron's call and dashed back to the living room, she was met by the oddest spectacle. The hyacinth macaw was circling about and squawking, clearly in a fuss. His flapping wings produced more breeze than the lone corner fan.

But the source of Milton Nascimento's agitation wasn't at all clear. Agitated by a ghost? Or by an occasional hiss Roberta could have sworn she heard rise above all the other ruckus?

"Am I too late?" Roberta anxiously mouthed without actually allowing any sound to leave her lips.

To which Ron responded by shaking his head and urgently stabbing a forefinger the direction of the nest shredded into the rattan sofa.

Sure enough, to Roberta's delighted relief, the wee little Carnotaurus head was still floating in mid-air, disembodied it seemed, from pecking its way out of an invisible egg, one had to assume. It bobbed about like any typical chicken or pigeon, bright yellow rings round its eyes, like around the hyacinth macaw's eyes.

Only then did Roberta remember to reactivate her retrieved camcorder, bound to her bandana.

None too soon, as only seconds later, the creature blurred and cleared, blurred and cleared, until it blurred out of sight altogether.

CHOMP!

"*Pobrezinho! (Poor little thing!) Meu Deus! (My God!)*" exclaimed Rosa. "Sounds like something ate our baby dinosaur, *after* it vanished!"

"Maybe Milton Nascimento's soul mate could think of nothing better to do than chow down their love child!" Ron speculated animately.

"SQUAWK!" went Milton Nascimento, suddenly taking a spiral flight path out onto the balcony.

Meanwhile, Roberta had to wonder whether surviving dinosaurs are so hard to pin down due to an extraordinary camouflage power. She found herself going back to Augie Matias's bizarre experience on New Britain Island off the coast of New Guinea. He swore an invisible presence with fetid warm breath tore the embarrassing big hole in his pants.

"Look! Look! Pay attention!" screamed Rosa, calling the zoologist's attention back to the present. "Our Milton Nascimento is leaving us! Following that invisible monster!"

By the time Ron and Roberta joined Rosa leaning over the balcony railing, Milton Nascimento's spiral glide path had already taken him several stories down.

"Whatever it is must be descending the wall like a gecko, as you'd expect some dinosaurs able to do," Ron laughed until most abruptly, he found himself looking into his sweetheart Rosa's eyes the same time she looked into his. They shouted simultaneously, "The *trem da alegria*!!"

*

"To review the bidding," Roberta addressed Ron and Rosa on the elevator ride to the ground floor, "you both believe... Well Ron, you thought you saw the tail of an enormous reptile wave hello from a landfill sinkhole the other side of the river..."

"Shortly after that," jumped in Rosa, "we were on the happy train, the *trem da alegria*, and there were these two Katydiddlys. That's the first time we ever see two of the same super-hero."

"And you thought that one of them, Ron, was camouflaged to look exactly like the other..."

"The teeth it bared were unlike any human teeth I know," Ron insisted. "They were too long and sharp, even sharper than Rosa's! Ouch!"

"Later on, I need to leave vampire marks on your neck, *meu amor!*" said Rosa. She twisted Ron's ear painfully much.

Roberta couldn't help a wistful smile. She regretted not being in a relationship as loving as Ron and Rosa's, at least not yet. Then she went on, "So after that, you heard Nascimento-"

"Milton Nascimento," corrected Ron.

"Okay, you heard Milton Nascimento with his mating call..."

"Oh, yes, there was so much longing in it," Rosa nodded emphatically. "Once it ended, we saw the Katydiddly with the extra sharp teeth, almost as sharp as mine," she playfully bared them. "She leapt from the train, and scaled nearby buildings in the direction of our condo like nobody's business."

"Can't believe I'm saying this," said Roberta, first to exit the elevator. "But it seems your hyacinth macaw mated with a large reptile, possibly even a relic dinosaur, of extraordinary camouflage powers. The reptile laid an egg, also with extraordinary camouflage powers, that hatched a creature that looks like a theropod dinosaur. And it's visible, at times, perhaps due to your macaw's very non-camouflaging DNA. Am I missing anything?"

Ron's eyes roamed the Belém night sky before he chuckled, "No, that sounds about right."

"*Sim*," nodded Rosa. "And what's so bizarre, so awful, is that it looks like the mama ate her own child right out of its nest!"

"Didn't necessarily eat her young," corrected Roberta, while Ron's attention to something way overhead distracted him from waiting in line for *trem da alegria* tickets. "Some alligators are known for holding baby gators in their mouths to protect them from predators, including other gators. It's very possible some dinosaurs evolved that same expression of maternal instinct."

By the time Dr. Quiñones finished her dissertation on a less-grisly explanation for their observations, she realized it was lost on Rosa and Ron, and anyone else who might have been listening as well.

There were finger-pointing "Oo"s and "Ahh"s galore, regarding the growing spectacle overhead.

Cloud Nine was hidden from view as usual by the large cumulus-style cloud its steam-powered locomotion always generated. However, it had quietly descended to a mere fifteen feet above street level, and Augie was already halfway down its rope ladder.

"Wow!" Ron couldn't help enthusing. "The dinosaur-searching cavalry has arrived in style!"

Hopping off, Augie asked Roberta as Scott descended behind him, "You saw a baby Carnotaurus head poke out of an invisible egg?"

"*Meu Deus!* You people don't even stop to say hello?" asked Rosa, stunned by how Augie Matias got right to the point without the least preliminary pleasantry.

Click...whirr... "No, we don't," answered Charly the artificial intelligence entity from his own stiffly mechanical climb down the ladder. Click...whirr... "'Hello' provides no useful data for finding a surviving non-avian dinosaur."

"Oh, yes!" enthused Ron. "I want him sitting beside me on the *trem da alegria!*"

"The happiness train?" said Augie. Contemplating the pickup-truck-sized replica of an old-fashion steam locomotive, he ignored the locals still ooing and ahhing over people's descent from Cloud Nine.

The happiness train included three flat-bed wheelers filled by rows of colorfully painted bleachers, and surmounted by equally colorful curved roofs as one would find atop an old-fashion caboose or rail passenger car. No train tracks were anywhere to be seen, though.

Standing side-by-side alongside the happy train, laboring to drum up passengers, were people dressed variously as stuffed animals or super heroes, including one, just one, Katydiddly. They were boogieing intensely to a disco version of "YMCA," such that Augie could easily imagine Bonsai Gator right beside them joining in, however dwarfed by their height.

"Is this where you thought a large, variably invisible reptile hitched a ride? Until it scrambled up a wall to your condo for an egg-laying night of passionate love-making with your pet macaw?"

"SQUAWK!! Mine is no disgrace! Mine is no disgrace!" squawked Milton Nascimento, flapping about.

"I think he just answered your question," laughed Ron, more amused than ever.

"We believe we saw his *cara* eat their love child," Rosa chimed in. "Although your Dr. Quiñones there thinks she could be protecting the little fellow inside her mouth, rather than actually having swallowed him. And now she might be hitching a ride on the *trem da alegria* to who-knows-where. Maybe she is camouflaged as one of those stuffed animals or superheroes."

While Rosa pointed at the line of dancing costumed characters, Augie noticed Ron nod emphatically to the music. The goofiest look in his eyes accompanied his blissed-out grin.

"What about Irene's gang and our time-traveling friends?" Roberta asked Scott. "Are they still keeping vigil near Kurupira?"

"Apparently a large reptilian creature left signature three-toed tracks in the mud out there. And it has demonstrated camouflage powers like your cannibalizing, or mouth-shielding, mama here. Made some hamster-like critter vanish in a single chomp."

"Whoa!" Roberta exclaimed, just imagining what Scott described.

"Anyway, they got a brief look at it crouched beside a waterfall. They described a very theropod dinosaur head with a horn above each eye."

"Just like the head that poked out of the invisible egg," said Ron, remarking on his realization as it struck him.

"A Carnotaurus head," chimed in Augie. "Next thing Irene knew, it melted away, and they saw a palm tree collapse into the waterfall."

"They're still reluctant to climb the rope ladder back aboard Cloud Ten," resumed Scott. "They fear there's a second one prowling about, maybe try a leaping pounce to tear off an arm or leg."

"*Meu Deus!*" sympathetically exclaimed Rosa for the umpteenth time. "They are waiting until the coast is clear, as your saying goes?"

"Correct," said Sherman, his chin ever-scrunched into his neck as he entered the conversation. "But regarding this head-melting-away camouflage business, maybe our prospective theropod dinosaur hypnotizes creatures into ceasing to perceive its presence. I am intrigued by the prospect of Charly being able to 'see'-" – finger quotation marks – "-what we cannot, even in video replays."

"Really?" said Ron beyond delighted and, Augie noticed, sustaining that wild look in his eyes.

"Indeed," nodded Sherman. "To assure myself Charly is not subject to such entrancement, the first time I activated him, I actually did try to hypnotize him."

"But you can't hypnotize a robot, well that's as I would have expected," nodded Laura.

"When I waved the iconic watch on a chain before him and said, 'You're getting sleepy,' he rebutted, 'No I'm not.'"

Click...whirr... "I am incapable of sleepiness. The closest thing to that would be if my battery charge ran out before Sherman replenished it."

"Do you ever fear your batteries might run out, and you'll never wake up?" Ron couldn't help mischievously asking.

Click...whirr... "I wouldn't want that, because then I would be unable to contribute to discovering indisputable evidence non-avian dinosaurs have survived to the present day."

"So, there is something you want to do!" exclaimed Sherman. Charly's remark excited him enough to lift his chin well off his neck. "Gentle people, sounds to me like our artificial intelligence entity might be making genuine progress towards genuine consciousness!"

Click...whirr... "No, I'm not." Click...whirr... "My employment of the word, 'want,' is an artifact of my empathy program, nothing more."

"Please listen to me, people, whether you possess a real consciousness or not," pled Rosa. She'd finally lost patience trying to draw attention by animatedly waving her arms, as even Ron ignored her. "The ticket master won't charge any of us to board the *trem da alegria*!"

"Really?!" said Ron, his attention captured, at last.

"Really! You explorers climbing down out of a cloud has him spooked. 'Everyone can board the train for free,' he told us. Milton Nascimento flying round about might also have helped."

"SQUAWK!!" squawked the hyacinth macaw as though to put an exclamation point on Rosa's explanation, Augie mused.

The big blue bird with a bright yellow circle round each eye continued to flap fussily about, just beyond anyone's reach.

On a hunch, Sherman once more addressed his artificial intelligence entity, "Tell us, Charly, do you see anything that bird might be agitated over, anything we're maybe not seeing?"

Click...whirr... "Whatever it is, is also not visible to me. Maybe he's chasing a bug too small to spot in the shadows..."...click...whirr..."...or a ghost..." ...click...whirr... "...or a floater in his eye..." ...click...whirr... "...or-"

"Stop that, Charly; you've provided us with plenty more speculation than we require," Sherman emphatically interrupted, tempted to shut down his artificial intelligence entity anew.

Click...whirr... "Maybe I don't want to stop that. Maybe I want to be my own man."

"Really?" Sherman did a doubletake.

Click...whirr... "Not really. Rather, as an implementation of the empathy program."

Toot! Toot!

"SQUAWK!!"

"I believe the train is telling us to finish boarding," warned Augie before Sherman could once again apologize for Charly.

Charly's empathy program still left loads to be desired. But Sherman was convinced he needed to keep putting him to these tests, however uncomfortably awkward the conversations turned out. Otherwise, there was no prayer that Charly could ever blend in with non-expedition people.

"Wait," said Scott. "Don't we need tickets?"

"That's what I tried to get your attention about while you were asking whether Charly can see things we can't see!"

shouted Rosa, evidencing a rare moment of frustration. "The ticket master said we can all board for free!"

"Whoa!" Scott exclaimed as he headed for the steps up onto one of the flatbeds.

"Again, I think you guys freaked out the ticket master, when you climbed down from a low-hanging cloud!"

Once Augie Matias took his seat on one of the bleachers beside Scott, he carefully scrutinized the costumed characters as they boarded.

Every last superhero and oversized stuffed animal eschewed the provided steps in favor of variously leaping, somersaulting, or swinging themselves up onto the *trem da alegria*. Among the stuffed animals were an alligator, a bear, a dolphin, and a pig. And rounding out the superheroes, besides Superman, was a single Katydiddly. No second one came into view, that Ron and Rosa would have insisted was the reptilian creature extraordinarily camouflaged. Who maybe had had a booty call, Milton Nascimento impregnating her some weeks earlier.

"What powers of camouflage could our creature of interest possibly have, that would make it appear to be one of those characters?!" Scott shouted to be heard.

A new tune, Barry White's "Can't Get Enough Of Your Love Baby," drowned out such night sounds as from the tree frogs, now that "YMCA" was finished.

"An excellent question!" said Sherman seated just ahead of Scott and Augie, beside his artificial intelligence creation. Once more, he lifted his chin off his neck, in this case to turn around to face Scott and Augie. Then turning back to Charly, he went on, "Charly, why don't you see if one of the people we think is dressed as a stuffed animal or a superhero is really a giant reptile, possibly dinosaurian?"

Click...whirr... "No particular reason why."

"To reframe my question, please tell us, Charly: Do any of the supposed costumed people aboard the *trem da alegria* look in reality like a large reptile?"

Charly's head stiffly rotated nearly a full 360 degrees. Along the way, he stopped to stare intently at each apparently costumed character.   Click...whirr...   "The answer is no. And from my data base, I would not expect a non-avian dinosaur to have the intelligence or inclination to put on a costume."

"But- Oh never mind!"

Click...whirr... "Oh never mind what?"

"Um, never mind what I was going to say."

"Wait," said Laura from behind Augie and Scott. "Don't camouflaging creatures like a chameleon usually simply blend in with something else nearby that they are crawling across? Such as grass that makes them turn green?"

"Remember what we told you about two Katydiddlys?" said Ron, seated with Rosa beside Scott and Augie.

"Oh, right!" said Augie. "Presumably our saurian quarry camouflaged as the other Katydiddly you saw! And even if Charly can't be hypnotized, he might still have difficulty discerning a camouflaged creature!"

"Well, there are no duplicate characters here now," observed Laura. "Maybe that means our saurian quarry, as you put it, Augie, never did board this happy train, and- Oh, too late!"

With a jolt, the *trem da alegria* got underway. Its multi-colored decorative lights again reminded Augie of Christmas lights. And progrock group Yes's "Owner of a Lonely Heart" replaced "Can't Get Enough of Your Love Baby."

"No, I'm sure the large reptile has boarded!" Rosa said most assertively. "You see how Milton Nascimento flies alongside?"

"Yeah!" said Ron, his silly grin seeming to Augie perpetually sealed onto his visage. "Too bad he can't tell us where she is exactly!"

"But why wouldn't Charly be able to spot her?" puzzled Laura.

"Remember that camouflage has an actual physical aspect to it," said Roberta seated beside Laura. She incidentally found herself regretting such an attractive woman wasn't lesbian like herself, a sure distraction from her mess with Daniela.

"I'm also thinking," added Augie, "maybe our quarry has some biochemical memory thingie. Too much stress can re-trigger the camouflage, even when the source material isn't present."

"Which means that lone Katydiddly might not be Katydiddly at all," Scott proposed.

"But it's also possible our so-called quarry might simply be blending in with the train car, and not camouflaging as anyone else at all," said Sherman, raising his point-of-order forefinger. "Charly, please rummage about here, see if you can accidentally on purpose bump into the camouflaging creature. I rather suspect your built-in machinery will allow you to climb about the train car, over the bleachers with their backrests, far more safely than any of us could. And should be found quite entertaining to our inescapable audience. Plus, your special vision might sleuth out the camouflage far faster than any of us could, anyway. Charly? I say, Charly, why aren't you moving?"

Click...whirr... "You told me to never mind what you say."

"Please, Charly! That was then! This is now! Forget what I said!"

Click...whirr... "Okay."

The person costumed as a furry pink pig hung upside down beside the bleacher where a young couple climbed amorously entangled all over each other. The spectacle distracted Augie from realizing Charly remained motionless, until Sherman said, "I say, Charly, you're still sitting here doing nothing! Please do as I ordered!"

Click...whirr... "I already did what you ordered. I forgot what you said."

Sherman Peabody proceeded to not only squish his chin back into his neck again. He pulled the front of his khaki shirt up over his head, then said in a loud if muffled voice, "Forget that I told you to forget what I said!"

Click...whirr... "In other words, don't forget."

"Yes!! Now stand up and step about! See what you can learn of the presence on board here of a living, breathing, non-avian dinosaur. Also, try blending in, wherever you can."

Click...whirr... "Got it."

Soon as Charly rose to his feet, he turned his attention to the ridiculously amorous couple while raising his right leg impossibly high up above the backrest of the bleacher before him. Then even more impossibly, his booted right foot projected ridiculous lengths from where it was attached to his right ankle, on a thin uncoiling metal strip like a stretched-out Slinky Toy, Augie mused. And with a thud, it came down on the blue-painted steel floor in front of the aforementioned bleacher behind which he stood.

"Interesting how he's focused on that smooching couple," Ron remarked to Scott and Augie. "Another couple behaved the same way when we think Milton Nascimento's lover camouflaged as a second Katydiddly."

"Maybe our, um, reptilian lover noticed that," said Augie. "And now instead of looking like a second Katydiddly again, it's camouflaging as those two smoochers."

Charly stiffly brought himself standing before said smoochers who Augie suddenly wasn't so sure about. They peeled their lips off each other just in time to watch him click...whirr... "Excuse me, I see you are very busy there." Click...whirr... "But can you fart for my flatus emission detector to tell whether you are a surviving non-avian dinosaur?" Charly asked while pointing at the microphone poking out of his pants once more.

The couple exchanged puzzled looks before the guy said angrily, "*Não entendo, pervertido!* (I don't understand, pervert!)," and they resumed their impassioned lip-lock...

...to which Charly reacted by embracing himself, then kiss-kiss-kiss down his right arm.

"Charly!!" Sherman shouted as loudly as he could while still whispering. "What on Earth are you doing?!?!"

Charly ceased the self-smooch most abruptly, stiffly looked up, and click...whirr... "I'm blending in."

"Well stop it! And about your question: Suppose one of them really is a non-avian dinosaur. Would she or he have understood your question?"

Click...whirr... "In Portuguese, the male did say he didn't understand the meaning of 'pervert.' But I never used that word."

"No, Charly!!" Sherman couldn't help screaming, so much for any whispers. "He said he didn't understand you, as in he doesn't understand English! And he was calling you a pervert!"

Click...whirr... "That was..." ...click...whirr... "...stupid on my part. I'm sorry."

"You're sorry?!" Sherman couldn't help bursting out, his angry frustration confusedly laced with positive excitement. *Could the Artificial Intelligence algorithms finally be stumbling his way into consciousness? With a conscience?*

Click...whirr... "Not really. The empathy program led me to say that."

"Well, it's quite alright," Sherman gently allowed as he resumed wedging his chin into his neck, fitting him like an old glove. Charly still might not have any genuine feelings. But Sherman couldn't help addressing him kindly due to his own genuine sensitivity, ashamed of having become so upset with him. "You just focus on discovering whether a non-avian dinosaur has stolen aboard this happy train."

Click...whirr... "Roger that." Charly actually saluted Sherman, but his hand totally missed his forehead, skimming his nylon thread hair.

By then, Augie noticed the stuffed animals, Superman, and the lone Katydiddly were leaning out both sides of the *trem da alegria* flatbed passenger cars, far as they could. They hung on to the colorfully painted iron supports for the arched roofs.

Augie sensed Katydiddly following Superman's example. But before he could make anything of that, he realized Charly was imitating the entertainers, hanging out one side just behind the pink pig. *Maybe he's still trying to fit in because he forgot Sherman's directive to stop trying to fit in. Though I'm not sure forgetfulness is a thing with artificial intelligence.*

Clang!

It seemed Superman hung his head too far out the side, and got smacked hard by a speed limit sign. Augie figured that had to be an optical illusion. The costumed character produced the clang without his head actually making contact with the sign. Otherwise, he surely would have been knocked senseless, left lying unconscious on the ground.

In case there was any doubt, clangs from other characters made clear a clever stunt at work, nothing more, while the speakers started pumping out Led Zeppelin's "Whole Lotta Love."

Augie puzzled over how the costumed entertainers were *not* giving themselves multiple concussions and dropping like flies off the *trem da alegria*. But before he could solve that mystery, the pink pig not only seemed to go clang! against another street sign. Her head flew off, and went bouncing alongside the *trem*. Which slowed down not-so-coincidentally, Augie figured, to keep pace with the furry pink pig head on its bounding course down the sidewalk.

The pig leapt from the train to go chasing after her head. She elicited howls of laughter and alarm, especially from children on board.

Charly followed suit. He leaned his head out far enough for the next street sign to knock it off as well, leaving it to also bounce down the sidewalk.

Sherman once again lifted his chin well off his neck, and he shouted, "I say, Charly, I hope you know what you're doing!!"

Charly's clicks and whirs hummed too far away for Sherman and company to hear. But his voice still carried loud and clear from his head bouncing down the sidewalk after the bouncing pig head. He shouted in his usual robotic monotone, "I know exactly what I'm doing!" Click...whirr... "But I have no idea whether it will work!"

Meantime, Charly's headless body leapt off the *trem da alegria*, then took impossibly long strides. His right leg stretched nearly rubber-band thin for his booted foot to come down not far behind the headless pig. His left leg followed suit. A mere two steps put him out well past the headless stuffed animal, rapidly approaching the bouncing, furry pink pig head. Another such stride by his right leg, and he was able to grab the pig head. He lodged it firmly onto his empty neck, and with another long stride of his left leg, he grabbed his own bouncing head...

...which he turned looking down into the neck of the headless stuffed pig, the woman wearing that costume having ground to a complete halt. She was intent on recovering the pig head from atop the torso of the artificial intelligence entity.

Click...whirr... "I see a fully clothed homo sapiens female hidden inside this costume!" loudly announced Charly's disembodied head, after Charly's hands lifted it back up like he could have been displaying a trophy, Augie found himself thinking unsettlingly. "No data to support the notion of a surviving non-avian dinosaur!"

By then, unnoticed by Charly, the *trem da alegria* had come to a full stop beside him and the furry pink headless pig.

With a showy flourish of his blue cape, the Superman character leapt down beside the artificial intelligence entity. He grabbed the furry pig head off the entity's neck, and handed it back to the woman posing as a headless pig.

Before resetting the pig head back atop her neck, the headless pig bowed graciously at the superhero.

Superman nodded acknowledgment of thunderous applause from both on and off the *trem da alegria*. Then he turned to Charly, who by that time had already reattached his head to his neck. And he said in somewhat stilted English, softly enough to avoid anyone else hearing, "Is one awesome costume you have there, *senhor*. When you joined the *trem da alegria*?"

Click...whirr... "Thank you, but I haven't joined the *trem da alegria*, especially if you're speaking in the conjugal sense. Please, can I remove your head to make sure-" Click...whirr... "Oh, that's right; a surviving non-avian dinosaur would be incapable of understanding English, unless its ancestors traveled unprecedented evolutionary pathways."

Toot! Toot! went the happy train.

Ring! Ring! went Superman's portable phone.

Charly, Pig Person, and Superman leapt back aboard the *trem da alegria* for its wild ride about to resume through the streets of Belém.

Augie strained to eavesdrop on Superman's end of his phone conversation above the Bee Gees' disco tune, "Stayin' Alive," pumped through the *trem*.

Meanwhile, the other stuffed animals plus some younger passengers danced up another storm.

"Sorry to hear that; hope you feel better soon," spoke Superman into his phone, in Portuguese. Augie didn't understand the specifics, but from the caped costume-goer's tone could tell he was expressing sympathy.

"So where did the new Katydiddly arrive here from?" Superman continued in Portuguese.

This time, Augie recognized the word, Katydiddly, and noticed Superman staring down that fellow superhero, dressed to look like a giant green grasshopper.

Katydiddly resumed swinging precariously from an iron support bar for one flatbed car's curved roof, while also boogieing to "Stayin' Alive."

"You have no idea the identity of this other Katydiddly?!" an agitated Superman asked whoever was on the other end of his phone line. "Maybe the same extra one who came here last week, but disappeared without saying a word to any of us?"

From Superman's frequent mention of Katydiddly, Augie gathered there was some question over that other costumed character's presence. Only then did he realize Superman had locked eye contact with Katydiddly...

...just in time to see Katydiddly open her mouth wide and, with a most reptilian hiss, reveal several needle-sharp fangs.

"There's our mystery reptile!!" Augie shouted and pointed as the creature camouflaged as Katydiddly leapt off the *trem da alegria*, and galloped on all fours, headed for cover inside a large open-air market.

Click...whirr... "My flatus emission detector has picked up a signature matching the noise Sherman Peabody recorded in Cameroon!" Charly announced. He joined Augie and company leaping off the *trem* in hot pursuit of the creature of interest.

Police car sirens rapidly grew louder and louder; the *trem* operator had had enough of goings-on far more bizarre than usual, and had called for help.

"SQUAWK!! Yours is no disgrace! SQUAWK!!"

Milton Nascimento flew high overhead, flitting in and out of floodlights for the open-air market.

The illumination lent Eclipso's crew a rough idea where the camouflaged beast headed while adults and children screamed, market stalls overturned, and an occasional hiss expressed both rage and fear.

"*Pare! Pare!* Stop! *Americanos!*" called out the police over bullhorns at the dinosaur searchers.

The smooching couple from aboard the *trem da alegria* ran past, the woman carrying the man, but both still engaged in a passionate lip-lock.

Meanwhile, Augie and company, including Charly, did heed the police officer's demand, and stopped.

"Can any of you explain what is going on here?"

Click...whirr... "It is like this, Officer," started in Charly without hesitation, drawing from a bundle of responses with which he was programmed for a vast variety of situations. "My flatus emission detector-" He pointed down at the mike still sticking out at an obscene angle from his pants. "-picked up the possible signature of a surviving non-avian dinosaur aboard the *trem da alegria*. But it leapt off, and is now running rampant through that open-air market."

"Oh my God!" screamed Laura before the police officer could insist Charly tuck away his flatus emission detector mike. "Over there!! Did you see that?!"

"You're talking about the sprinting cashew nut the size of a kangaroo?" Augie asked while experiencing out-of-body detachment. *Has our dinosaur search really come to this?*

"I could actually use some honey-roasted cashews about now," mused Ron as he joined the general rush between market stalls in the direction of the monster cashew sighting.

"We might require ambulances equipped with several straitjackets," the officer who spoke to Charly meanwhile reported over his walkie-talkie in Portuguese. "An insane person spoke like a robot, something about 'flatus emission' from a dinosaur. He had a robotic sex organ sticking out of his pants, while someone else- *Meu Deus,* forget it! There *is* a monster cashew on the rampage!" concluded the officer as he joined the pursuit.

What extraordinary power of camouflage is this? Augie wondered as he saw what looked like an eight-foot-tall honey-roasted cashew tip over a market stall featuring stuffed-animal versions of a cartoon giraffe. *Our creature of interest can look like a cashew that large, after having merely glimpsed a bag full of them?*

Near the *Guamá* River bank, Charly suddenly extended his right leg to an incredible length again. He easily stepped over a pile of market stall rubble left in the camouflaging creature's wake.

The spectacle halted the police officers' pursuit. They crossed themselves fearfully, sweat pouring down their faces.

No matter.

The creature camouflaging as the biggest cashew nut, ever, made a running leap with a big splash into the river. There, open air market floodlights revealed it dashing across smoothly running waters like a stone skipping an impossibly long way without sinking, Augie marveled. He was reminded of a nature video that captured a small lizard running across water on its hind legs.

Click...whirr... "Whoever wants to board me before I resume my pursuit better hurry soon!" warned Charly. Everyone distracted by the camouflaged creature, nobody noticed when he once again reconfigured his torso and limbs to transform into a motorboat. This was exactly what he did near the *Yanomami* village, when he propelled himself across the flooded furrow, propelled by his robotically repurposed rear end.

No sooner did Augie climb aboard than Charly was on his way, chasing what still looked like a giant cashew skimming the river's surface like the ultimate skipping stone.

Seated beside Augie were Scott, Laura, Ron, and the guy from the *trem da alegria* dressed like a stuffed-animal dolphin. *Guess I shouldn't be surprised the non-stop amorous couple didn't also make it on board!*

Next thing Augie knew, Furry Dolphin Man leapt into the *Guamá*. His dorsal fin curved gracefully in and out of the water like a real dolphin, plenty visible thanks to the floodlights from the open-air market back on shore. All too quickly, though, numerous small fish were splashing all around him.

"Piranha!" gasped Ron, the silly grin off his face for the first time since they boarded the *trem da alegria*. "They'll eat him alive before he can make it back to shore!" he shouted, beyond alarmed.

Cries and screams from on shore expressed like sentiment.

Only seconds later, though, the entertainer ran ashore, down to his underpants and heroically pumping his fists in the air while the fiercely carnivorous little fish finished tearing his costume to shreds.

My God! He's still trying to amuse the passengers from aboard the trem da alegria! That's real dedication! Augie couldn't help thinking as the crowd back on shore burst into applause, and the near-naked man took numerous bows. *They ought to tip him extra for that!*

"SQUAWK!!"

Flapping overhead and keeping pace with the monster cashew, the hyacinth macaw with his complaining chirp returned Augie's attention to the main matter at hand.

The mysterious quarry raced ashore the opposite side of the river as effortlessly as it first plunged in. Still looking like a behemoth cashew, it scaled a mangrove barrier with the same ease Charly stepped over the market stall ruins. Moreover, a fleeting glint of wetness had a distinctly scaly, reptilian character to it for Augie. *Is the cashew mimicry wearing off?*

By then, the four humans were disembarked from Charly, and he was transformed back to human appearance. All five characters continued their pursuit of the creature of interest back on dry if underbrush-y land.

Augie hoped Sherman's special pest repellant hadn't been rinsed or sweated off too much. That it would still protect them adequately from whatever poisonous snakes and bugs lurked in the tropical darkness. He wanted to rest assured that pinches, scratches, and clothing tears came from nothing more than twigs and thorns and the like. But he just had to keep his fingers crossed.

Security floodlights around the sink-holed landfill illuminated the hoped-for saurian quarry such that its chameleon-like camouflaging kicked in, again. Presently, the creature no longer looked like Katydiddly, or a monster cashew. Rather, it took on the appearance of whatever rusted-out car, palm tree or palmetto bush it scampered past. That appearance changed as rapidly as it moved from one object to the next. Far as Augie was concerned, it might as well have been a creature with window-like transparency

At the last, the mysterious entity scaled the crater rim of the sink-holed landfill. And the same as Ron saw weeks ago, a reptilian-looking tail swayed side to side on its disappearance down inside.

"SQUAWK!! SQUAWK!! SQUAWK!!" Milton Nascimento couldn't help squawking repeatedly, clearly upset as he circled and swooped about overhead.

Before Augie and company could reach the crater rim themselves, a quaking rumble threw them off their feet, left them sprawled about on gravelly ground, Charly included.

What they could not have known, would not learn until later, was what happened that very moment, hundreds of miles north at the base of the tabletop mountain, Kurupira. The same rumble also threw Irene and company off *their* feet.

Poor Alistair cowered with his head tucked into his long-sleeve khaki shirt. But Irene, Harriet, Fred, and Stephen kept their wits enough to notice something most extraordinary.

They could still hear the pulsing ebb and flow of water even though darkness fully concealed the water itself. More importantly, though, was what Irene and Fred's flashlights picked up on the precipice of the collapsed cliffside wound in one side of Kurupira. Two coconut palms where there had been no trees of any kind before looked like they hopped over the precipice, out of sight into the wound. No sooner that than a second quake initiated a new landslide, and more collapsed rocky cliffside covered over the wound.

The ground did settle quickly. And all the chirps and other nature noises resumed, minus the occasional loud reptilian-type hiss from before.

"Unless I fatally miss my guess," said Irene, "I believe it's safe for us now to take the rope ladder back up into Cloud Ten. No need to worry about some saurian predator picking off one of us."

"There was *never* any need to worry about that," scoffed Stephen disparagingly.

"I know you have a reputation to maintain as prime skeptic," said Fred while Irene called on Kevin aboard Cloud Ten to lower the ladder. "But you will have to admit that since the big rumble has subsided – how's that for freakin' impressive vocabulary? – we no longer hear that special hiss from somewhere out there in the primeval gloom!"

"Yes, the snake is probably too busy swallowing an agouti whole."

*

The noise grew so deafening loud, Augie and company had to press hands over ears for what seemed an eternity.

After the ground-shaking tremor that threw everyone off their feet, there was a tremendous, surging rush of water Augie feared might be overflowing the banks of the Guamá River. But he quickly realized that continuing racket came from inside the sink-holed landfill. Moreover, Cloud Nine wasn't in descent mode for a rescue. Nor was anyone on board there communicating through his earpiece about any sort of imminent danger, spotted from overhead.

Nevertheless, neither Augie nor any of the others dared venture up the side of the sinkhole crater, not even Charly with his survival logarithm having kicked in. But through all the tumult, they kept a close eye in case any water did start slopping over the crater's rim.

After endless-seeming minutes, the surging noise evolved into what Augie could only understand as what one might hear, connecting an amplifier to a water drain, then turning the volume up all the way.

At long last, with a final, distinct slurp!, it sounded like every final drop had emptied. That's when Augie and company climbed the rim, ever confident that Bernie and

Harry looking down from Cloud Nine overhead would warn them off, did they notice any real peril.

For sure, the creature that camouflaged itself variously as Katydiddly, then a giant cashew, didn't exhibit any prior interest in attacking humans, even during its rampage through the open-air market. Augie guessed that would be the furthest thing from the creature's mind, if indeed it was protectively carrying her and Milton Nascimento's love child inside her mouth.

Click...whirr... "The flatus emission detector no longer picks up a possibly non-avian dinosaur gaseous expulsion," reported Charly in his usual robotic monotone. "And I don't see movement down inside there."

"Unless it's camouflaged as a rusted-out pickup truck, and is playing dead," said Augie, although he seriously doubted that. Yes, amidst all the other floral and garbage scents, a distinctive, fetid odor still lingered. It was akin to what he remembered from inside the reptile house at the National Zoo in Washington, D.C. But his sixth sense told him the creature traveled down the drain at the bottom of the landfill crater, even allowed itself to be swept there. And the drain had since closed up, rusted-out vehicles left lying in a circle round where it had been. *Rubber duckies round a bathtub drain?*

Chapter 20

Here we go again, lamented Victoria Copplestone as she entered Diane Mueller's office early Monday morning, the first day of the new school year. Once more, Green Pasture Elementary's curriculum adviser grinned on the verge of a bust-out guffaw. Once more, she could hardly conceal her delight over hope that at long last, she'd found a way to give Vicky the boot. Diane could avert her eyes all she wanted; her mirth was plain to see.

Nevertheless, one simple fact kept Augie's wife from experiencing anew that familiar hole in the pit of her stomach. The reclusive, most eccentric Eclipso Sunray Smith was paying her husband a small fortune for his dinosaur-seeking efforts. Vicky could afford to tell Diane where to stick her unemployment threats, and then storm out of her office, if she so chose.

"Well first off, Vicky," Diane tapped the edge of her desk with a sense of finality, "I must express appreciation for your arrival extra early today, on the official opening of the new school year."

Seated before her, Vicky made a pronounced inhale and exhale not without a bit of exasperation. *Here we go again, for absolute certain.*

"Now, am not sure whether to term it dedication, or stubborn persistence. Whatever it is, one can't but be impressed by your allowing students and parents to remain in your classroom well into Friday night for your husband's curious exploits...in Brazil, was he?"

"Upriver on the Amazon from the port city of Belém, yes, Brazil."

"How late were you here?"

"Everyone left by nine, after the Pteranodon turned out to be yet another faked prehistoric reptile."

"Yes," Diane cleared her throat. "How very surprising that was. So, here's the situation, Vicky. No matter the number of people packed into your classroom for an enterprise one might argue exhibits either admirable tenacity, or extreme foolhardiness. Once the curiosity seekers are peeled away, the numbers of children enrolled in your, um, supposedly educational experience are way too small for us to justify offering that elective even part-time.

"Don't worry; we are well aware of the contractual obligations, and fully intend to honor them," Diane rushed to add defensively. She raised her hands before her, palms facing out, while Vicky crossed her arms, stone-faced in her regard. "We want to present you with options. Any one of which you can do full-time, or mix and match for the variety although that will put you on the road a lot. To continue hands-on with children, you could become an instructional assistant in classrooms experiencing overflow. Or you could devote your days to much-needed clerical work at Central Office. Or as I said, you could do both, driving from one to the other each day."

Or I could tell you to go straight to hell. Have to have a lawyer check if this is even legal what you're proposing.

Knock! Knock!

"Oh, let's see who that is," said Diane quickly rising from her chair to make for the door, in her as-if-I-didn't-know-already voice.

Vicky figured it would be the principal, Dr. Klondike, to pile on about her options by turns humiliating and disgraceful, if not legally sketchy. *By the by, did you ever consider resigning so you could explore other opportunities out there while you're still young enough? Maybe even tag along on your husband's expeditions?*

"Marsha!" squealed Diane most ebulliently, spreading her arms wide to welcome Marsha Klondike into her office. "So very glad you could join us! I was just going over Vicky's options with her!"

"Yes," Marsha reacted curtly as she pulled up a second chair beside the one Vicky took. She labored not to let the contents of the stuffed file she was carrying spill all over the floor. "Vicky, you should know that a large group of our parents have been very active this past weekend."

"Oh?"

"Oh yes; they've been expressing their discontent after dropping in on your unconventional orientation session Friday," Marsha went on, making poker-faced eye contact with Vicky Copplestone only. "One mother even called the superintendent, and boy did he ever give me an earful."

"Sorry to hear that," reacted Vicky, straining not to bristle while Diane thought to herself: *Wow, this could not be going any better, even if I had made more of an effort to fan the flames than I already did! Any luck at all, Vicky only has one choice now, and that's to get the hell out of MY school!!*

"Here's the bottom line, then I'll fill in the details on how we got there. I know we raised the specter of your only having enough students signed up for your cryptozoology special to justify your teaching half days, at best. The other half would be given over to either clerical work in Central Office, or teaching assistant or some such here. Are you okay, Diane?"

Turning her face aside, Diane Mueller had made a peculiar grunting noise that resulted from her having suppressed what would otherwise have been a gleeful cackle. But what she said was, "I'm fine; accidentally swallowed the wrong way."

As opposed to having intentionally swallowed the wrong way, Vicky had to stifle herself from snarking.

"Ooookay," reacted Marsha as in, *That doesn't make any sense since you weren't eating, but whatever.* "What I'm getting to, Vicky, is...would you be willing to continue teaching full time, after all? I know this is awfully short notice..."

"Yes, it is," snapped Diane. "How can she do that with only a few days before the specials officially start?!" as in *How can you do that?!?! Not again!!! What, does this woman have nine professional lives like a cat?!?!*

"It's fine. I'll manage. Though I do appreciate your concern, Diane." Vicky reached out a hand to appreciatively pat the back of Diane's hand...or rub salt in the wound if she was being honest about it.

Diane found most conveniently she had to scratch at the nape of her neck. She lifted her hand away to do that in just the nick of time to avoid Vicky's touch.

"What brought this on, Marsha?" Ms. Copplestone went on to ask, undaunted.

"A group of parents drew up a petition saying it was unfair to make students choose between your multi-disciplinary class, and either physical education, art, or music. They argued for your class as an extra science elective, and got over one-hundred-fifty signatures. During expedition days, when you follow your husband's exploits televised live- How does he do that, again?"

"He keeps a camcorder mounted on his bandana," Vicky explained, while unable to help but notice Diane Mueller's thin-lipped mouth take a crooked path across her face, like a meandering stream.

"Ah, thought it was something like that. Well on those days when he sends you live feeds, the parents would like to see a combined-group assembly in the all-purpose room so nobody in the upper grades misses out."

"That sounds terrific!"

"But one other thing, Ms. Copplestone," said Marsha, it not lost on Vicky that the principal suddenly resorted to addressing her more formally. "The parents, as well as Central Office including myself, of course, would deeply appreciate keeping your class from turning into a media circus. For now, it seems your husband's search has been a lesson in not getting taken in by hoaxers, more than anything else. That's of little interest to reporters. But should a Tyrannosaurus that isn't some mechanical contraption suddenly pop up on your TV..."

"Augie and his crew delight in our children learning scientific methodology, fun nature facts, and the importance of tempering an open mind with a healthy dose of skepticism. But believe me, they are also worried about the safety of any discovered creature formerly thought extinct for millions of years. They don't want me welcoming reporter types into my classroom to cover that, any more than you do."

"I trust you will also adhere to a policy of not calling any more attention to Vicky's class than is absolutely necessary, Ms. Mueller?"

"That's the furthest thing from my mind. Oh, look," Diane went on, looking down at her left-hand wrist hidden well beneath her desk, at the watch that still wasn't there. "Getting so close to bus duty, and I really have a lot of paperwork to wade through..." By this point Diane was up from her desk and halfway out the door.

"Isn't that odd?" asked Marsha while Diane's high heels went click-click-clicking down the hall.

"Isn't what odd? Oh, you're right!" Vicky added with her dawning realization. "Isn't this her office where she'd be doing that paperwork?"

Chapter 21

Augie and company, including three time travelers from 2064 still stuck in 1982, filed into Eclipso's conference room on the first floor of his mansion redesigned to look like a palace-sized Ankylosaurus. They found themselves accompanied by the Beatles' "Twist and Shout," the reggae version recorded by the Beatles reggae cover band, Yellow Dubmarine.

As usual, Bonsai Gator made a small spectacle of himself dancing to the music on Eclipso's massively sized, swamp-embedded conference table.

"Now I get it," Sergeant Fred Frankly muttered softly to fellow time travelers Kevin Smith-Park and Ali Magabu, officers from aboard the starship Smoke and Mirrors. "We're part of the processional for a special ceremony to honor having lost our minds to the point we think there might be dinosaurs round every corner!"

"C'mon c'mon c'mon BABY now!" sang a member of Yellow Dubmarine, aping perfectly Beatle John Lennon's raspy voice, just as Scott McDonald and Irene McDowell made eye contact. They'd been out of touch for days, Irene aboard Cloud Ten to Kurupira and Scott part of the Cloud Nine contingent. Scott already seated at the conference table, Irene was still filing in. Who knows? Maybe she would have braved sitting down beside him. But the "c'mon baby" coincided precisely with their noticing each other. As if they weren't already experiencing no small amount of anticipation.

Anyway, the lyrics proved so irrationally embarrassing to both, Irene and Scott looked away from each other. And Irene sought a chair the far side of the table from where

Scott sat. They could have been two magnetized objects repulsed by like charges, Augie imagined.

Gotta hope Bonsai Gator's manic boogie has distracted everyone from noticing how red Scott's ears have turned, Irene found herself fretting, as her embarrassed turning-away from Scott did not prevent her stealing another glance his direction. *And mine as well, for all I know!*

"Welcome back, one and all," Eclipso spread his arms effusively. "You can see how excited Bonsai is, over the prospect of reviewing so much promising evidence of non-avian dinosaur survival. Don't think I've ever seen him dance so intently."

"He's probably preparing to pounce on a tempting pigmy dragonfly," pushed back Stephen Feldman with his authoritatively deep voice. "Doesn't look that different to me from your typical Anatole lizard's pushups before it tongues an ant into its mouth."

As though to rub Stephen's face in just how wrong he was, Augie mused, Bonsai Gator turned his back on everyone, and made an unmistakably boogie-inspired butt wiggle. That wiggle coordinated perfectly with the "shake it shake it shake it" part of "Twist and Shout" while Bonsai raised the roof with his forelegs.

"Okay, maybe the pulsing bass rhythm does awaken some primordial element deep inside him," Stephen grudgingly conceded.

By then, Charly had stood stiffly out of his own seat, and turned his back on the conference table. But before he could mimic Bonsai Gator's butt wiggle dance moves, Sherman advised him, "No need to make common cause with Bonsai Gator, Charly. Stay focused on discerning evidence of surviving non-avian dinosaurs."

Click...whirr... "Sorry; I thought Bonsai Gator might be demonstrating a manner by which to insightfully analyze the video data for evidence of non-avian dinosaur survival."

"Think some more, Charly: Does that even make any sense?" Sherman asked, clearly unable to hide his irritation.

Click...whirr... "As per my reason-for-being program, I pursue every possible avenue, including those I do not currently understand."

"Here's the thing, Charly: If you don't understand it, if it makes no logical sense, don't pursue it."

Click...whirr... "Done." With that, the artificial intelligence entity known as Charly took his seat.

"Careful, there, Sherman," advised Stephen, "telling Charly not to pursue any avenue that doesn't make sense. Where surviving non-avian dinosaurs are concerned, you'll leave him with nothing to do."

Before Sherman could push back on Stephen's usual skeptical snark, the reggae "Twist and Shout" cut off abruptly, the dino searchers having finished filing in and making themselves comfortable round the swamp-embedded conference table.

Eclipso said, to his mother's cross-armed approving nod standing right behind him, "I think Charly will have his hands full, indeed, with the videos we are about to examine and discuss...except for perhaps the first one, unless he notices something there that has escaped my attention."

Irene had to stifle herself to keep from remarking on the difficulty Harriet and Harry appeared to have, restraining themselves from crawling all over each other like the young couple on the *trem da alegria*. They were finally reunited after their time apart, Harry aboard Cloud Nine, and Harriet in the field joining Irene and company on Cloud Ten for the trip to the base of Kurupira. They held hands, tenderly stroking each other's fingers while looking directly Eclipso's way with silly grins on their faces. Not turning to each other for fear they wouldn't be able to resist passionate kisses even one second longer?

Good God, Irene wanted to say, *forget about Charly having his hands full! Harriet and Harry look like they're about to have their hands full of each other! And I don't think they're going to come up with any evidence of surviving non-avian dinosaurs by exploring each other's mouths with their tongues!*

"What I've done," went on Eclipso, oblivious to Harriet and Harry's blush-stoking finger fondling, "is curate only the most intriguing videos from the countless hours recorded. Again, we will begin with something that, though clearly not dinosaurian, might be a most significant discovery in its own right. I believe this was taken from your bandana camcorder, Dr. Matias."

"It sent some of my wife's students poring through books on prehistoric mammals to pin down the identity."

"Where does that project stand? Or should we just roll the film?"

"No consensus was reached due to a curious issue I didn't consider at the time. So yes, let's see what we've got first."

"If you'll do the honors, Samuel," Eclipso motioned towards his all-sorts assistant, Samuel Longbottom.

Against one wall, a framed enlargement of a *Turok* comic book cover depicted a Native American member of the Mandan tribe aiming an arrow at an attacking Tyrannosaurus Rex. It slid up into the ceiling, revealing a movie screen.

Augie noticed Eclipso's mother, arms still crossed, once more nodding approval...and Bonsai Gator doing the exact same thing, down to the crossed forelegs while he stood up to his waist in the conference table's embedded swamp.

"I seriously doubt Bonsai Gator is doing what it looks like he's doing," Stephen whispered to Laura. "Untold millions of years evolving on an isolated atoll in the South Pacific must have proven especially beneficial, to develop such extraordinarily flexible articulation of his forelimbs that he can cross them like that. But not to express smug satisfaction as Eclipso's mom is doing. Far more likely he's instinctively protecting his upper torso from being stung by that small dragonfly buzzing-"

"Sh!" Laura shh-ed Stephen sharply. She wanted to go on about Bonsai's crossed forelegs. How could they prove at all effective for blocking insect stings, when crossing them still left a good part of his torso unprotected? She really wanted to go after Stephen over his increasingly tiresome skepticism. But even more, she wanted to focus her full attention on the first video clip Eclipso would share.

Back in Brazil while his bandana-mounted camcorder was filming, Augie scrambled to keep out of the way of the huge creature that emerged from a cave-like burrow. Consequently, the picture jumped about quite a bit.

Nevertheless, everyone could clearly make out the creature's back. Fat and muscles rippled mightily beneath its thick coat of coarse mahogany-brown fur as it made a panicky climb up one side of the steeply-walled deep furrow. Also obvious was how it clawed away a blanket of light green moss, revealing streaks of reddish-brown sandstone clay.

"Wow!" sighed Dr. Roberta Quiñones. "Really wish I had been there to see that thing up close! For all the world it looks like an overgrown groundhog!"

"I really respect your assessment as a professional trained zoologist," Stephen said pointedly before going on, "but are you certain that's not just a slightly-larger-than-normal groundhog, or some such local animal, made to appear grizzly-bear-sized by an atmospheric inversion layer?

Wasn't it very damp and misty inside that furrow? That's how it looks in the video."

"True," conceded Roberta. "However, no creature I know of there, comparable to the groundhog, such as the capybara, could claw away the moss like that."

"There's also the question of why the locals would have fled in such a panic. That is, if it was only some familiar local creature such as the capybara," added Sherman. Then piling on further, "And surely, they would have had more than just a passing acquaintance with ground-level inversion layers exaggerating creatures' sizes."

"Well, I wasn't there to see for myself," snipped Stephen.

"Regarding the capybara, that's the one question my wife tells me came up in her class, that honestly didn't occur to me. Could the creature we filmed have been an extra-large capybara rather than a Megatherium?"

"Not to bog ourselves down too much over the matter," suggested Eclipso in diplomatic mode. "The only real contribution to our quest, at best, would be to suggest it's not necessarily impossible for large surviving prehistoric relics to have escaped notice. Including a monster capybara which I believe was named Phoberomys."

"Escaped notice, except by the locals. They've spoken of the *mapinguari* being part of their ecology going back thousands of years," bristled Irene.

Which got Scott to thinking, *I must stop being such a cowardly fool. I simply have to tell Irene how much I missed her, and worried for her safety when she joined Bernie to survey where he might have seen a Carnotaurus prowling about, some years ago.*

"Point well taken, Ms. McDowell," said Eclipso. "I should have known better than to have slipped back into that prejudiced assumption you documented so well in your most thoughtful book. Where too many people are concerned, no creature officially exists until explorers from Western civilization, mostly white-skinned, confirm it."

"Perhaps," grudgingly admitted Stephen. "However, can we at least concede that precise identification of whatever creature, its taxonomy, is the domain of such trained experienced professionals as yourself, Dr. Quiñones?"

"More than 'perhaps.' But as for the other: Yes, of course," nodded Roberta. She would have had to also concede that, as irritating as she found Stephen, dealing with him proved a pleasant experience compared to facing her lover, Daniel.

"Let's move on to another video clip from Augie," said Eclipso.

Bonsai Gator appeared to nod approvingly again, mirrored by Eclipso's mother.

Stephen wanted to push back on what he knew everyone else was thinking... and feared contaminated his own mind as well. But he decided, *No; better save that for later, how Bonsai simply had to be imitating Eclipso's mom.*

"This one is unlike the Megatherium ground sloth or giant prehistoric capybara or okay, maybe some smaller creature magnified to appear many times larger by water vapor," Eclipso nodded Stephen's direction. "Augie's camcorder was the only one that captured what you're about to see."

"Maybe because I was the only one to notice it," Augie added.

Again, circumstances resulted in Augie's video clip jumping about like he was on a ship in rough seas. But twice, each time lasting mere seconds, two green eyes appeared to stare out from the pitch-black interior of a cavernously large burrow. They were so large, and so far apart, the head would have had to have been massive.

Something on the order of a blue whale's head, Augie reckoned, dwarfing even the largest known Triceratops or Tyrannosaurus Rex skull.

Eclipso replayed the short clip multiple times before anyone commented, starting with Laura in full journalist mode. "If those were eyes," she said, "either they blinked, or their owner looked down then back up."

"Blinking might rule out a surviving Titanoboa," weighed in Sherman, his chin ever-scrunched into his neck. "Whether or not he was blinking would be difficult to assess without getting awkwardly, or what some might call dangerously close. Snakes don't have eyelids as we commonly refer to them. But dinosaurs most certainly would have sported them, if they followed the lead of their avian descendants. And the same as birds, they would have included an extra film that moved sideways like a windshield washer to brush away dirt and particles and such."

If she writes me off as a nutjob, so be it. I've got to confess, see if there's any hope.

"What are your thoughts on this, Scott?" Eclipso asked. He noticed Scott's attention adrift, pondering something not necessarily the video clip at issue.

How to begin? "Irene, please don't take offense..." Naw; why should I apologize for my feelings? It's not like I've assaulted her or anything like that!

"Dr. Scott McDonald!"

"Oh, yeah! Sorry," apologized Scott, nearly slipping off his conference table chair in a combo of surprise and embarrassment.

"Do we need to rerun Dr. Matias's video clip a fifth time?"

"No, that won't be necessary. I did notice one thing," said Scott as he forced himself not to sneak a glimpse, between bonsai-sized coconut palms, of Irene seated across the swamp-embedded conference table from him.

And he hoped his ears weren't glowing red enough to light up the room in case of a power failure. "After you see those presumed eyes a second time, they appear to rapidly diminish in size rather than blink shut. The creature must have been backing off deeper into the furrow," he concluded. "And unless I miss my guess, shortly after that was when we heard a tremendous splash in the general direction of the Amazon tributary running behind the furrow. Something enormous taking a dive?"

"Oh c'mon," scoffed Stephen as usual. "Two eyes on something where the head alone would have to be the size of an elephant? Before we go there, we must consider the possibility two fireflies were glowing on and off. Or lightning from that storm you mentioned reflected off something glistening..."

"Such as two eyes," Irene inserted snarkily.

"I was thinking rather of two plants growing either side of the burrow," Stephen couldn't help bristling.

"Two plants. Deep inside a dark burrow, away from any sunlight. Exactly opposite each other. Got it," Irene reacted.

"And remember, there's also the matter, like I said, of that tremendous splash back behind where the burrow might lead," Scott piled on.

"Okay, I surrender," Stephen lifted his hands, palms facing out. "It's got to be a snake or a dinosaur the size of a subway train. No, wait; it blinked its eyes, so it could only have been a dinosaur."

With a heavy sigh, Eclipso finally remarked, "No other clips from the Amazon reveal anything pertinent I can see. But maybe after your close examination... Anyway, unless one of you has something more to add...and I am well aware of the positive sign from Charly's flatus emission detector, Sherman."

"If you believe in that sort of thing."

"I'm sorry, are you casting aspersions on my flatus emission detector?" Sherman bristled for the first time Augie could ever recall. Sherman lifted his chin off his neck to confront Stephen directly.

"If I'm perfectly honest about it, I am. And that's despite my immense respect for your successful repurposing of advanced technology left in the place of absconded weapons worldwide. There's the REAL mystery. Anyway, yes, I've been dubious from the start. With so much background noise typical of a lushly vegetated wilderness, how could any device successfully tease out various animal farts, down to a firefly's even?"

"Well, there you go," said Sherman with a finality that continued to show off his considerable irritation. "I never said my flatus emission detector was fool-proof! In fact, in fact," he sputtered as he returned to scrunching his chin into his neck, as though really addressing his own belly button, Augie never tired of musing, "there is a specific reason we have only that 'positive sign' Eclipso so accurately referenced! Rather than a firm signature identical to our famously intriguing mystery fart from Cameroon! What I'm talking about is the volume of ambient noise from the rainforest shower! If you'd like, I could walk you through the exact mechanics of my detector. You will come away with loads more knowledge of what you're judging so harshly, than you obviously have at the moment."

"I can't be bothered."

"Oh, steady on, mates!" boisterously intervened Alistair Frump. He spread his arms wide as he stood up right beside Eclipso. To Augie, he appeared ready to hug the whole world. "I know we're feeling stressed by so much smoke without clearly definitively seeing the fire, i.e. the creature that's been our goal! But there's no need to become snippy!"

"I'm afraid all that smoke is actually a fog of wishful thinking. The only fire is figurative, from fevered burning imaginations," glumly pronounced Stephen his grim judgment.

"Having been at Kurupira yourself, I am amazed by your own fog of fevered skepticism. Okay, I'm out!" Alistair tossed his hands in surrender.

"What's that, Bonsai Gator?" asked Eclipso, cupping his hand over his ear Bonsai's direction. "You feel like a boogie to 'You're Going to Lose That Girl'? Samuel?"

"Got it, sir," said Samuel Longbottom as he pressed some buttons on a walkie-talkie-looking device he carried.

Quickly thereafter, a reggae-fied version of another Beatles classic filled the conference room. As usual, an infectiously syncopated reggae beat led the way. And Bonsai Gator was moving to the rhythms again, his lower half swaying before his upper torso joined in.

Bonsai's petite spectacle provided such welcome relief to the building tension, most people round the conference table burst into giggles.

Even Stephen couldn't help a small snort, himself. How absurd, anyone believing the pencil-sized gator was actually dancing rather than simply reacting instinctively to the rhythms. Or completely unrelated to the music, preparing to snap at a small dragonfly! Which in fact Bonsai did do, on the end of the Beatles' lyric, "I'll make a point of taking her away from you."

Shortly after Bonsai ate the hapless midget dragonfly, Samuel faded off the music, at Eclipso's nonverbal behest.

Eclipso slapped his hands against the edge of the conference table. This sharp action oddly coincided with his mother slapping her hands together in seeming rapturous appreciation of the latest little show Bonsai put on.

"Well now that we're in a much better mood," Eclipso enthused, "let's continue our review of the most tantalizing video clips from other locales, shall we?"

The next clip run by Samuel Longbottom came from Harriet's bandana-camcorder. At the outset, it featured a lingering view of the tabletop mountain Kurupira's full majesty. A lightning flash highlighted where one cliffside had partially collapsed, creating stairstep levels of vegetation.

"We are skipping the faux Pteranodon footage; I'll circle back to that, including its implications for our future moves," explained Eclipso, punctuated by a distinct chomp! on a humus-lathered pretzel. "But for now…"

For now, Harriet's camcorder footage shifted to a patch of soft, clayey soil in front of ruins from the collapsed *Yanomami*-type *shabono*. A large, three-toed foot track figured prominently, accompanied by background hubbub including Irene's distinctive, "That wasn't there a second ago!" and Stephen's equally distinctive, dismissive, "Oh c'mon."

Irene especially wished she'd made a plaster cast. At the time, she feared a surviving theropod dinosaur might try to take a bite out of her.

In any event, out the corner of her eye Harriet had noticed movement near the ruins. Turning her full attention there, her camcorder filmed a large agouti rodent emerging. It sniffed about, like rodents were wont to do in their perpetual search for food or a mate or, as Augie liked to think, out of sheer joie-de-vivre curiosity.

In a literal flash, a second lightning flash, it was gone.

"Jesus Houdini Christ where'd it go?!" Sergeant Fred Frankly could be heard animatedly asking.

"I know what we're *supposed* to have seen," said Stephen while the video ran a second time. "That was Bernie's stoa aka surviving Carnotaurus, exercising paranormal powers of camouflage. When he ate the agouti in one bite, he made it look like that hapless creature vanished into thin air."

"Don't forget about the conventional explanation you're about to regale us with, concerning the three-toed foot track, Prince Skeptic," drily advised Irene.

"Oh, I rather like the idea of being a prince," jovially reacted Stephen, back in his unflappable place. "And no, I haven't forgotten about the 'foot track' (finger quotation marks) at all. I am reminded," Stephen plowed on, "of certain photos from lunar and Martian surfaces, taken by our unmanned spacecraft. Sensationalist tabloid newspapers read all sorts of amazing things into rock formations and erosion signatures. Much like seeing a floating monster bunny or some-such in passing cloud formations. Remember those Martian hills that looked like facial features?"

"So, you believe that impression in the clay was- What? Soil splitting apart in the shape of a foot track?" asked Laura in a sincerely inquisitive, ready-to-give-any-suggestion-a-fair-hearing tone of voice, like the impartially open-minded journalist she was.

"Maybe that," said Stephen appreciatively. Especially so, since he found himself rather attracted to Laura, and wondered whether it might be mutual. "But I was thinking a trick of light from the approaching thunderstorm played across the ground from between tree branches. Who knows? My point is, we shouldn't postulate a relic dinosaur's foot track having suddenly magically appeared until we've exhausted other possibilities. Moreover," he went on, feeling on a roll, about to deliver the final, devastating blow to the foot track notion, "why is there only one? If it is a foot track, why only one? Did your Carnotaurus hop out into the open on one leg, snatch up the agouti, then make its one-legged hop back into the rubble or underbrush?"

"You've been rather quiet, Dr. Matias," said Eclipso, putting Augie on the spot. "Perhaps you'd like to add something? Something you've been holding back?"

The way Eclipso eyed Augie Matias whilst ruminating, seemingly, on another piece of humus-lathered pretzel, Augie strained not to appear anything other than his usual, absent-minded self. This, even while his brain churned, *Holy freakatoly! Is his extrasensory perception so powerful, he can sense my holding back on sharing with him about that cloth fragment blown out of the cavernous burrow? No wonder he speaks with such confidence about what's going through Bonsai Gator's head. No, wait; he had to have known from the video clips about Raul telling me to drop what I was holding, thinking it was gold...* "I was pondering what Stephen said about a single foot track. There are so many different reasons there would only be one. Maybe the others were lost in the shadows. Or maybe the ground was too hard in other places the creature stepped, for much of an impression to have been made. Or impressions that would have shown up all that well in the combo of fading sunset and imminent thunderstorm."

Augie faded off, himself, albeit satisfied he rose to Eclipso's challenge to contribute something meaningful to the conversation.

Nevertheless, Eclipso did a doubletake, then unnervingly, where Augie was concerned, eyed him most intently. Did he notice some peculiar blemish on Augie's face, and was squinting to make sure it wasn't his imagination before he commented? "I know I'm backtracking here, Augustine," he spoke at last. "But something still bothers me from the video during your standoff with the gold miners and those young *Yanomami* gentlemen. I clearly heard you told to drop, let go, whatever that was you picked off your face after it got blown there. What was it exactly? Even if it had nothing to do with our quest?"

"I'll be perfectly honest with you, Eclipso," started Augie, losing his appetite for continued avoidance of the subject any longer. Despite his concern over how painful it might prove for Eclipso to hear...or cruelly lend him a slender thread of hope where there ought not to be any... "The plain fact is that I *have* been holding something back. And had exactly to do with what blew against my face from inside the monster burrow. There was nothing else along with it, to bring us any closer to what is obviously very close to your heart. So..."

"Well out with it! What was it?!"

Augie made eye contact with Bonsai Gator.

Bonsai Gator darted his eyes Eclipso's way, then back to Augie, as though to say, *You heard the man; how about it?*

"Okay, then," said Augie. *You asked for it.* "It was a fragment of cotton cloth imprinted with the very same Styracosaurus design I noticed in a photo of your wife, on her bandana scarf. That was from when she posed beside that environmental activist, Aninha Floresta. Sadly, it was lost in the rain shower flooding of the furrow after Raul told me to let it go. Before I could give it another thought, we had to be on our way pursuing the Pteranodon."

"Okay, I know all the rest," Eclipso batted both hands before his face to put off Augie from saying another word. Irene imagined he was waving off some swarming insect pest. "Let's consider a second video from Kurupira that's maybe harder to explain away than your vanishing agouti."

"Before you do," leapt in Stephen, "I had one more thing to say about the vanishing agouti. Some snakes attack their prey with lightning speed. Isn't it possible that from one second to the next, that's what happened to the agouti? Whatever local large snake shot out from underneath a nearby fern? Then retracted its head with our hapless rodent acquaintance firmly lodged between its fanged jaws? Too fast for the human eye?"

"Maybe too fast for the *human* eye. But not for a frame-by-frame analysis to pick up at fifty frames per second," said Sherman, as usual with chin scrunched into his neck, *like he's having a sidebar conversation with his belly button.* "I've already run such an analysis, and sorry. There's no snake head that appears in any of the frames."

"You're assuming the combined darkness from both storm and sunset didn't cloak anything," rebutted Stephen, back to sounding defensive to Augie.

"Okay, so from one one-fiftieth of a second to the next, our agouti friend went from clearly visible to totally lost in shadow."

"And the only alternative is to believe a surviving theropod dinosaur with supernatural camouflage powers gobbled him up in one bite."

"Please stifle yourselves, both of you!" snapped Eclipso. "At least long enough to carefully consider this other video clip."

"Oh, yeah," nodded Irene, immediately recognizing the partially collapsed cliffside of Kurupira. The "wound" revealed an underground waterfall strangely ebbing and flowing between falling downwards, and appearing to defy gravity falling upwards.

"Now I think we can all agree, at least, that that partially visible water stayed a very unusual course," said Eclipso hopefully. Albeit, his voice sounded to Augie more nasal than usual.

"Strange tricks of light reflecting-" was far as Stephen got before a collective groan stifled him.

Jesus Porcupine Christ, he's like a dog with his skepticism bone! Sergeant Frankly cursed to himself. *Wish he'd bury it for a while, until it actually would come in handy when one of these other clowns claims a dinosaur gave them a blow job or something!*

Let's suppose Irene really does not have any interest in me, in that way, Scott meanwhile took the opportunity to conjure with, before he might be put on the spot again, like Augie, about having so little to say. *Isn't it better if I establish that fact with perfect clarity sooner rather than later? Then I can get back to giving my full attention to the quest? And maybe also end the awkwardness between us? Apart from a little humiliation, what's the worst that can happen?*

"There!" suddenly exclaimed Harriet, pointing at the screen.

"I must have missed it like I did the first time, back when we were viewing Kurupira in real time," deadpanned Stephen.

"Wo! How did those palm trees suddenly show up?" Augie couldn't help exclaiming as he pointed at the screen as well.

"Like any other plant, I imagine," Stephen continued with his deadpan affect. "They grew out of the ground."

"Oh yeah; those palms grew full-grown out of the ground, instantaneously. Then they hopped into that flowing underground water for a swim. Like any other plant, I reckon," Irene deadpanned right back.

The video clip had already moved on to where an earth tremor made for a jumpy look at the additional cliffside collapse that totally concealed from view the mysteriously ebbing and flowing waterway.

"Oh c'mon," Stephen scoffed for his umpteenth time.

"But you know what, Mr. Feldman?" said Eclipso. "We're going to put you in the docket with this particular video, by freezing it at two particular spots I really do think test your skeptical dismissiveness. Samuel, you know what I'm talking about for spot one."

"Indeed, I do," confirmed Samuel Longbottom. He lost no time returning the video to a frame that, if only for an instant, did appear to show a distinctively reptilian head looking out away from the open cliffside wound behind it. With a small horn above each eye.

"So just what do you suggest that is, Stephen Feldman, other than a surviving Carnotaurus?"

"From our perspective analysis, Harry and I established it had to have been the size of an alligator's head," added Harriet.

"In other words," piled on Harry, "large enough to have swallowed an agouti in one bite."

"That's assuming you've got your perspective measurements correct, and there wasn't some optical illusion," animatedly, defensively spoke up Stephen finally. "A close-up distorted view of certain insects could look very dinosaurian, indeed, I should think. If you would, Samuel, how about running the following few seconds from this clip?"

What transpired on the film over those next seconds happened so fast, Samuel reran it slowed down to a frame at a time. Clearly, something bug-sized did fly off from being extra close to the camcorder lens, the same time the reptilian-looking head either vanished, or blended in with its shadowed surroundings.

"Okay, something obviously did fly off from being very close to the lens," conceded Roberta Quiñones, ever grateful for this distraction from torturing herself over what to do about her relationship with Daniela. "And I have seen some really bizarre-looking bug heads. But I don't recall any that reminded me of a reptile. More the stuff of sci-fi aliens."

"So, it was just a coincidence your dinosaur head vanished the same time that bug flew away from the camera?" Stephen asked most dubiously.

"Far as coincidences go, I think there are far stranger ones than that to be had," Scott remarked. "And coincidences do happen."

"Agreed," Sherman nodded his chin into his neck, as though he was responding to a comment by his belly button, Augie mused. "The odds for that have to be far less than astronomical."

"Okay, assume that's true. We're still left with the very plausible possibility that so-called head is really just a trick of light," Stephen responded without missing a beat. He pretended not being the least rattled where his world view was concerned. "As with other such illusions, soon as the lighting changed with approaching sunset, the illusion vanished far faster than your typical rainbow."

"And what an extraordinary coincidence *that* is, then," piped up Bernie Coleman. He sounded far more animated, less soft-spoken, than Augie ever remembered hearing him before. "Such a marvelous illusion took on the exact same characteristics of the creature sighted around there, albeit on rare, rare occasion, including by myself."

"Which might indicate a combination of local vegetation with special lighting conditions rather favors recurrences of that particular illusion?"

Bonsai Gator gave Stephen his arched eye regard, shaking his head in marveling disgust.

Eclipso said, "Samuel, let's have the next clip, and see how that fits in with Stephen Feldman's nothing-to-see-here narrative, shall we?"

"Right-o," said Samuel ever agreeably as he ran the next selected segment.

Taking place not too long after the controversial Carnotaurus head, the next short clip featured the sudden presence of palm trees around where the head was last seen. They appeared to leap into the ebbing and flowing partially exposed underground stream behind them. Pursuant to which, the latest tremor on the nineteen-day cycle caused that stream's re-concealment via additional cliff wall collapse, as captured very jiggly on the video. The camcorder's bearer, Irene, had been jostled about by the tremor, as one would expect.

"I'm delighted to be a figurative fly on the wall, to hear how you're going to explain away those palm trees, Stephen," chortled Irene.

"What's there to explain?" Stephen spread open his arms innocently. "The tremor obviously dislodged them from their precarious position we couldn't see from where we were. And as the ground kept quaking, well that sent them sliding into the waterfall."

"And they managed to remain upright the entire freakin' time," snidely added Fred Frankly. He required every last ounce of self-control not to hurl a string of profanities Stephen's way.

"What, you think those trees got up and moved of their own volition?" scoffed Stephen. "What if their root balls were dislodged by the tremors where they were clinging to the hillside, and went sliding? Wouldn't that be enough to keep them upright all the way over the precipice into the stream?"

"Believe it or not, back in the future from where we arrived, we dealt with extraterrestrial tree creatures who DO move of their own volition," said Fred with the kind of matter-of-fact tone that had Augie, at least, totally convinced. "Two of them accompany us on our starship, in an advisory capacity."

Sure they do, Stephen wanted to respond, followed by, *You really ARE doubling down on this time travel bull dookey, aren't you?* But he feared Fred was that delusional, rather than making up the whole thing. And he certainly looked strong enough to beat the crap out of anyone who ridiculed him. So, Stephen reacted instead with an I-give-up tossing of his hands in the air.

"To backpedal a smidge," went on Frank, "I don't think any of those particular beings is likely to have made their way to Earth on their own. But I do know that what I saw looked for all the world like two trees taking a leap. And it does seem your surviving dinosaurs, or some other large reptiles, could have f-n' beyond-the-beyond camouflage abilities. MY best guess is we actually saw our agouti-eater, and his mate, share a swim."

"Only, from what we discussed before, there are other more conventional explanations for our observation. They do not require resorting to such incredible assertions."

"But you haven't produced any real evidence to back up those explanations," Bernie Coleman pushed back, though returned to his disarmingly soft-spoken voice. "All you've given us has been an assortment of 'ifs' and 'mights.'"

While Stephen bent forehead into hand, Eclipso bulldozed on, "Speaking of 'mights,' far as definitively establishing the existence of any such extraordinary camouflage powers: It *might* be useful to consider Dr. Quiñones's camcorder videos from that condo of interest overlooking the Guamá River in Belém."

So many bizarre adventures, Scott found himself thinking with a dreadful sinking feeling. *It can't be that we've been so desperate to succeed, we've read extraordinary possibilities that aren't really there into a host of mundane occurrences, can it? That our resident skeptic has been correct all along? No, suggesting the giant ground sloth was just an overgrown rodent... Well, what does this mean for whatever signals I've believed, have wanted to believe, Irene is giving off, of interest in me? More wishful thinking? All the more reason to unload my feelings for her sooner rather than later? Have done with the disappointment so I can keep my focus on the dinosaur quest? And ultimately get that disappointment over with, as well?*

"I'm telling you in no uncertain terms," Roberta Quiñones bristled preemptively with an eye towards Stephen. "As you're about to see, a baby reptile bearing a striking resemblance to a Carnotaurus appears hatched out of an invisible egg, before it turns invisible also! Extraordinary camouflage would be the only explanation, I should think!"

Roberta was late getting her camcorder to the party, focused on the haunted nest shorn into Rosa and Ron's living room sofa. The creature had already pecked its tiny reptilian head through a stubbornly unseeable egg. And not long after the video started running, it vanished, followed by a distinct chomp!

All that while, the hyacinth macaw, Milton Nascimento, made a fluttering squawking fuss, circling round about. Then its spiral path took it flying down off the balcony.

"Okay, rerun that, and stop right after your supposed baby Carnotaurus supposedly disappears," insisted Stephen. "There," he went on after Samuel obliged. He rose from his seat and circled around others to walk right up to the screen behind where Eclipso sat. "You see that small speck?" Stephen asked, pointing adamantly at a small detail. "Samuel, if you will please continue the replay at very slow speed," he asked more politely this time. "Now keep a close eye," he went on, tracing the speck's erratic movement with his forefinger. It finally came to rest on Rosa's centerpiece plant, a tall bromeliad, bright red at the top, and situated in a colorfully decorative ceramic bowl on the rattan coffee table in front of the nested sofa. "There's your baby Carnotaurus. It's some generic bug that flew too close to the camera before making its way onto that house plant."

"But where's the transition?" asked Eclipso in a tone suggestive to Augie he might have had just about enough of this constant skeptical poo-pooing he'd asked for in the first place.

"What transition?" asked Stephen, also sounding supremely irritated.

"If what you're suggesting is true, Mr. Feldman, your bug shouldn't have suddenly gone from something that sizeable to a difficult-to-see speck."

"Ahh, but if it were close to the camera, then flew to one side, not flying back into view until it was much further away..."

"Okay, I get it," Eclipso conceded, though no less bothered. "But what particular bug in closeup would look so reptilian rather than outer-space-alien?"

"I'll do a search, see if I can present some candidates," reacted Stephen, satisfied enough with Eclipso's concession for the time being.

"You also have to explain how it wasn't simply the camera view. It was my own view as well," bristled Roberta. "What, my desperation to spot a living dinosaur had me believing a bug that flew in my face was several feet away? And then just by coincidence, after the hyacinth macaw appeared to chase something down off the balcony of our friends' condo, it made a beeline for where a Katydiddly showed up at the Happy Train? Even though the person playing Katydiddly called in sick?"

"Okay, so it could only have been a surviving Carnotaurus that bears a striking resemblance to a costumed Katydiddly. That is, when it's not altogether invisible due to its camouflage superpowers," heartily snarked Stephen.

"I'm not saying I necessarily buy this magic dino stuff yet. Though as mentioned before, we've seen far stranger on other planets," said Fred Frankly. "But gotta admit that after Katydiddly galloped out of sight into an outdoor market, the next thing we knew, we saw this cashew the size of a grizzly bear leap into the river! Gotta be spooked by that!"

"You've never heard of someone dressed as Mr. Peanut?"

"Well while we're at it, then," Fred couldn't help snarling, "why should I believe you're really you, Stephen? How do I know you're not a Cashew-odon disguised as a human being?"

"Maybe you should roll up one of my shirt sleeves, make sure I'm not honey-roasted."

"We need to agree to disagree about the strength of our videotape evidence from this most recent expedition," broke in Eclipso. He wanted to avoid any more testiness than there already was. "Much as I regret having to admit it, the net result is: strongly suggestive, yet still inconclusive. However, there is an even bigger problem."

"That the object of your quest doesn't really exist in the first place?"

After giving Stephen one of his intensely long, withering stares, replicated by Bonsai Gator down to the crossed arms, Eclipso announced, "From here on out, I shall anoint you 'Honey-Roasted Feldman.'"

"I'm flattered."

"Of course you are. But here's our bigger problem: I made an effort supreme to keep the hoaxers, whoever they are, from knowing our next move in enough time to once more plague us with another elaborate fraud. Despite that, they quite obviously did find out where we were headed, in more than enough time to set up their most elaborate prank, yet."

"The remote-controlled Pteranodon that fell apart mid-flight, just to rub our noses in it," said Irene, still disgusted by the very thought.

"All the more reason to regard any future thing that looks like it might be your impossible dream dinosaur with extreme suspicion," cautioned Stephen aka Honey-Roasted Feldman.

"That small shiny object that flew away, that looked like it might be some oversized beetle," said Augie when Stephen interrupted, snarking, "Wait, you're not going to suggest that was a disembodied Carnotaurus head, are you?"

"No, Mr. Honey-Roasted Feldman, I am not!" Augie couldn't help snarling. "My point is: How unfortunate we didn't track it. I suspect it was the brains for operating that contraption that- Didn't the wreckage turn out to be mostly wood?"

"Including cedar planks that were shaved leathery thin to look like oversized bat wings," Eclipso confirmed. "But here's what's even more curious: Our rainforest activist friend, Aninha, said that in the wake of the Pteranodon fiasco, her land-developing nemesis, Raul, complained to her about two gentlemen from the states. They told him they set off detonations every nineteen days near the *Yanomami* village you visited, for gold mining purposes."

"There you go, then; mystery solved," Stephen declared, patting the conference table with both hands in see-I-told-you-so satisfaction.

"That's not the whole story, Honey-Roasted Feldman," Eclipso shook his head. "According to what Raul told Aninha, the alleged foreign gold miners asked several young *Yanomami* men to show up at the notoriously deep furrow. And they also extended this invitation to those gold prospectors who worked a small quarry. That is, those prospectors who abandoned the dig site near where the behemoth-sized dinosaur head was seen eating a smaller dino."

"Of course, the incident that led to our exploring the Amazon rainforest basin in the first place," Bernie reminded himself as much as anyone else.

"Correct," nodded Eclipso. "Apparently, those two mystery gentlemen promised their next detonation would produce streams running through the deep furrow, aglitter with gold flecks. After that, certainly, the prospectors would mine there intensively, expecting abundant gold nuggets on a scale far larger than the other sites yielded. Plus, you had those young *Yanomamis*, impatient to leave living-off-the-land ancestral ways for the glam and glitter of big city life. They would be that much more enthused about converting rainforest land to grazing pastures, on the strong chance they'd also unearth untold mineral wealth."

"But instead of glittering gold flecks, there was a hoaxed mock-up of a sleeping dragon, roused to action by intruders come too close to the fortune it hoarded," guessed Irene. "That's assuming dragon mythology here runs similar to many other parts of the world. The giant sloth and those two eyes set deep into the one burrow were non-hoaxed bonuses."

"Whatever their local legends, Ms. McDowell," said Eclipso, "it would appear Raul's mysterious acquaintances wanted your audience at the furrow for the exact opposite purpose they claimed. Rather than lure them into further mining, plus forest-clearing landscaping, they wanted to scare them away permanently from such environmentally degrading activities."

"Have they succeeded?" Stephen asked.

"On all counts, apparently. The young *Yanomamis* even went before their village leader, the *Macawoyano*, to apologize for their intended land-pillaging transgression.

They presented to him fragments of leathery-type shell found lying about the furrow after the rain shower floods diminished to a trickle. Parts of the shell the would-be Pteranodon hatched from, they supposed."

"There's something about that *verdadeiramente incrível*, truly incredible, *senhor* Eclipso," Aninha told Eclipso over a cell phone, the day before he'd reassembled his search team at Ankylosaurus Mansion. "The *Macawoyano*, himself, quickly determined the shell fragments were not fragments at all. Rather, they were pieces of bleached and dried leather intended as part of the hoax. Yet his young subjects said that really didn't matter, because of what they saw deep inside the burrow. Two green eyes stared out that had to have been from something the size of their entire *shabono*. There was no way they would risk disturbing it."

"Coincidentally," went on Eclipso presently, "when the nineteen-day rumble took place, not only did Kurupira experience another landslide, and that landfill sinkhole flood to full."

"After which, a guy in a cashew suit just happened to leap into it," Irene couldn't help interrupting.

"If my life boiled down to dressing up as a huge cashew, not sure I wouldn't have taken a running leap into the nearest deep hole, as well," Stephen just had to push back.

"What I'm trying to tell you," Eclipso plowed on impatiently, "is that at the same time as those two events, both mining pits I mentioned were completely flooded out."

"So effectively, not only have we been stymied in our non-avian dinosaur quest," observed the soft-spoken Bernie Coleman. "Those who would, as some protests go, rape the environment for material gain, have also been totally frustrated. A good thing, I would venture to say."

"Maybe those two mystery men Raul met are the ones who have been stalking us round the world with their hoaxes," said Laura with dawning realization.

"There's a definite pattern," said Harry.

"Beyond the hoaxed prehistoric reptiles, themselves," added Harriet, hand in hand with Harry.

"She completes- No," Harry shook his head, catching himself before he could finish sticking his foot in his mouth. "She's a complete person all by herself, with her own special interests."

"The same for you, my sweetie pie," Harriet patted him gently on his hand. "You should see the watercolor paintings he worked on while I was away. Sunsets in Brazil!"

"Something to do while we waited on Bernie's return from Kurupira," Harry confirmed, his ears turning red as he nodded.

"You should see them," repeated Harriet.

"Looking forward to that," Laura raced to say before Harry could also repeat what he said. "But for now I think we would all like to hear about that pattern you two noticed, Harriet and Harry."

"Yes, of course," said Harry, pushing the bridge of his thick-rimmed spectacles back up his nose. "On all three of our expeditions in search of living non-avian dinosaurs, the hoaxers did things that either helped the environment, or at least were not hurtful."

Squeezing Harry's hand as in, *I'll take over from there*, Harriet went on, "There was the robot that left foot tracks in the sand, and was painted to look like the lower half of an ornithopod dinosaur such as a Trachodon or an Iguanodon. Where it was left to rust off shore in Papua, New Guinea makes the perfect base for new coral reef growth."

"And the sauropod balloon that flew around us like a dragon," Harry excitedly continued, "we found was made of completely biodegradable material. It added helpful nutrients to the Sangha River as it decayed."

"Yes, I see your point," broke in Sherman. His chin ever scrunched into his neck made it appear he addressed his belly button as having made the point. "The hoaxers' Brazilian hi-jinx has been perhaps their most environmentally protective gambit, yet. They not only left a wooden Pteranodon replica to rot innocently in rainforest jungle, apart from an electric motor at its core. They scared off the locals from clearcutting forests and digging the land for valuable gems."

"Which suggests huge potential, were we to establish formal contact with them!" piped up would-be golf course resort developer Alistair Frump. His eyes sparkled wide open with fresh inspiration. "Maybe we could make common cause with them! By convincing them that the sooner we confirm the persistence of living non-avian dinosaurs into the present day, the sooner we can protect such marvelous creatures from extinction! And what better way to do that than to protect their environment! Which is where the golf comes in, pumping all kinds of money into that effort!"

"And pumping all kinds of wayward-hit golf balls into those dinosaur habitats. The dinos can choke on them directly, or their rotting-out chemicals can leach into their environment. Sounds like a winner," sarcastically muttered Irene.

"Steady on, mate!" protested Alistair defensively while Scott's admiring heart went out to Irene.

Scott resolved, *She's so wonderful, and I'm just so in love with her; if I make a fool out of admitting how I feel, so be it! At least I get it over with!*

"There is such a thing as the completely biodegradable golf ball!" Alistair meantime went on. "It's all I ever hit in wilderness areas in case they do get lost!"

"I actually like that idea, Alistair," Eclipso nodded. "And I believe Bonsai Gator wants to dance out his likewise enthusiasm. Samuel, will you play Yellow Dubmarine's version of that Beatles' classic, 'We Can Work It Out'? Though what am I saying? They are all classics!"

"Yessirree you've got it," Samuel Longbottom announced in his usual genial mood after pushing a few buttons on his smart phone.

As yet another Beatles song got going reggae style, opening with, "Gotta see it my way," Eclipso went on, "But there's a problem. The hoaxers continue to confound our efforts to thwart them from advance knowledge of where-to next. So long as that's the case, it is not clear to me they will have any interest in letting down their guard enough for such a negotiation. Why risk our using that to halt their mischief? In their estimation, can't they just keep on protecting the environment and scaring us away from what they see as ecologically degrading intrusions? And I hate to say it, Alistair, but..."

"I know," Alistair raised both hands defensively. "That polystyrene golf equipment for children I left littering a beach on New Britain Island. Never again! Always biodegradable clubs, biodegradable everything!"

"It's a small ask," nodded Eclipso approvingly. "Anyway," he paused to admire Bonsai Gator's dance moves to the quirkier-than-usual reggae rhythms of "We Can Work It Out." Those moves reminded him of the elaborately fluid arm motions of hula dancers. "I'd love to resume our investigation in Brazil," he proceeded finally, "going more in-depth as I'd promised and envisioned. But I am anxious to finally succeed in eluding the hoaxers, thereby driving them to the negotiating table with us. As well, can't quite put my finger on it, but Bonsai agrees don't you, Bonsai?"

Bonsai Gator appeared to Augie to work an affirmative nod in amidst his latest reggae working-out, most appropriate for "We Can Work It Out."

"Of course he does!" Eclipso insisted. "There's something going on that feels like it encompasses far more than non-avian dinosaur survival in multiple locations."

"You can lose your mind all over the world if you want. No need to limit the crazy to just one place," snarked Stephen. For the first time, Eclipso had him wondering whether the dinosaur quest was a lame excuse to simply hopscotch his circus act every place his curiosity took him.

"What about you, Charly?" Eclipso asked Sherman's artificial intelligence entity, blowing off his resident skeptic's latest barb. "You've remained remarkably quiet for the longest while since we first met. Or have you shut him down temporarily, Sherman?" he turned to ask Charly's creator.

Charly had been sitting perfectly dead still for several minutes counting, like he might as well have been a lifeless statue.

Click...whirr... Charly's sudden stiff head motions, in addition to noises abruptly if typically issuing from him, gave everyone a start. "There has been nothing for me to add here," he replied in his monotone robotic voice, "because no additional data relevant to the surviving non-avian dinosaur possibility has been presented, of which I was not already aware." Click...whirr... "The single most provocative bit of evidence we have garnered from the Brazil expedition remains a recording on my flatus emission detector. It is consistent with the recording from Cameroon of a gaseous expulsion with an unknown signature. Which was coincident with the sighting of what might have been a sauropod dinosaur, lost in the rainforest haze of trans-evaporation."

"In other words, the strongest evidence stinks," Stephen had to snark.

*

Okay, this is it, this is it, Scott MacDonald anxiously told himself. He'd just stored his knapsack underneath his seat in the Turok Tours bus, bound for a terminal near Baltimore Washington International Airport, south of Baltimore, Maryland. He was distracted taking out a *Turok* comic book, a granola bar and a drink from his knapsack before he packed the rest under his seat. But he was fairly certain he saw Irene take a seat directly in front of him, unaccompanied by anyone else.

As the bus got rolling, the chance was upon him to make a long-overdue confession, any ridicule he might face be damned.

"Hello, it's me, Scott, sitting right behind you. I-I really have no idea how to go about this, because I've never quite felt this way before...about anyone! But from the time we first met, I've- I've cherished every last interaction. I have feelings for you. I'd like to get to know you lots better. I'm well aware this might be hitting you from a completely unwanted place. And that's why I can't hold it in any longer. If none of this is reciprocal, well that's as important to know as if it *is* reciprocal, so I can take extra care not to bother you. For all I know, there's already someone extra special in your life, someone extra fortunate as well. I certainly want to respect that."

Just then, Scott felt cut off by the bang of the bathroom door, rear of the bus, well back behind him. *Well, this is appropriate,* he thought grimly. *I've gone on like this without a peep coming from Irene up in front of me. Maybe her cold stone silence is actually her gentle way of letting me down without rubbing my nose in it. And that door shutting so loudly is the universe beating me over the head with- Oh, crap!*

To Scott's horror, when he twisted around in his seat to see who had accidentally, he was sure, let the bathroom door spring back shut too hard, he found himself looking at Irene. She was returning up the aisle, latching onto headrest after headrest on her cautious way forward, given how the bus was bumpety-bump across a semi-crumbled patch of highway. Her eyes clearly focused way past him, on Laura waving at her from near the front of the bus.

So, who's that sitting just ahead of me?

Click...whirr...

To Scott's even greater, extra-wide-eyed horror, Charly stiffly rose out of the seat directly before him. He turned his head, only, around, the rest of his body still facing forward. "None of what you said is reciprocated, because I feel nothing for anybody," he robotically remarked. "For that same reason..." ...click...whirr... "...I am not bothered. I am incapable of being bothered, except as a logarithmic response from my empathy program."

"Tell us, Charly," leapt in Fred Frankly, turning about in his aisle seat a row past Charly to say, "you wouldn't be bothered, or disappointed or whatever, were someone to dismantle you so you could not complete your mission to uncover evidence of surviving non-avian dinosaurs?"

Click...whirr... "No, I would not."

"So even though that mission is your sole motivating force, you really don't give a rat's ass about it, do you? Cause you're basically just a robot? Um, hope that doesn't hurt your feelings, my putting it that way."

Click...whirr... "I have no feelings to be hurt, except, again, as a logarithmic response from my empathy program. However..." ...click...whirr... "...were I in possession of a rat's ass, and advised that giving it away would result in my receiving definitive proof of non-avian dinosaur survival to the present day, then yes, I would most certainly give a rat's ass."

"Well Jesus Diplodocus Christ, isn't that a comfort to know! But as for you, Dr. Scott MacDonald," Fred turned his attention back behind Charly to Scott, also in an aisle seat. "It's f-n' obvious you didn't think you were confessing your puppy love crush to Charly. Who is the lucky lady? Or man?"

"Sergeant, I truly don't think it's appropriate-"

"I should step in here to explain," broke in Sherman Peabody seated beside Charly before Ali Magabu could finish. He wanted to call off Fred's effort to embarrass Scott even more than already felt, while Scott made a concerted effort not to make eye contact with Irene.

Irene was looking back down the aisle with a sympathetic frown embedded in her as-usual snarky grin, her chin nevertheless lifted regally high.

"Scott," Sherman went on, "I want to thank you for providing me with especially useful data in regards to Charly's empathy program."

"Wait, so you *wanted* Scott to come on to your 'Artificial Intelligence Entity'? Who I'd term an artificial something else; sorry, Charly, don't mean to rile up those logarithms."

"When Eclipso judges our quest can continue, we might well find ourselves in a situation where it becomes essential Charly be regarded as a typical human."

Click...whirr... "If that is programmed as a secondary goal," ...click...whirr... "then I should also be willing to donate any rat's ass that might fall into my possession, in matters other than the search for surviving non-avian dinosaurs."

"Thank you," Scott whispered to Sherman in between the two seats ahead of him.

Chapter 22: North Coast of Pembrokeshire, Wales, near Strumblehead

Year four primary school student David Taylor felt quite full of himself. He'd just finished kick-digging a Tyrannosaurus Rex three-toed foot track into pebbly beach sand at the base of a steep cliff surmounted by Strumblehead Lighthouse. Sure, further down the coast other school children stumbled across fossilized imprints made by long-necked, elephant-bodied Diplodocus-type dinosaurs, some hundred-eighty-million years earlier. But he was going to leave behind what he hoped would fool coastal hikers into believing was a freshly made track from a legendarily ferocious, fifty-foot-long carnivore.

David's plan to sneak away from fellow students on the coastal field trip went perfectly. The geology lesson concerned a natural look-out hill, Garn Fawr, or Great Rock, the remnant from a volcanic eruption that didn't quite surface, four-hundred-fifty-million years ago. After that field instruction, year four team teachers Ms. Jones and Ms. Anstee turned their young charges loose. They could hunt for everything from those aforementioned dinosaur tracks, to flint spearheads chiseled mere thousands of years ago, to odd burrows left in the lush hills overlooking the Irish Sea, burrows among the earliest signs of human habitation left anywhere in the entire United Kingdom.

It was the easiest thing for David to scurry off and make his way down a narrow footpath to the beach. Only now that his dirty-work was done, figured he better hustle hard to rejoin-

Slosh!

The ebb and flow of surf had been a constant companion to the nine-year-old from the time he stepped off the school bus near Garn Fawr. But this particular slosh proved far louder, more distinctively insistent than the rest. And was accompanied by a tremor so slight underfoot, he might have made nothing of it otherwise.

Glancing seaward, David noticed a late morning fog rolling in quickly. Behind him, from well up the cliff, he could hear the teachers call students back together before they were lost in the low cloud bank.

But his real concern had nothing to do with either anxious adults or impending thick mists. Rather, there was an enormous, dark brown shape offshore, already fading into the fog. Its long, long neck and whale-sized body produced additional loud sloshes as it appeared headed directly out to sea.

"David Taylor!" shouted Ms. Jones hurrying down the last stretch of footpath to the beach. "What have you been doing here? We have to leave like ten minutes ago to- Oh, I see. Committing a wee bit of a hoax with that dinosaur track, are we? If you would only-"

"Look out to sea, Ms. Jones!" David shouted, pointing.

"*Bobol bach!*" Kay Jones gasped in a Welsh expression of surprise. She caught the remaining instant of what David got a good look at before it disappeared altogether in the rapidly thickening fog.

All too soon, the distinctive sloshing faded into the din of the gentle surf.

"Oh!" Kay gasped anew, surprised by a sudden splash back very close to shore.

There was the very familiar "Arf! Arf! Arf!" of a local sea lion, and the fog thin enough close to shore for clearly discerning that creature's sleek, dark-brown hide arcing gracefully between wavelets.

"Ahh!" Kay laughed relievedly, "there's our prehistoric sea monster. C'mon now, let's tell the others all about it before this *haar* rolls in too thick for me to see you when I have to shout at you to behave! David Taylor! *Talu sylw!* Pay attention! You're going to drown in those waves the way you keep staring at them from shore! It was just a seal, I'm telling you! No amount of your starin' is going to turn it into a dinosaur!"

"Now in a minute, mum!" spilled from David's mouth. The way he raised his nose so high reminded his teacher of a dog sticking his head out a car window. He was satisfying himself that well beyond the usual, oddly comforting sea air brine, he detected a special pungence. More than of anything else, it reminded him of the odors inside the reptile house of a zoo where his parents took him in north Wales.

David would have sworn that a short while earlier, as they spotted the seal, he'd heard a distinct Psst! from well offshore, where the monstrous, long-necked phantom seemed to dissolve into the billowing fog bank. *Was that the biggest fart, ever?*

Chapter 23

Augie Matias didn't expect to suddenly be wandering down a dark passageway with Houdini Chicken by his side, the bird who nested atop him in Cameroon, West Africa. But there she was, bobbing her head about...the same as he felt himself doing.

Clunk!

Ouch! Must have been a stalactite! Have to be more careful, but what's this in my mouth? Down the end of this passageway, where I'm carrying a suffocated furry creature to feed...whatever has those glowing eyes must be impossibly-

Clunk!

Augie thought he opened his eyes, and found himself standing on his bed with a pillow in his mouth. *Phew! Just a bad, if over-the-top bizarre nightmare...*

Ring! Ring!

"It's for you, Augie-Doggie," Augie thought he heard his wife Vicky say as she handed him the phone.

"Hello? Who is this calling at such a late hour?"

"Buk-buk-buk-buk-BUK!!"

Clunk!

At last, Augie really *did* wake up. He just missed bumping his head into the ceiling fan a third time. Not a stalactite, after all.

But his pillow really was partially stuffed in his mouth, and he really was standing tall on his and Vicky's bed.

"Good grief, Augie-Doggie! What crazy nightmare led to your standing there eating your pillow? Didn't you have enough for dinner?" asked Vicky. Her grogginess from being woken by Augie's noise-making the middle of the night rapidly dissipated when she turned over and saw what he was doing.

By then, daughter Liz had rushed in, flicking on the light. "Jeezy-peezy, Daddy!" she exclaimed. "Is this what seeing a dinosaur disguise itself as a monster cashew did to you?"

Nearly gagging as he pulled pillow stuffing from his mouth, where he'd torn through the fabric in his sleep, Augie admitted, "This actually had to do with, you remember Houdini Chicken?"

"OMG!"

"Yeah, I was accompanying her towards this monster at the end of a deep tunnel, like those eyes I saw in Brazil..."

"To wed you in holy matrimony? Should you be jealous, Mumsy?"

"Better Houdini Chicken than one of his fellow explorers."

"As that old song goes, Vicky, 'I only have eyes for you.'"

"Oh, yuk; that's my exit cue," Liz announced, already spun around on her way back to bed.

"Um, this might be as good a time, or bad a time, as any, to admit something," said Vicky as she joined Augie sitting down on the edge of their bed. "Um, I've had a clandestine communication with Samuel Longbottom, your expedition chauffeur."

"Say what?! You're not going to build a nest on his head, or anything like that, are you?" Augie forced himself to joke, even though his heart raced a mile a minute.

"Why, Augustine William Matias," said Vicky, giving him an affectionate, comforting pat on his pajama-covered leg. "Do I detect a hint of jealousy? Let me assure you; I hardly know the man, and his cardigan sweater is more sedative than arousing. But figured he'd be the fastest conduit for a photocopy of your great grandpa's booklet to Eclipso behind your back. I wanted to throw that into the pot of prospective expedition spots, since he's ruled out a return to Brazil for now despite all that unfinished business there. Hope you're not angry, but I should think the dragon passage..."

"You're right, of course."

"Sorry, Augie, I should have admitted this earlier. Now was not the time, especially after your Houdini Chicken fantasy."

"It was a nightmare I assure you."

"But maybe you can get back to sleep? We can talk more in the morning?"

"I'm a bit too wound up; think I'll try settling down with telly on the adventure channel."

"A rerun of *Cryptomonster Hunt*? Mind if I join you for a cuddle?" Vicky followed Augie off their bed headed for the hallway down to the living room.

"I would mind if you didn't; just have to keep the volume low so we don't wake up Liz again," Augie whispered as they passed their daughter's shut bedroom door. "Keep down the TV volume also, of course."

Vicky slapped Augie playfully.

Turned out, though, Augie was soon ready to scream like a banshee, but not out of passion for Vicky. Rather, over a certain TV commercial.

"Everyone knows about fossils left behind by monsters that ruled the Earth millions of years before us humans came on the scene. But ever since their discovery, some of us have dreamed of finding one of those prehistoric wonders of nature still roaming some remote, unexplored area," went a voice that sounded strikingly familiar to Augie. He couldn't quite place it yet, especially in his agitated state trying to mellow down from such a notably bizarre nightmare.

Anyway, lots of images flashed across the TV screen for the first part of the commercial teaser. There were skeletons of dinosaurs, and of such large, extinct mammals as the Wooly Mammoth. Included, ironically enough, was the giant ground sloth, Megatherium. Augie would have sworn he saw it alive and well, scrambling out of a furrow carved into the Amazon rainforest, for all anyone knew, by a snake the size of four subway cars.

"Unfortunately for our would-be history-making explorers," went on the familiar voice, "there are certain bad actors with dreams of their own. They want to fool the whole world via forged evidence."

For this part of the narration, several more images flashed across the screen. There was a famous faked photo of the Loch Ness Monster, a photo of a mermaid corpse made by splicing together a giant fish's tail with a chimpanzee's upper torso, and a video clip of a guy in a Bigfoot suit scampering across a field.

"There have been plenty of shows about searches for surviving prehistoric monsters. They produced very little, if any, promising results. So maybe it's time to go after the charlatans, the pranksters who would fool us into believing things that don't exist. Join me, Jake Rumblehouse,-" The camera angle pulled back from a television screen inside Vicky and Augie's television screen. Revealed standing beside it was the guy Augie used to work for on the defunct *Cryptomonster Hunt* series. "-as we go after monster hoaxers the world over, on *Crypto-fake-ology*. Premiering Monday night at nine, right here on the Amazing Adventure Channel. Our first stop: Papua, New Guinea, where the locals thought they might be invaded by an Iguanodon. You won't believe the lengths someone went to!"

The camera zeroed back in on the screen beside Jake. There, a photo showed the robotic contraption Augie and company found left in emerald green shallows off the coast of New Britain Island, made up to look like the lower half of a dinosaur. Presumably, it would have become the base for a new coral reef. Only it was shown standing on shore.

Before or after we found it? Augie seethed in a boiling rage.

Ring! Ring! Ring! Ring!

Augie and Vicky exchanged looks as in, *Who would be calling at this time? Please not one of our moms with a medical emergency!*

"Who is this?" Augie raced to answer, not hiding his irritation as he figured it more than likely to be some prank call.

"Buk-buk-buk-buk-BUK!!"